PUBLIC OFFERINGS

Book Three

Killer Priest

A novel by

Bob LiVolsi

Copyright © 2014 by Robert F. LiVolsi

ISBN: 978-0-9769446-7-6

Trade Paperback Version

Cover design by Kana LiVolsi

Published by Fifth Book Press: December 2016

www.PublicOfferings.Net

Follow at www.Facebook.com/PublicOfferings

NOTICE

This is a work of fiction. Names, characters, places, events, and incidents are either products of the author's imagination or used fictitiously. Any resemblance to actual persons, living or dead, is purely coincidental.

DEDICATION

To Susan who has patiently believed in me and encouraged me for far too long for her own good. Thank you, my darling wife, for being there always and for loving me. I love you always.

To all the people in generous communities of caring around the world who continue to sacrifice their comfort and often risk their lives to bring hope to our peers in less fortunate corners of the world. And to the people of Sierra Leone whose misery at the hands of warlords and power brokers informed the very first draft of this book all those years ago in 1995.

To all those who cling to and proclaim a faith of compassion for human beings, built on service not conquest, built on hope not rules, and encompassed by love – at all times recognizing a much greater force that transcends our personal demands and yet embraces our free will and individuality.

TABLE OF CONTENTS

BOOK THREE – Killer Priest

Summary of Public Offerings Books One & Two

Summary of Birthright: Book One

In a secret lab high up in Cameron Pass in the Colorado Rockies, Sheila Stratemeier, a drug developer for the Aldrich Institute, believes the Aldrich no longer focuses on a mission to save lives. She knows now that the Institute's executives do not plan to use their new malaria vaccine to cure people – at least not in the short term. Instead, they plan to first cull the population in a twisted eugenics plot that will kill as many as a million. As she prepares to blow the whistle on her company, Sheila is killed at her desk

Dave Clement works covertly with Sheila to identify a cure for his daughter's drug resistant HIV. While Dave is passionate about his work, finding a cure for his daughter tops his priority list. Five weeks before Sheila's demise, Dave travels on a business trip to Nigeria and then Sierra Leone in West Africa. He is the Vice President of Operations and Business Development for Prodeus, a partner of the Aldrich Institute where Sheila works. Prodeus makes a Portable DNA Analyzer (PDNA) that can quickly test an individual's blood and DNA to ascertain if they have the genetic make-up to benefit from the new malaria vaccine developed by Sheila's team at the Aldrich.

To fund a pilot program for the vaccine and deployment of his PDNAs in Sierra Leone, Dave works closely with Evan Conger, the World Health Organization Assistant Director-General for HIV/AIDS and Malaria, and Adrian Guerra, the West African Country Director for the World Bank. They recruit the Lokoma tribe of northwestern Sierra Leone to be the first recipients of the new vaccine in the pilot program. All of Sierra Leone still suffers in the aftermath of the Ebola pandemic; the economy is devastated and its people struggle with high malnutrition levels, making them more vulnerable to death from malaria, the biggest single killer of children.

Hamara Karanja, the tribe's chief, has lost one daughter to malaria already and wants to protect his two remaining children, Jacob and Emma. Hamara works closely with Father Jim Reilly, an Irish missionary priest who brings anti-malarial drugs and outside medical missions to Lokoma village. Father Jim first introduced Hamara to Dave Clement years earlier as part of a medical mission to the village. The long-term relationship between Father Jim, Dave and Hamara is the connection that results in the final decision to move the malaria vaccine pilot program from Nigeria, beset by the Boko Haram, to Sierra Leone, starting with the Lokoma tribe.

At home in Fort Collins, Colorado, Dave's daughter struggles with illusions induced by medication she is taking to manage her HIV. At 15, Liv Clement has allegedly engaged in no risky behaviors to cause her to become infected with AIDS. Liv's HIV is a secret only her immediate family, doctors and Sheila know. Dave suspects that Liv must have had some intimate encounter that led to her infection. As a result of that suspicion and his preoccupation with work over family, Mel Clement, Dave's wife, throws him out of the house. They are now separated. Liv, in particular, struggles with the family situation as she copes with her secret disease and with HIV drugs to which her disease quickly builds resistance. She fears she is facing a death sentence. Because of the nature of HIV, Liv keeps it from even her closest friends who she fears will shame her.

Claire McQuaid is executive director of the Aldrich Institute. She has extensive scarring on her body from an unspecified incident in her youth. The scarring and the unspecified incident that caused it preoccupy her and somehow help her focus on her mission to eradicate malaria. She seems obsessed with terror attacks and genocides, occasionally watching a video compilation on her computer to remind herself of the horrors.

In Lokoma village, five-year-old Sara Karanja contracts malaria. Fr. Jim is bringing anti-malarial medication to her, but gets kidnapped on the mountain road between Freetown to Lokoma. He never gets there with the drugs.

Jennifer Winter once worked alongside Sheila Stratemeier when both were protégés of Claire at the Aldrich. When Claire helped Ed Hepp set up Prodeus to manufacture PDNAs to enable optimized delivery of the malaria vaccine, Claire arranged for Jennifer to go to work at Prodeus as project manager for the PDNA development. Jennifer works directly for Dave Clement. She is up to something with Dave, seeming to encourage his separation from Mel and making a play for him to be her lover. Dave rebuffs her advances, insisting he is happily married and that he will put things back together with Mel.

Dave has a chance to get back with Mel by joining her at Liv's volleyball game, but he gets delayed by a meeting with Jennifer and Brian Middleton, the Prodeus VP of Engineering. He shows up late to the game. Thought upset with him, Mel and Liv join him for dinner afterward. There, he tells them the good news that his quest for a cure for Liv is finally bearing fruit. Through their covert cloud account, Sheila has told him she has found a path to a cure. Sheila plans to meet with him in person the following week to give him the details. Unfortunately, Dave needs to leave dinner early to catch a flight. He has agreed to meet Evan Conger at the Admirals Club at the Denver International Airport before boarding. Evan needs to tell him about something that affects the malaria project and Liv. Both men are on the same flight to Geneva and the WHO conference there. Dave's early departure from dinner reinforces his family's feeling that work is more important to Dave than they are. Mel is angry with him. Liv is very hurt; she misses her Dad and wants her parents to get back together. At the same time, they want him to learn more about Sheila's discovery.

The Geneva flight has trouble over Nova Scotia and smoke pours into the cabin. On Evan's visit to the Aldrich lab in Denver, Sheila slipped him a flash drive with information that shows that Claire McQuaid and the Aldrich are willing to risk genocide in West Africa as part of their deployment of the malaria vaccine. It's part of complicated chemistry that hides proteins that will cause an HIV mutation inside the vaccine. Anyone with HIV who receives the vaccine will get the mutation. The mutation is much more deadly than the regular strain of HIV in Sierra Leone. It kills in months instead of a decade and there are no drugs that can stop it. The Aldrich, however, has a way of eradicating the mutation once antibodies are collected from its victims. But while the Aldrich waits to collect antibodies, those with the mutation will drop by the tens of thousands, potentially up to a million losing their lives before the Aldrich is able to use the antibodies to deploy the HIV vaccine that will stop it.

Evan, sitting in business class on the Geneva flight, thinks of Dave in the coach section of the plane. He had hoped Dave and he would stop the Aldrich plot, but now he realizes the plane is not going to stay in the air. He also now knows that the plot specifically endangers Dave's daughter. He quickly types a note into his phone, secure in a waterproof and shockproof case, to try to find a way to get Sheila's information to someone else. The plane crashes into the Atlantic, with everyone on board presumed dead.

In Fort Collins, Mel Clement sees the news of the plane crash on CNN. She realizes it's Dave's flight and immediately leaves a message on his mobile phone, telling him that she wants him back home and that she loves him. Hearing the news that the crash has no survivors, Mel breaks down in sobs.

At the Aldrich Mountain Lab, Eldridge Perry, head of drug development and Sheila's boss, speaks with Claire on the phone. He realizes that Claire's security force has somehow arranged for the Geneva-bound plane to go down. He is not happy with the thuggish tactics of Mike Farley, the IRA-trained security chief, but does not argue with Claire, recognizing that the mission of the Aldrich is bigger than all of them. He thinks about the chess pieces the Aldrich yet has available to ensure successful implementation of the plan in West Africa. He focuses on Liv Clement, recognizing that she is a key pawn in keeping the plan on course, all because she is Dave's daughter. Thinking about Liv and the threat to her, Eldridge mumbles aloud: "Helluva birthright."

Summary of The Price of a Life: Book Two

As Book 2 begins, Dave Clement's plane has crashed with all aboard lost. Evan Conger, sitting in first class on the flight, is dead, and Sheila has now lost her outside relationships that could stop the Aldrich's genocidal plan. While Sheila apparently has some way to bring help to Liv Clement for her HIV, the crash of the Geneva-bound plane and Eldridge Perry's targeting of Liv Clement as a doomed pawn in the Aldrich conspiracy change everything, promising deadly trouble ahead for Sheila, Liv and the people of Lokoma Village.

In the Kono district in southeastern in Sierra Leone, a Doctors Without Borders volunteer physician hikes to a village on a medical mission. Dr Warren Sturbridge, a friend of Evan Conger, has discovered that the predominant HIV form (or clade) in Sierra Leone is the same as that of the rest of the Sub-Saharan Africa region. Sturbridge provided a faxed handwritten copy of the report to Evan Conger, but does not yet know that Conger died in the air disaster in Nova Scotia. He is waiting for Adrian Guerra's World Bank office in Freetown to transcribe and print a final copy for distribution. On the trail in the rain, one of the clerks from the office appears in the distance, taunting him and waving the original handwritten copy of the report in the air. The man lures Sturbridge into a clearing where a landmine explodes and kills him.

At 5:02 a.m. in Chicago's O'Hare International Airport, an exhausted Dave is waiting for his next connection en route to Geneva. He missed his original flight out of Denver due to a security snafu at Denver International Airport where he was pulled out of the security line and unnecessarily delayed by TSA. In the airline club, he sees news of the Geneva flight's crash. He realizes Evan is gone and that he dodged a bullet. He returns to Fort Collins. There, he meets Mel for breakfast at the Silver Grill. Mel is tearful, having nearly lost Dave. She invites him to move back home, but he surprises her. Though he professes his love for her and Liv, he says he has been spared for a reason. He feels called to focus 100% on getting the malaria vaccine deployed. She tells him that if there's a reason, it's so that he finally realizes he is called to come home and spend quality time with his family. When he remains stubborn, she tells him that he has an overblown opinion of his own importance in God's plan – as always. As she leaves him, she says, "You're breaking your daughter's heart."

At the Prodeus headquarters at 3 a.m., Jennifer puts an encryption CD in her computer's CD tray and encrypts emails with confidential Prodeus attachments. When she finishes and leaves, she forgets the incriminating CD, leaving it in her computer.

At Evan Conger's memorial service, Sheila Stratemeier approaches Dave. Increased security at the Aldrich Institute caused Sheila to postpone a breakfast meeting with him early that morning. She thinks she is being followed and investigated by the "IRA thugs" running Aldrich security. She had promised Dave evidence of a cure for Liv's HIV. But Sheila has more to tell him about Liv than that. Before she can confide anything, Mike Farley, the Aldrich security chief, interrupts them and escorts Dave to Claire's limo. Claire wants to know what Sheila wanted. Dave tells her she only wanted to be introduced. Claire invites Dave to join her for lunch to discuss the impact of Evan's death on the malaria vaccine project. At lunch, Claire comments on Dave's good fortune in missing the flight. When he says God was watching out for him, she tells him, "God or not, someone was definitely looking out for you" – as though she knows something. Claire tells him she wants him to take on a bigger role in partnering with the World Health Organization now that Evan is gone. She tells him she is confident Jennifer can back him up at the Prodeus plant in Loveland. Knowing that Sheila intended to tell him about an HIV cure in the works at the Aldrich, Dave tells Claire about Liv's HIV and confronts her about the Aldrich cure. Claire denies it exists. He pushes back, but she insists that she and the Aldrich cannot help.

In Peggy's Cove, Nova Scotia, scene of the Geneva flight's crash, ten-year-old Marie is playing on the beach against her abusive father's orders. She finds a mobile phone in a waterproof case. Though it's battery is very low, Marie is able to read some notes on it before it dies. The note says the plane may have been sabotaged and the phone's contents need to be given to someone responsible that is not under the influence of US authorities. Marie runs back to the house and quickly hides the sandy phone to make sure her father doesn't know she disobeyed him by going to the beach.

In Lokoma, Sara's condition worsens. Hamara decides to take her over the mountain to the hospital in Freetown. His wife, Mariama, accompanies him, but Jacob refuses, choosing to stay behind with Ani, his birth mother. Jacob is concerned that bandits might raid the village, but Hamara assures him it will not happen.

At Rome's Leonardo DaVinci Airport, Father Jim is found barely alive in a coffin inside the cargo of a flight from Freetown. A note to deliver him to the Pope is pinned to his shirt. Sara's medication is still in his shirt pocket. As the coffin lid opens, Fr Jim, delusional from his ordeal, flashes back to his childhood on the streets of Belfast. There, as Sean Farley, he helps his brother Mike and the IRA set off a car bomb on a Protestant landlord. He did not know that the landlord's wife and two daughters, one teenager and one toddler, would be joining him in the limo. Before the teenager enters the car, her emerald eyes meet Sean's eyes in his hiding place in an alley across the street. Suddenly struck by the enormity of what's about to happen, Sean tries to warn her. As he runs toward the street, his brother hits him over the head with a cudgel, knocking him to down the cobblestones. When he looks up, it is too late. Somehow the father survives the fiery eruption and Sean, running from the scene, hears the man's anguished wailing behind him.

Jacob Karanja hears something in the dark as he sleeps beside his mother. Quietly going outside, he follows the sound about a kilometer out of the village, but finds only animals. He falls asleep on a rock and returns to the village just after daybreak. By then, his mother has been kidnapped in a bloody raid by child soldiers that killed both her parents and others. Jacob blames his father for not being there. He runs away into the jungle.

At the Aldrich mountain lab, Sheila again works deep into the night. She knows of horrifying flaws in the plan to use the malaria vaccine to introduce a manufactured HIV mutation into people already infected with a natural form of HIV. The plan calls for the synthetic drug to cause the natural HIV to mutate to the new synthetic form. While the mutation is much more deadly with a much shorter incubation period, the Aldrich also knows how to completely cure the manufactured mutation, unlike the natural form of HIV. Animal testing has already proven the science. Another Aldrich drug – a synthetic protein - introduced after the mutation will enable the body's self-defense system to completely defeat the mutation, thus eradicating HIV. The only problem is that there is an issue getting the synthetic protein designed to attach to human antibodies. As it stands, the cure that worked in animals will not work in humans. Confident her team will ultimately solve the problem, Sheila insists Claire McQuaid delay the planned deployment of the malaria vaccine which secretly contains the HIV mutator. Claire refuses. When Sheila challenges that hundreds of thousands, or even more, could die within months as a consequence of deploying before the protein design is fixed, Claire tells her to back off. Claire says, "We're in the business of life and death. And I'm the only that gets to play God."

Liv Clement struggles with sleep because of both the HIV and the absence of her father. At school, she researches in the library. Everything tells her HIV is at best a life sentence and likely a death sentence. Her friends do not know about Liv's illness, but when they talk about AIDS, her friends think of it as a gay disease and say unkind things about people who have it. Liv hides in a stall in the girls' restroom sobbing.

Teenaged bandits kidnap Jacob outside Lokoma. They keep him drugged and indoctrinate him with Rambo films. They convince the drugged Jacob that his father betrayed him and the Lokoma people. Soon, he is no longer a captive but a child soldier, his captors now his commanders. They claim to be rebels, not bandits, and assure Jacob that the bandits that attacked Lokoma are a different and evil group. He is also told that if his mother survived her kidnapping, surviving might be worse for her.

Dave gets the first orders for PDNAs from Claire and the Aldrich. He is excited about the prospect of the initial public offering that Prodeus is planning as a result of the success of the PDNA. It will provide the funds needed to afford experimental treatments for Liv and free him to spend more time at home. His excitement, however, is tempered in that he remains unable to reach Sheila Stratemeier about Liv's cure. Meanwhile, Liv's CD4 T-cell count is dropping, increasing the odds that her HIV might seroconvert to deadly AIDS.

The Karanjas and the Lokoma tribe are in a refugee camp run by the Catholic Church on the southern edge of Freetown. Sara stays in the clinic there where she is treated for malaria with medication and IVs. Hamara, Mariama and three-year-old Emma live in a temporary tent while they collect wood, concrete blocks and tin to build a more stable, albeit tiny, structure. At the clinic, the doctor tells them that Sara has AIDS. As they leave the infirmary, the crosshairs of a rifle scope, hidden in the hills above, zero in on Hamara. The assassin is Jacob under orders from teenage commanders that stand over him. But Jacob hesitates and his parents disappear into their makeshift home. The commanders violently kick Jacob over his failure, taking his AK-47 away from him, leaving him armed only with a machete as they and their platoon of boy soldiers slip back into the jungle.

Several hours later, under cover of darkness, the platoon returns to the camp where they attack a group of nuns who are leaving for the night. They mutilate the nuns with machetes, deliberately leaving one survivor to stay on with her scars as a reminder of the rebels' power. Jacob is the only boy who stands back and does not participate in the attack. The commander calls Jacob a coward and tells him that if they did not need him to get to Hamara, Jacob would be dead.

Meanwhile, back in Fort Collins, Liv's HIV has stabilized. She remains on the volleyball team and has a new romantic interest in Michael Winston who, through encounters at school, seems to like her, too.

Jennifer meets with Dave to tell him that the PDNA has passed in-house engineering verification testing (EVT). It looks like the PDNA's will deliver before Thanksgiving as Claire requested. Jennifer asks after Liv and talks about how Mel does not appreciate him. She surprises Dave with an aggressive kiss. He pushes her away and hurries out of the building to get to Liv's volleyball match, for which Jennifer's interruption had now made him late – again. Dave arrives only to find a crowd around Liv. She passed out on the last play of the match, dropping as she reached to hit the ball. Mel is pissed at Dave for being late again, but is far more concerned about Liv than fighting with her husband. Mel and Liv go to the hospital in an ambulance while Dave follows behind in his car. Liv seems to be feeling little more than tired in the exam room, but they learn that her T-cell count has dropped again. While Liv's count is still not dangerously low, the trend is not good. With her medications, the count should be going up. The doctor feels that Liv's current medications should be changed. They will get with the infectious disease specialist in the morning for further evaluation. After the evening's trauma, Dave thinks it's time to move back home. Mel hugs him, but when he hints at returning home, she steps back. "Too soon," she says as she walks off, wiping away a tear. Subsequently, she contacts him several times, leaning on him to find out more about the alleged Aldrich cure.

In Sierra Leone, Ani, Jacob's mother, is a wife of one of the teenage rebel commanders. She is regularly raped by him and his drug-addled comrades. Tonight, she hides behind a tree in the dark after they finish with her. She prays and thinks she wants to die, but she decides to stay alive to find Jacob. Her captors tell her Jacob is now a soldier, too, killing as they kill. She prays it's not the case, and if it is the case, she contemplates praying for his death.

After missing several days, Liv returns to school only to be surprised by her best friend Chelsea's claim on Michael Winston. While Michael has not talked to Chelsea, she now "claims" him. Since Liv never confided her feelings for Michael to Chelsea, she now cannot go to Michael herself without looking like a disloyal friend.

At Prodeus, Jennifer brings Dave the engineering authorization from The Aldrich, meaning Prodeus can now begin manufacture. Jennifer tries to kiss him again. He firmly rejects her. Jennifer notices a book about AIDS stashed in Dave's office. She insists on knowing about it. Dave realizes that Jennifer, who worked at the Aldrich side by side with Sheila for years before coming to Prodeus, might have some idea about the cure. Still unable to reach Sheila, he decides to risk asking Jennifer about a cure and disclosing the situation with Liv. She tells Dave the AIDS cure is a major secret undertaking at the Aldrich and that Sheila is the chief scientist on the project. Jennifer seems surprised when Dave tells her Claire would not tell him about it. She tells him he needs to go back to Claire again, but to not tell her that he heard anything about it from Jennifer. Dave leaves a message for Claire, asking for another meeting urgently. Dave doesn't hear back from Claire, but he hears from Mel and finally moves back home the next night. He is happy to fall asleep beside Mel again and regrets all the nights he missed. His heart is wrenched over the fact that he has been so unavailable for Liv, both through the separation and all the years of prioritizing work ahead of her and Mel.

When Claire gets back to Dave, she stonewalls him again on an AIDS cure. Meanwhile, Dave and the executive staff discuss the public offering. Thatcher Ripley, one of the most prestigious underwriters of IPOs, has bid but it's a lowball bid. For some reason, no other firms are bidding. Dan Dorfmann, the CFO, suspects that Pamela Thatcher, possibly conflicted by her role as a board member at the Aldrich, might be actively "discouraging" her competitors from bidding. Dorfmann and Ed Hepp, the CEO, wonder if Pamela might want to keep the IPO price down to get Prodeus more willing to sell out to the Aldrich instead —for an undervalued price.

Hepp and Dorfmann decide it's critical to meet a pre-Thanksgiving ship date for the PDNAs to get a big humanitarian story out by Christmas on the malaria vaccine effort. They feel that the PR would strengthen their hand in attracting more investment bankers and a higher offering price. After the meeting, Jennifer asks Dave if Claire told him anything. He tells her that Claire said Jennifer probably drew incorrect assumptions from old product roadmaps the Aldrich used when Jennifer was still there. Jennifer is angry. Dave promised he would not tell Claire she was his source. Dave explains Claire drew her own conclusions. Jennifer says the damage is done. Dave thinks that this is a good outcome. If Claire had been suspicious that Sheila leaked to him, she now knows it's Jennifer instead – a useful diversion. Plus, Dave can protect Jennifer's job at Prodeus. Jennifer tries to use Dave's guilt to interest him in a hug and a kiss. He walks away. After he leaves, Jennifer tears up. She is deeply touched by the man's love of his wife and family. She is also disheartened that her plan has failed. Claire will be disappointed in her. Now, she has no alternative but to go on to "Plan B". That night, Jennifer emails Sheila from her apartment and they agree to meet for breakfast at the Silver Grill in Fort Collins the next morning. She writes Sheila that it's time to move on to the "next drastic step". She writes she wants to give Sheila some fresh perspective to keep her from blowing the whistle.

In Rome, Fr. Jim walks outside the Vatican walls where he meets a young Irish woman who is fascinated with him. She poses for pictures with him on the Ponte Sant'Angelo, surprising him with a quick kiss as shutters snap. Then, over coffee, he acknowledges that became a priest in part to do penance for past sins. she calls him Sean, a name no one has called him in twenty years. Growing hostile, she says, "Your secrets are catchin' up to ya, Sean." When he challenges her to find out what she knows, she runs off.

At the Aldrich mountain lab, Sheila works late into the night again. This time, however, she prepares to blow the whistle on Claire McQuaid and the deadly Aldrich plan. She believes Claire is on the verge of genocide, playing God with the lives of millions. She prepares an email to the board of directors in hopes of making them aware and stopping Claire. If the board does not respond, Sheila plans to quickly go to the press. As midnight approaches in the empty lab, Sheila goes to press "enter" to send the email. Instead, she is yanked out of her chair by a garrote around her neck. Across the country in Pittsburgh, Sheila's brother, a priest and member of the secret Christus Society, contemplates a phone conversation with Sheila earlier that evening. He calls Christus to report the conspiracy of a fast acting AIDS hidden inside a malaria vaccine even though he suspects his sister is being paranoid. The story seems unlikely. Then, as he walks in the parish garden smoking his pipe under the stars in the chilly night air, he is stabbed to death.

Jennifer waits for Sheila at the Silver Grill the next morning. While she waits, she writes a cryptic note to herself to "prepare Liv for clinical trial." Sipping coffee, she thinks about how to talk Sheila into not blowing the whistle. Finally, Jennifer orders cinnamon rolls and hash browns for herself.

When she finishes eating, she gets a newspaper and reads about a woman's body found murdered in a motel in Walton, very near the mountain lab, early that morning. When she still cannot reach Sheila, she drives to Walton where she learns the woman had a tattoo on her upper thigh identical to Sheila's. It says Rocky 28714.

Back at the Prodeus office, Dave signs into the covert cloud he and Sheila use. He discovers that Sheila has sent him a folder, updating the files for the first time in weeks. The new folder is password protected. Happy that Sheila is finally communicating out again, he is frustrated since he does not know the password.

At the Thatcher estate in the Tidewater region of Virginia, Pamela Thatcher meets in her library with a group of key partners: Joseph Mossoumou, president of the Middle African Democracy (MAD), Tony Wayne, US Undersecretary of State for African Affairs, and Claire McQuaid. Wayne and Mossoumou are lifelong friends, having been roommates at Harvard's JFK School of Government years ago. Mossoumou is a close ally of the West, his country on the border of the Islamic north and the Christian south in Africa. Time magazine declared him the African continent's most important political leader. They discuss the strategy and logistics of the malaria vaccine deployment, sharing updates on their individual roles. Pamela tells Mossoumou that MAD will have sea and air access for food and supplies through Sierra Leone. Undersecretary Wayne assures President Mossoumou that the US will let him operate without impediment. "We're too entangled in the Middle East for that," Wayne says. He also confirms that the US Navy will facilitate a clear sea route for MAD shipping between Freetown, Sierra Leone, and Douala, Cameroon.

They talk about slipping the plan's schedule into January, but Mossoumou is adamant that the plan launch before Christmas. Extremists are building strength in the northeast region of MAD and his army needs to act sooner rather than later. The MAD President says he would rather have access through Nigeria as it's closer to MAD, providing easier logistics. Pamela says Nigeria is off limits, an ally with a large standing army. More importantly, the HIV clade or mutation there has long been identified. If the plan is to work, they must operate where the HIV clade has not yet been pinned down. Sierra Leone with its long civil war and impoverished system has poor medical records, inadequate in the first place and many of them destroyed in the war. Wayne points out that Sierra Leone opens access to the westernmost portion of the oil-rich Sierra Leone trench, a huge undersea oil field filled with sweet crude and easily accessed with today's technology. All are clear that they must also minimize growing Chinese influence in West Africa and stabilize the region. Increasing productivity and managing disease are critical to stabilization. By eradicating malaria and eliminating the overhead of caring for millions of AIDS victims, productivity will skyrocket. Claire gives everyone an update on the malaria vaccine, the HIV Trojan horse in it, and the role of the PDNAs in hiding what the plotters are doing.

Later that same night, Pamela goes to Claire's bedroom in the estate. She asks her if she's dealing all right with the decision on Sheila. Claire says she is, but she needs to get Jennifer back to the lab to cover Sheila's work. Pamela tells her she's confident that Jennifer will come back as long as she doesn't learn what happened to Sheila. They talk about Dave Clement, expressing that he is "clueless about the subterfuge," and that they need him to work with them to keep the critical relationships in the plan working.

Claire, talking about Dave, tells Pamela, "Who knew a man existed that couldn't be compromised by either a beautiful young woman or kickbacks? He left us no choice. Jennifer completed the first phase months ago. We hoped it would be enough to drive a wedge in the family and focus him on making money above all else. It turns out it wasn't. So we have to raise the stakes on him. Jennifer needs to finish the job before she comes back to the Aldrich."

"Ironic," Pamela said. "Clement's going to pay a dear price because he does the right thing. Makes you wonder who's really on the side of the angels."

In the conversation, Claire calls Pamela "aunt" and Pamela calls her "Joanne". Claire says, "Never call me that. Joanne is gone…When this is over, I'm going to feel like I finally buried Joanne once and for all."

Claire asks about other news. Pamela tells her, "Steady progress. Holy Mother Church is really a very simple thing to manage once you understand its combination of bureaucracy and naiveté."

As she drifts off to sleep that night, Claire dreams of seeing her reflection as a red-headed, freckled teenager in a limousine window. Then Liv Clement's face super-imposes over her own. Beside her, her mother and her baby sister appear on a damp Belfast sidewalk. Like Liv, Claire is still an innocent teenager caught in life's deadly crossfire. Suddenly white light fills her dream and searing heat overwhelms her. Enormous pressure threatens to make her head explode. She reaches for her mother and sister, but they are gone.

Book Two concludes: *Claire awoke trembling in the black night of the bedroom. For a brief moment, she did not know where she was. Gradually, the nightmare faded and the terror subsided as her eyes adjusted to the darkness. She was alone. Pamela had long since retreated to her own bedroom. Claire pulled the blanket up to her chin and rolled on to her side.*

"Dad, help me to see this through," she whispered into the dark. She felt no response. Instead, she felt completely alone. She hugged her pillow. The empty void around her mushroomed into a desolate wasteland of endless blackness. No hands reached out to comfort. No

God existed to render hope. A profound fear gripped her, squeezing her heart so tight that she gasped for breath.

"Dad," she pleaded. "I miss you." She still did not feel a response. She steeled herself, slowly taking deep breaths.

"By Christmas," she said. "I promise. We will make them pay."

Pulling the covers tighter, she drew her knees up toward her chest as though to make herself smaller. She prayed for dreamless sleep that did not come.

PUBLIC OFFERINGS

BOOK THREE

Killer Priest

CHAPTER 1

Fort Collins: Clement Home
November 24, 9:25 p.m. Mountain Time

The emptiness. The nagging fear of loss. They scratched at his soul like thorns slowly dragged up and down. But more than his soul ached. The hollow pain touched him physically, relentlessly.

Finally home. Finally able to spend time with his daughter after months away. Then an hour ago, he undermined everything. Fussed at her for no good reason. Because she wanted to spend time alone. He thought she wanted to be away from him. He wanted her to just sit down with him. Watch television. Play Clue or Monopoly. Anything to be together. But Liv just wanted to be by herself, perfectly normal for a fifteen year old, especially one wrestling with a deadly illness. Why couldn't he understand that?

In the middle of his minor eruption, Mel told him to back down. He told her not to get between "me and my daughter."

"Don't undermine me, Mel," he said to his wife under his breath.

"What's with your attitude?" he demanded of Liv. "I just want you to spend some time down here with us. You're all pouts and snorts. And short answers. I'm sick and tired of your short answers. You have no respect. Do you realize the sacrifices I make for you?"

She just stared at him, curled back into her chair, her body turned away from him, tears building in reddening eyes.

"Not that I mind the sacrifices," he continued. "Not that I mind breaking my ass. But I do mind when it's for an ingrate. At least you can show a little respect. Spend a little time with us. Instead, you'd rather hide up in your room, feeling sorry for yourself. Or texting your friends. I'll take your phone away and pull the plug on that damned computer if you don't straighten up."

As his explosion of comments ended their string, he started to hear himself. Started to see that he had frightened Liv, hurt her. Pushed her away when all he wanted to do was draw her closer. She had no idea that she had hurt him. He was Dad, the guy who could always take care of himself and everyone else. She just wanted him home. Wanted to know he was there. She had argued with her mother over it. Now, he had turned on her. Angrily. Hatefully. She felt certain that he hated her.

He recognized all that in the pain in her eyes. He recognized it in her determination not to let tears pour out, tears that brimmed on her eyelids, crying that caused the muscles to tremor around her half-open pout.

"Can I go upstairs now?" she asked in a quiet voice after a thirty second break in her father's tirade.

Mel looked at Dave. He could not answer.

"Yes," she answered for him. "Give us a kiss good night."

Liv bent down and kissed her mother.

"I love you, Liv," Mel said, pressing her hands on the side of her daughter's head.

Liv started to walk by Dave's chair.

"Liv," Mel said.

Liv turned and kissed her father on the forehead.

"I love you, too, Liv," he said.

"Okay," she mumbled.

She went up the stairs. Dave stared at his hands for a moment. "Dear God, Mel. What's wrong with me?"

"You tell me," she quietly demanded.

"I want to be with her more than anything in the world. She and you. Sometimes, she's the only thing that gives me peace."

"Me, too. Please, please, don't undermine that."

"I'm sorry. Will you talk to her?"

"Let's give her some time to deal with it herself. She did lip off. And she has been rude. But you overreacted."

He felt an urge to argue, but found no basis other than pride. "I agree," he said. "Lord knows, she has more to be stressed about than any other kid her age. At least, around here."

"We shouldn't just let the attitude go, though. But we shouldn't treat her like a serial killer either."

"I feel so damned horrible. The poor kid. She's been so strong through all this garbage."

Mel tilted her head slightly and looked hard at him. "Stop beating yourself up, Dave. She'll get over it. And you'll get plenty of time to show her you love her. One person feeling sorry for herself around here is enough."

Now he stood alone on the back deck as Fort Collins autumn chill knocked temperatures down into the low 40s. As he started to shiver, a product of anxiety as much as the air temperature, he folded his arms to ward off the cold. Mel had gone upstairs to console Liv. He awaited her return with a verdict.

He stared at the sky, at the limitless expanse of space. He noticed how empty it felt amidst those billions of stars, how he related only to the darkness and not the distant twinkling glimmers – related to the void. And he feared the void, the hard, hard emptiness of a world without Liv. He only wanted to feel her warmth tonight, hold her like he did when she was still so little, her head tucked into the small of his neck, her hand warm in his, his soul calmed and peaceful, his heart knowing that he brought tranquil security to her, enfolding her in his love, protecting her from that very void.

Tonight, he had launched her into the void all alone. Launched her with his desperation just when she needed him most. She would get over it by morning, leave it behind as one of the quirks of parenthood. Mel assured him of that when she finally returned downstairs after what seemed a lifetime.

It would be different for him. He would always worry about the damage done short and long-term to her self-worth by the degrading tape he drilled into her head.

He would never forget.

CHAPTER 2

November 25, 8:45 a.m. Central European Time

Lovers and tourists crowded the steep Spanish Steps just up the street from the Trevi Fountain where the same lovers might make a wish and toss a coin over their shoulder. Around the corner in an eight-story building covered in ancient plaster and shuttered windows, a group of twelve men met in the dining room of the Ignatian College's residence hall.

The interior of the building belied its plain exterior of thick plastered stone walls. Entering from the noisy hustle and bustle of Rome's hectic streets, a crescendo of quiet besieged the visitor as the heavy oak doors closed behind him. In the center of the building, Italian hawk moths, similar from a distance in appearance and behavior to American hummingbirds, hovered over lavender blooms in a fragrant open courtyard filled with tall junipers and bright flowers.

In a gloomy dining room of tapestries and elaborately carved wood, the ancient furnishings and dark paneling absorbed the final word on much of the information discussed and exchanged. The Apostles of Christus knew that anything less than complete secrecy might alter both their earthly and eternal destinies.

The chairman, a slender man in the red cassock of a cardinal, stirred his tea as he began. "Good fathers, it appears the devil is raising the stakes. We have urgent news from the United States this morning. A priest from our society called the US center warning of a genocidal plan birthed in the mountains of Colorado. Within hours of his call, someone stabbed him to death outside his rectory in Pittsburgh."

He paused and rubbed the side of his long aquiline nose with his manicured index finger. Watching the faces, he waited until the group had absorbed his words. He sipped his tea, peering over the rim of his cup. He continued, "There is strong evidence that a splinter IRA faction is in the middle of this, running security for the operation. Information provided by the murdered pastor aligns with innuendo gathered from pastoral counseling over the last few months."

A young monsignor, destined for much higher office in the church, leaned forward to be seen. An American, Stan Zabinski came from a well-to-do Chicago family. Such men rarely came to the church these days. Different stakeholders within the Vatican bureaucracy all wanted a piece of him, but Christus had won out.

The loss of his fiancée in the World Trade Center bombing in 2001 had affected him deeply, ultimately altering his life plan. On a three-month internship with a brokerage firm there, Patricia called him back in Chicago twice a day expressing how much she missed him and how homesick she was for Chicago. She did not work in the World Trade Center, but had, after months of persistence, secured a job interview there with one of the biggest bond traders on the globe. That morning, she called Stan from the lobby of the North Tower, getting one last pep talk from him before taking the elevator to the 98th floor. She told Stan she loved him and that she could not wait to see him back home in Chicago in just two days. The 8 a.m. interview was supposed to last only 30 minutes. But the interviewer must have been impressed because she was still there when the first plane came in at 8:46. It would be ten weeks before they identified her body in the rubble.

At first he cursed God, completely immersing himself in his work at an investment banking firm, but months of sleepless nights drove him into downtown Chicago's Holy Name Cathedral one morning. Dropping to his knees beneath the massive Romanesque arches of the church, he began an earnest conversation with the Lord. He started praying to be rid of his anger, but then realized he did not need God to end his anger, but instead to help him know at whom to be angry. Jesus, after all, showed anger at the moneychangers in the Temple. It felt like a breakthrough to Zabinski. But he knew the anger and the deep hatred building inside him could not serve God unless he channeled it constructively. He wrote a letter to the Trib in response to an editorial portraying the Afghan invasion and the plan to eradicate Al Qaeda as a panacea for what happened at the World Trade Center. He wrote that poverty, desperation and power provided fertile ground for despots like Osama Bin Laden to build their radical visions. Eliminating that desperation and its breeding grounds, he wrote, presented the only real hope for an ultimate end to terrorism and its champions.

The Trib published the letter. Then, twelve days later, he received a call from an aid to Pamela Thatcher. The great lady herself planned to be in Chicago. Did he have time to meet with her? He did. And that meeting opened his eyes and re-directed his course.

Less than a year later, he matriculated in a seminary. Six years of prior undergraduate and graduate school fast-tracked him there. He also had spent a year as superintendent for one of his father's shopping center developments between undergrad and business school. The hardball of the metro Chicago construction business grounded him in strong street-level experience to complement his academic training. And throughout his time in seminary, he knew Pamela Thatcher kept an eye on him. Contributions from wealthy donors, attributed to his work as an assistant pastor in inner city Chicago, led to his coming to the attention of the leaders of the Church all the way to Rome. A whispered campaign within the hierarchy touted his background and experience, fast-tracking him to assignment in Rome and ultimately his selection by the Apostles of Christus.

"The news is very disturbing, eminence," Monsignor Zabinski said. "So what's the bottom line?

The cardinal bowed his head over his teacup, organizing his thoughts before speaking. "We know," he said, slowly lifting his head, "that there is very likely a plot afoot to commit genocide via some kind of genetic intervention. What we don't know is specifically how that will happen."

"There is one thing of utmost interest," said Father Adam, a trusted American septuagenarian with a slight southern accent and a perpetual smell of cigarettes on his clothes. "This latest information triangulates with rumors we have been hearing for some time, rumors we could not act on because many came in veiled messages culled from the confessional. But…" Father Adam looked hard at Zabinski. "…we know that IRA extremists went to Colorado months ago to protect a research site of some kind. This may be the site in question."

The chair grew impatient. "So how do we get inside this research site?"

"That, eminence, I cannot answer."

"But you do have the answer, Father Adam," Monsignor Zabinski interrupted.

Adam turned to face Zabinski. "I don't understand."

"Our miracle man from Sierra Leone."

The cardinal and the priests knew immediately who the miracle man was. Though kept out of the press, Fr. Jim Reilly's dramatic return to Rome quickly became legend in the halls of the Vatican. Many insiders considered his survival in a coffin over 9 hours at high altitude to be nothing less than direct intervention from heaven. While the kidnappers thought he would survive, scientists consulted by the Vatican said the kidnappers clearly lacked an understanding of what happens to oxygen in that environment. Fr. Jim should have died en route. Vatican priests of all ranks, often embittered and hardened by the politics and administrivia of the Catholic Church's immense bureaucracy, found respite from their anger and ambitions in the miracle of the Irish missionary.

Fr. Adam tensed. "Don't," he said to Zabinski.

"He's no longer your student, Father," the Monsignor said. "The Church needs him. Don't you think the Lord saved him for a reason?"

"I should never have told you. I confided in you as friend and confessor."

"And when I recruited you to join Christus here in Rome, the Holy Spirit laid down a path I could not have foreseen," Zabinski responded. "Fr. Jim doesn't need your protection any more. The Lord has good hold of him."

Zabinski leaned back and scanned the room. "The IRA faction in Colorado," he said. "The one we think may guard the secrets of the genocide – its leader is an old IRA hand named Michael Farley."

Adam's face paled, his jaw slackening as his eyes widened.

"Fr. Adam, do you want to tell them?" Zabinski continued.

"Mike Farley is Fr. Jim's brother," Father Adam said quietly.

"Fr. Reilly's brother?" the cardinal asked looking back and forth at the two men.

Zabinski explained. "Jim Reilly is an alias assumed when the man we know as Fr. Reilly turned his back on the IRA life to enter the seminary. His birth name was Sean Farley. Priests in Ireland have easy access to birth and death certificates, y'know."

The priests around the table leaned in a little further. Only the Lord could provide such a "coincidence." A few blessed themselves with the sign of the cross.

"What's your connection to this man, Father?" The cardinal asked Fr. Adam.

Adam folded his hands and contemplated them before lifting his head and speaking. "He's very special to me. Like a son. He escaped IRA thugs in Ireland as a child. I protected him as my student in the monastery in Georgia for many years."

The cardinal smiled. "Then your charity has blessed us. The Lord saw today's problems coming far in advance. Through you, he prepared part of our solution. Decades ago."

"I hope you're right, Eminence," Fr. Adam said.

"Are the brothers still in touch with one another?" the cardinal asked.

"As Father Adam can tell you, they haven't spoken in years," Zabinski explained. "Fr. Jim Reilly prays every day for his brother Mike to repent. The brother, on the other hand, waits for the priest to tire of holy rollers and return to the field of combat."

"Reilly never really left it, did he?" the cardinal asked rhetorically. "From what I hear, he seems drawn to trouble spots."

"He did leave his own violence behind," Zabinski said. "By his own choice, he has been a missionary in the roughest spots on the globe. And he is completely non-violent."

Father Adam interrupted, "He has given almost every moment to our Lord since he was twelve. Through his guilt, he struggles hard to find God's peace. If anyone can, his brother could destroy that hope for peace once and for all. Fr. Jim's soul would be at risk."

The cardinal focused hard on the old man. "Would he kill again, Father? If he needed to save others. Does he have the will to defend himself and others with lethal force?"

Fr. Adam slowly shook his head from side to side. "I don't really know. I'm certain it's the last thing he wants to face. Jim lives a life of perpetual penance, more so than anyone else I have ever known. He may stand up so bravely to danger because part of him wants to make amends by being martyred."

"So would he pull the trigger or just stand there and die?" Zabinski pressed.

"He would let the Holy Spirit guide him at that moment."

"Let's hope the Holy Spirit talks fast if he should find himself in that situation. In the extreme, the fate of millions could rely on him to transcend his piety and self-pity."

Fr. Adam's face reddened. "Would you have him kill his own brother?" the priest countered.

Zabinski spoke without hesitation, "Of course. We're all brothers. His mission is to help the entire brotherhood of mankind."

"Enough, gentlemen," the cardinal interrupted. "Argument enough for me is that we have been provided by inexplicable miracle with the brother of this enemy. The Lord has singled out Fr. Jim Reilly. It is not for us to fathom the reasons, only to be obedient to God's will."

Twenty minutes later, Zabinski dropped into the chair behind his desk at the Vatican. He pressed his fingers to his forehead. Rage churned inside him as he thought about the hypocritical saintly posturing of some of the ambitious men at the meeting. The pompous pious, he thought. As if an almighty Creator would waste his time on their churchy details. They would learn the price of their misplaced trust. They would learn who provided this "inexplicable miracle."

Smug self-satisfaction replaced rage inside him. Pamela will be pleased, he thought.

CHAPTER 3

Boulder, Colorado: Aldrich Institute
November 26, 7:50 a.m. Mountain Time

Claire's face burned crimson.

"What does she know? How the hell did she find out in the first place?"

She listened as the person on the other end of the phone connection explained himself in a thick Irish brogue.

"You don't go to Walden, Colorado, by accident, Farley," she said heatedly.

She drummed her fingers on the desk as the man continued to explain himself.

"Look, I hired you people because I thought you knew what you were doing," Claire said. "Did she identify the body for the police?"

She nodded as she listened. "Good. That's our girl. Always a team player."

Her eyes widened as a she listened to the man's proposal. "No. Absolutely not. Don't you dare. She did not identify the body. If she was working against us, she would have told that cop. She knew enough to leave it be. I'll take it from here myself. Jennifer can be trusted. She just needs to understand."

She listened as the man concurred, apparently happy to get the monkey off his back.

"Good, we're in agreement. I'll let you know if anything goes wrong."

She hung up without even saying good-bye. She opened her favorites on her phone and tapped Jennifer's name.

"Jennifer? It's Claire."

In her cubicle at Prodeus, Jennifer's eyes widened when she saw the caller ID on her mobile phone. She quickly walked to an empty conference room and closed the door before answering.

"What's up, Claire?" Jennifer struggled to sound casual as she slid into a chair at the conference room table. She had been Claire's biggest defender. Now, she suspected her of having Sheila murdered. Sheila had replied to Jennifer's e-mail at one Friday morning from her desk in the lab, the only place Sheila had e-mail access because the mountain lab prohibited the use of mobile phones for both email and texting for security reasons.

Yet a housekeeper found her body in a motel room in Walden early Friday morning. How and why did she go to Walden between 1 a.m. and 9 a.m.? Jennifer knew she would not have gone willingly. Something happened in the lab that night.

"I'm calling to see if you're okay," Claire said.

"I'm good. You?"

"Sheila left us."

She knows that I know, Jennifer thought. Claire always seemed to know everything. "That's a blow to our effort," Jennifer said.

"Probably never hear from her again. I don't think she was very happy with some of our decisions on the mountain."

Jennifer had to be careful. If Claire did have Sheila killed, the same fate could be in store for Jennifer if she let on that she knew about it. Any form of disloyalty might risk a death penalty.

"Look, Jennifer. I'll cut to the chase."

Jennifer tapped the end of a pen on her desk as she listened.

"We need you back at the Aldrich. You're our best hope to fill in for Sheila."

Jennifer stopped tapping her pen. Her mouth went dry and she felt herself shrivel inside. She could not go back into the lab. That would make her as vulnerable as Sheila. "No, Claire. Find someone else. I have a good deal here. When Prodeus goes public, I'm going to make more money than I ever dreamed of."

"Jennifer. Do you hear yourself? Have you lost sight of the big picture? You helped architect it."

Jennifer's hand tightened around the pen. "I helped with a plan to save lives, not take them."

"I don't know what you think you know, but you don't anything about what has to be done. We will be saving lives for generations."

"I can't do it, Claire. I can't leave. My future's here now. That was the plan of record last time I looked." Jennifer rolled the pen between her fingers.

"If you're counting on a public offering of Prodeus stock, I won't let that happen. You'll make your money with us."

"Not a very good idea," Jennifer said.

"You'll be safe here. Think about it."

"I feel safe at Prodeus." The pen snapped in her grip.

"Make this easy. You don't have a choice. It's my decision. You and the boys at Prodeus exist because I let you exist. I can change that in a minute."

Jennifer quivered as she watched the ink run over her fingers. "Why are you threatening me? I've only been loyal to you."

"I'm not threatening. I'm imploring you. The Aldrich mission is bigger than both of us. We need to do what's best for everyone."

"I'm not going back."

Claire did not respond right away. Jennifer tucked the phone between her chin and her shoulder to hold it while she grabbed a tissue from her purse. She wiped her hand while she waited, trying not to be frantic.

"And what about the next step with the Clements?" Claire asked. "Will you do what you have to do, what you committed you would do if necessary?"

The tissue only smeared the ink on Jennifer's hand. She reached for more, but knocked the tissue box to the floor. When she reached for it, her phone dropped to the floor. Balling her hands into fists, she felt like screaming. Taking deep breaths, she calmed herself and picked up the phone.

"Neither one of us ever really believed it would come to that, Claire," she said.

"We both did."

"I didn't. They're good people."

"What we're doing is bigger than a few good people. With Sheila gone, the outcome's ultimately in your hands. You can break it. And you can fix it."

"If I come back to the Aldrich, I can fix it. But so can Eldridge. I won't do it. Not now. And I won't break anything else for you. I've done enough already."

Claire said nothing.

"You have to understand," Jennifer said. "We're doing this to help people, not hurt them. That's how you taught us."

Still nothing from Claire.

"Please don't do this to me, Claire." This time, Jennifer waited for Claire to say something. She looked at the second hand on the wall clock in the conference room. She watched it tick off 40 seconds and felt like she did not breathe the entire time.

Finally, Claire spoke. "I'm sure you'll re-consider."

The phone clicked as Claire hung up. Jennifer rolled the chair away from the conference table and hunched over, grabbing her legs behind the knees and shaking like a leaf. At times like these, she wished she still had some kind of religion. Who could she turn to? She couldn't very well call her mother in Texas with this one.

Picking up her briefcase, she left the building, reassuring herself that she would be back. She walked to the parking lot in a surrealistic daze. Someone had murdered her closest friend and her mentor had fundamentally just threatened her. Trembling, she dropped her keys on the floor of the car three times before finally shoving them in the ignition.

CHAPTER 4

Freetown: Outside refugee camp
November 26, 3:10 p.m. Greenwich Mean Time

Dust filled the air as the crowd, smelling of sweat and old fruit, gathered around the journalists near the camp's small makeshift market at the main gate. The markets' stalls were lean-to's made of cracked, rotten wood. Scavenged from the remains of buildings destroyed in the fighting in town, the wood formed jigsaw puzzles of irregular shapes nailed together in creative necessity. The items offered by vendors included fruit picked from the nearby jungle, children's clothing items that had been outgrown by the vendors' children, and fresh wood for cooking chopped from a now nearly defoliated field south of the camp. Some of the items, like the rice cooked at a small stand that sold handfuls of it, had been carried in by arriving refugees in the manner traditional in the region: on their heads.

Mariama Karanja, wearing a loose-fitting dark green caftan that kept slipping off her shoulders, stayed back from the journalists and the pleaders surrounding them. Her grip tightened on the hand of her three-year-old daughter Emma. She kept her away from crowds, fearful that close contact might weaken her immune system. That could either make her sick like Sara or make her unable to visit Sara for fear of worsening Sara's condition.

The little girl shuffled her pink plastic sandals in the dust as her mother coaxed her to a shady spot made available by the crowd's rush to tell stories to the journalists. Two slender twin trunks, reaching high above the camp's security fencing, cast flimsy but welcome shade between two of the lean-tos. Many of the native trees had been bulldozed to make room for the camp. Enterprising refugees who sold logs for fuel had long since chopped down those of any substance that remained unscathed by the original clearing effort. The leafy tree over Mariama and Emma had likely survived because of its anorexic trunk and branches.

"You get over here, woman!"

Appearing suddenly from behind the ramshackle medical clinic, the man wore a soiled white t-shirt and khaki shorts. He sucked on a beer can, the foam dribbling down the curly, black stubble on his unshaven chin.

"Where the hell are you?" he shouted. Spotting the object of his rage, he plowed into the crowd. He re-surfaced a moment later, pulling a small woman behind him. Neither came from the Karanjas' village.

"I expected my rice by now. You are a wife. You will do as I ask."

"Let me go, you pig," she yelled, swatting at him.

He slammed her in the back with his forearm and she stumbled to the ground. He kicked her repeatedly in the side, yelling for her to get up.

The frightened Emma clung to her mother, but Mariama knew she could not let the man keep beating his wife. Bending down to her daughter's ear, Mariama said, "You wait here and hold on to this tree, Emma. I have to help that woman."

"No, mama. Don't. He'll hurt you."

Mariama pressed a finger on her daughter's lips and smiled gently. She then turned and walked over to stand beside the cowering woman.

"Sir, leave her be," Mariama demanded, standing up straight with her hands on her hips.

"You be gone, lady, before I do the same to you."

"You don't want to be doing this, Mister."

"The hell you say. This is a private matter."

The man kicked his wife again. Mariama stepped over the woman and into the face of the man.

"If you want to kick someone, you can kick me, Mister. My husband is a paramount chief. Kick me and our entire village will be your enemy."

The man turned his face away, taking another swig of his beer. He used a forearm to wipe sweat off his unshaven face. He faced Mariama now, his eyes widening and his chest swelling with fresh rage.

"Mama!" Emma screamed and ran toward the man.

At the same time, the man swung his beer can around and slammed it into Mariama. Warned by Emma's scream, she ducked just enough to receive the first blow on the shoulder instead of the face. As his next blow came down toward her head, his hips suddenly caved in and he stumbled over the prone, sobbing body of his wife. He fell backward over her. Emma stood huffing on the spot from which she had pushed him. The man started to get back up and the little girl ran into her mother's arms.

He reached down, picked up his wife and threw her to the side. Turning to Mariama, he yelled, "You and your little brat are dead!" He stepped over to a fruit vendor and grabbed his knife. Waving the knife, he charged at Mariama. A faint crack echoed in the distance. Blood exploded from the man's neck, his momentum thrusting him at Mariama's feet. More gunfire followed and the crowd scattered. Mariama and Emma ran toward the infirmary. As they did, the little girl blessed herself. Uncertain as to who was shooting who, Mariama did likewise.

From behind an abandoned car outside the main gate, Jacob took careful aim one more time, but the man did not get back up. Jacob could not let the rest of his family die. They were victims of Hamara's betrayal, just as he was. It was for Hamara and the other village chiefs they had come. For weeks, his commanders drummed into him the story that Hamara had betrayed his people. In his drug-induced state, Jacob became convinced it was true. Today, he again carried an AK-47, given one more chance to prove himself to the thugs that had become his masters.

Using a pick-up truck 20 yards behind Jacob for cover, the teenaged commander yelled, "Go now! Go! Go!"

Fifteen young boys ran toward the gate, rifles nearly as big as them swinging at their sides. Jacob held back. They were to hit and run, returning to the jungle and then coming back again at a different spot, each time firing into the camp for effect.

"What are you doing?" he called to the commander. "This is suicide!"

The teenager, uniformed in a black Nike t-shirt and Old Navy skater shorts, pointed his pistol toward Jacob. "I am the commander here, boy. You do as I say or this time I'll do more than just take away your rifle."

Jacob had seen the teenager kill ruthlessly before. He got up from his knees and ran toward the camp. He mumbled a quick prayer that the Lord protect him and then he started screaming like the other boys.

Several armed men suddenly appeared at the gate. They were camp constabulary, meant to keep order within the camp, not fight rebel units. The boys fired inaccurately while on the run, giving the men inside time to aim. Two boys fell in front of Jacob. He dodged them and ran to the side, taking cover behind a trash dumpster.

From behind safe cover, the young commander and the three other teenagers he brought with him yelled at the boys to keep going, but several of the boys had turned to run away. As one of the retreating boys ran past the pick-up truck where the teens took cover, the commander fired at him, dropping the boy instantly.

The remaining boys reversed course again, yelling that the commander was killing them. One of them fell to fire from the camp.

Jacob peered through his scope and squeezed. A red hole appeared in the rebel commander's forehead, his eyes still wide open as he fell forward. The other three teens looked around in confusion. They did not know where the shot came from.

Jacob fired again. Another teen fell. Now the other younger boys, all pinned down behind varying forms of cover from palm trees to trash piles, watched Jacob. They saw what he was doing. Several of them now turned their rifles in the same direction as Jacob's was pointed. The remaining teens died in a flurry of bullets.

"Follow me!" Jacob yelled as he ran up the hill into the jungle.

Confused by what they had seen, the constabulary held their fire while they watched the boys run off.

Back in the jungle, Jacob rallied the boys in the deep foliage. They were all panting, all frightened.

"We have no friends," he said. "And now we can't go back to the rebels."

"We can say the commander and his friends were killed by the constabulary," one of the boys suggested.

"Even if they believe us and even if one of you doesn't tell, how long do you think it will be before another stupid commander asks us to kill ourselves?" Jacob said. "Look what just happened. They don't care about us. They use us."

Consensus quickly surfaced among the group. Though Jacob had become their peer leader, one of them suggested formally electing him their captain. All but three of the surviving 11 boys voted for him.

"So, sir, Chief Karanja still lives," one of the dissenters said, his tone surly. "Will we return to the camp to finish our job and kill him?"

Jacob glared at the boy and then grabbed him by the hair. "No. Did you see those guns? They're ready for us. We need to be smarter about where we attack."

"All I want is food and a good place to sleep," said another boy.

Jacob peered at him and then back at the boy he had by the hair. "Any other questions?" he said.

Obstinate with his pride on the line now, the boy challenged, "What about your father?"

"He's my business," Jacob fumed. "Mine only."

Suddenly, the now familiar drug-fired rage rose inside him. He hefted his rifle into the air and hit the boy in the head with the stock.

Another boy moved toward Jacob to keep him from striking again. Jacob turned toward him, his angry eyes discouraging the boy from taking another step. On the ground, the first boy moaned, blood matting on the side of his head.

Jacob crouched beside him. "I heard that moan," he said. "I guess that means you've changed your vote."

The other boys laughed nervously, even the wounded dissenter.

CHAPTER 5

Prodeus: Ed Hepp's office
November 26, 8:45 a.m. Mountain Time

Chunky forearms lay across his desk in front of him, beefy fingers interlaced in folded hands to hide their tremors, Ed Hepp peered over the top of his bi-focals at Dave. Behind him rolled the pastoral backdrop of a snow-covered horse pasture and the white-capped peaks of the Front Range.

"I'm going to do you a favor, Dave. How about I authorize you to get rid of one of your biggest headaches? What if I tell you I want you to fire Jennifer Winter?"

Dave lifted a disbelieving eyebrow. "How's that a favor? She's an enormous asset."

"She's a pain in the butt and you know it. C'mon, Dave. It's no secret that she's got a thing for you. Can't be comfortable."

Dave's face turned pale. "What's that have to do with keeping her or not?"

"You two were seen in the boardroom after the impromptu meeting last week. I'm told that you were very clear in saying no."

"How were we seen?"

Ed threw his beefy hands up and looked to the ceiling. "The door was open. You think the employees around here don't follow the execs like we're celebrities. Of course, they do. And Dave…" He leaned forward and whispered, "Jennifer's little escapades with you make for great stories."

"I can't believe this. So we're going to fire the kid because she came on to me."

Ed contorted his face. "No. I thought that would be an enticement, though. You're firing her because she pissed off Claire McQuaid. And the main justification for her existence has been her relationship with Claire."

Dave's belly gnawed at him. His call to Claire did this. He protected Sheila, but underestimated Claire's ability to reach into Prodeus. Claire did not want him or anyone to know about the Aldrich HIV research. She was delivering a message to both Dave and Jennifer while closing the door on Liv. He slipped back in his seat and looked out the window past Ed.

"How will we cover her work for the launch?"

The additional workload and disruption risked by her departure would be both stressful and risky, he thought. And thus far, Sheila had not found a way to get the password to him for her newest cloud folder. Jennifer could be his only line on that. Dave felt certain she knew more than she had already said.

"Hire somebody else."

"We're not going to find someone and train him or her in a few weeks. Jennifer gets this stuff. She understands the code, the statistics, and the trial guidelines."

"So do you."

"I don't have enough hours in the day as it is."

"Find them."

And kiss my marriage good-bye once and for all, he thought. It would be months before he could do more than catch a few hours' sleep at home. "Did Claire say why she was pissed?"

"Said Jennifer's too pig-headed, that she almost killed the negotiations last month. She complimented you, by the way. You, my friend, are the reason that she rolled over for us."

"Ed," he said, looking back to his boss, "that's not the way it was at all..."

"Dave? I'm surprised you're fighting me on this. Sounds like maybe you really do having something going with Jennifer."

"Hell, no. She's just an important asset around here. We can't afford to lose her. Not now."

"McQuaid is pissed with her. Middleton can't stand her. She's trying to wreck your marriage. Am I missing something?"

Dave exhaled in exasperation. "Yes, Ed. You are."

"Mind telling me what?"

"I do. I do mind."

"Unless you plan to fire her, you don't have a lot of choice."

Dave's mind whirled. Ed's heavy-handedness had him seething. He tried to calm himself, to think this through. Whether he fired her or not, McQuaid's attitude would ultimately push Jennifer out. Unless Dave just stood by her. How would that look? If Mel even had a clue about Jennifer's come-on's, odds on keeping the marriage intact imploded. Not to mention that she would kill him for not firing her when he had the chance. And if he did fire her, Mel would be all over him for living at the office and on the road. A complete no-win situation. But, with Sheila not communicating, Jenn's insight on the prospect of a cure for Liv would trump with Mel. That would transcend everything – if Jennifer was telling the truth.

So Jennifer ends up on the street for her apparent willingness to risk her relationship with McQuaid to help Liv. He could not let her go down for trying to help his daughter. Mel might even understand that.

"I need complete confidentiality on this, Ed."

"Sure."

"McQuaid's pissed at Jennifer because she thinks she told me the Aldrich has a cure for AIDS."

Ed tilted his head, narrowed his eyes. "What?"

Dave spoke slowly. "Liv's tested HIV positive,"

"Liv? Your daughter? How the heck did that happen?"

Squeezing his lips together, Dave shook his head. "We don't know."

"She's not that old, is she?"

"Fifteen."

Ed said nothing for a moment, his eyes boring into his top VP and likely successor. He tapped his hands on the arms of his chair.

Shifting in his chair uneasily, Dave filled the silence. "I told Claire that I'd heard the Aldrich had a cure in the oven. She denied it, but she insisted that Jennifer had told me something."

"Did she?"

"She hinted."

Ed looked at him questioningly.

"Okay, she did," Dave said. "But she was very careful. She did not say it was a certainty."

"I understand Claire's position. If one of my former employees broke a confidentiality agreement, I'd be pissed off, too. Why didn't Claire just tell me that's what this was about?"

"Maybe because that would be admitting that there is a cure in the works."

"Wouldn't that be good news for Liv?" Ed asked.

"I hope so, but I don't understand why she wouldn't tell me about it."

"C'mon, Dave. She has confidentiality issues, too. She can't tell you. I'll bet she'd probably love to help Liv."

"Why?"

"I know her. She's full of passion for her work. She lives to help people. And she thinks the world of you. But she's also a professional who knows you have to live by a set of rules to stay in position to help."

Dave sighed.

Ed continued, "Doesn't change the fact that Jennifer broke confidentiality and put Claire, and you I might add, in a very awkward spot."

Ed let this sink in while Dave pondered the mountains and considered. Jennifer thought she was helping. Plus Dave had a complete confidentiality package with the Aldrich. At worst, it was a judgment call. Firing her was inappropriate, but Ed seemed to have made up his mind, probably goaded on by comments made by Middleton. Middleton had jumped at every opportunity to get one-on-one with Ed recently, actively trying to work around Dave.

"I'm not going to fire her over this..."

Ed interrupted, "Assuming that you have the right reason for Claire's attitude."

"Right. But even without that, we're too far into this with too much at stake to cause that kind of disruption now."

"Okay, Dave. It's your call. You're important to this company. I promised you I would never micro-manage you. I'm not going to start with this issue. That's what I'll tell Claire."

Dave tapped his palms on the side of his thighs as he stood up. "Thanks, Ed. Maybe she'll tell you what's really going on."

"Maybe."

Dave started out the door.

"One other thing, Clement," Ed said. "Be a little more discreet in your meetings with this woman. No more one-on-one's in your office after most of us have gone home. And slug her next time she tries to hug you or even touch you."

The two men exchanged understanding grins.

As soon as Dave left the office, Hepp dialed Claire. He knew she would not be happy. He could barely get his fingers to hit the right buttons on the dial pad. Every moment of every day had become an effort. He did not have much time left to be effective. He and Claire agreed that Dave was still the best choice. Yet they sure as hell could not afford to let him blow it all on them now.

CHAPTER 6

Cameron Pass: Aldrich High Altitude Facility
November 27, 2:40 p.m. Mountain Time

A swirling dust of snow flung a biting chill at Mike's exposed face and hands. He ducked, a forearm over his eyes for protection as he ran to the door of the chopper. In a tight brown leather coat with faux fur collar, Claire reached out to him with a gloved hand as she stepped down on to the heated helipad. The two walked quickly to the building, greeted by warm air as they entered.

"So, Farley, do you have things under control up here?"

"Yes, ma'am," Mike replied. "The boys love their work."

"No repercussions?"

"None," he said, his Irish lilt still strong after nearly a decade based in the United States.

"How are you keeping the lid on?"

"No one gets to see local papers for starters, print or online. And no one's allowed off premises. We justified that with the run-up to the late December benchmark."

Claire pulled off her gloves as she walked, her two-inch leather boot heels clicking on the concrete floor. "No whining about being here Thanksgiving?"

"Sure, but they're startin' to understand that this is a bit like a military operation. We let 'em write and talk on the phone. Keyword eavesdroppin' is workin' well."

"Did you find any infractions?"

"Minor stuff. Nothin' deliberate. Nothin' threatenin' to us. Not like Sheila."

As they entered Claire's office with its enormous window filled with white mountain peaks and snow, the aroma of fresh brewed coffee filled their senses. On one wall, an enormous stone fireplace blazed.

"Feels like home," Claire commented. "Thank you, Mike."

They sat in two overstuffed wingbacks beside the fire and Mike poured the coffee which sat on an end table.

"I've not done a thing about Jennifer. Are ya sure that's what ya want? Nothin'?"

Claire leaned forward to put cream in her coffee. She drank it black in Boulder, but for some reason she liked it with cream up here at 10,000 feet "So far. She should never have learned about Sheila. So now she's frightened. And pissed off. She's been away from the big picture for too long. Not enough perspective."

"She thinks she could end up like Sheila if she comes back," Mike said.

"If she turns on us, she could end up like Sheila whether or not she comes back. She was completely insubordinate when I spoke with her on the phone. She could put the whole project in jeopardy."

"You're a cold one, Claire. Your practically raised those two."

Claire sipped her coffee and then spoke over the rim. "I'd have myself killed if I thought I was impeding the mission. It's all about the mission."

"I'll take that as fair warning. So how do you want me to handle it?"

"She still has work to do with the Clements. Now more than ever. She's close to Dave. What if she tells him about Sheila? We need him – probably more than her - and we have to be able to control him. She has to finish tightening the circle around him. Make sure she does."

"You have my word."

"Did you crack Sheila's latest cloud upload?"

"No. It's password protected, but she didn't give Clement the password either."

"Hack it and find out what's in it."

"It's in the Amazon cloud, ma'am. It's tough to crack. Then, if we do hack it, we're inviting scrutiny from a very large corporate animal."

"What's that mean?"

"We shouldn't poke the bear. The risk associated with the potential scrutiny far outweighs the likelihood of Clement hacking her password."

Claire steepled her fingers and thought for a moment. "Okay," she said. "Do it your way. Leave it alone. In any event, if Jennifer gets her job done, we'll have Dave well in hand before he figures it out."

"If he figures it out. Meanwhile, we can hope that Jennifer's a good actor and pulls off the next stage."

"Don't rely on her acting. Make her believe."

"Very interesting." Mike took a swig of his coffee. "You're tough on your protégés. I'll handle her personally."

"For the greater good," she said.

"Yes ma'am. The team will be waiting for you in the executive boardroom at 10:30. I'll go make sure things are ready."

Reaching into her small briefcase, she said, "Not yet. I have something for you."

"Oh," he said, sitting back down. "What's that?"

"There's a priest in Rome that seems a bit disenchanted with the priesthood."

"Ya found him?" Mike responded. "I'll be damned."

"That you will," Claire said without cracking a smile. She spread a handful of pictures on the coffee table. One showed Father Jim Reilly on the Pont Sant Angelo with a short, slender brunette. Another showed him pressing lire into the hand of a known member of the Red Brigade. Another placed him at a café bar chatting with the same dark-headed woman as in the first shot.

"It is him. Would ya look at that! My little brother. All dressed in his black priestly splendor."

"Pay more attention, Mike."

Mike studied the three pictures again. Things began to dawn on him. "Why is he with this woman?"

"Good question. Do you recognize the guy he's paying off?"

"No."

"Francesco Vitello. Red Brigade."

"Mother of mercy."

"Priesthood's over for him. He's trying to find you and get back to the life. The skinny girl is one of mine. She's kept us informed. He thinks he's in love with her so he tells her everything. Or at least he did. We had her break up with him to further disillusion him. She told him she could not have an affair with a priest. Said she needed something out in the open of which she could be proud. He's crestfallen. In complete denial."

"Can we get him here?"

"He paid to find out you're in the States. We'll get him that far. The rest is up to you."

"The mountain air will do him good."

Claire beamed. "You owe me, Farley," she said.

"You're a darlin', Ms. McQuaid," he said as he got up to hug her. She patted his back perfunctorily.

As Mike left the office, her eyes stared right through the back of him. When he shrugged his shoulders as though to shake her off, she knew she had him under control.

From the wingback, Claire opened a small compartment and pressed three buttons in succession. The first closed and latched the door. The second caused great metal blinds to slide down over the massive windows. And the third opened a large panel in the opposite wall, disclosing a 65" HDTV plasma screen. A menu appeared on the screen. She navigated it until she found what she wanted.

A few moments later, she renewed her resolve as she watched the growing video montage of terror.

CHAPTER 7

Prodeus Headquarters: Office of Human Resources Manager
November 29, 10:15 a.m. Mountain Time

No smile crossed Judy Baines' thin lips as she guided Jennifer into her office. As the human resources manager for Prodeus, she seemed well suited for the company's wet work.

"What's up, Judy? You said paperwork. I'm really busy today, y'know."

"Sit down, Jennifer."

Judy, her light brown hair tucked in a tight bun, waved to a low chair in front of her desk as she sat in a much higher one behind it. As soon as Jennifer sat down, she started speaking, just like the training manual said.

"Jennifer, we're terminating your employment as of today."

Jennifer's neck popped forward. "You're what?"

"Your employment is terminated."

Jennifer's mouth rounded with an unformed word.

Judy continued. "If you help us with transition information the balance of today, you'll receive two months' severance."

Jennifer massaged her temples as though to stimulate a change in reality. "My God, Judy," she said. "It's the day after Thanksgiving."

Judy maintained eye contact, but did not respond.

"What if I don't?" Jennifer said after a long pause.

"Don't what?"

"Sign."

"You get nada," Judy said.

"You can't do this. Where's Dave Clement? I don't even know what you think is wrong."

"Colorado is an employment at-will state. We can do whatever we want."

"This is unbelievable. What the hell is this about? Clement did this. That bastard."

Judy remained very even, her lips pursed, eyes narrow. She wrote down each of Jennifer's comments. Ed had warned Judy that Jennifer would blame Dave because she tried unsuccessfully to compromise his marriage.

"Jennifer, I need a decision from you. If you don't give me one, I'll assume you want to leave immediately and that there will be no severance."

Jennifer responded with very crisp enunciation. "This company needs me. Without me, we don't get this far."

Judy remained focused, sitting perfectly still. "Your decision, Jennifer?"

"Really? That's all you can say?"

"Yes," Judy said, implacable.

"Are you people friggin' crazy!?" Jennifer's eyes widened, her face redder than her hair. "How will I pay my rent? You don't want to make me desperate. It won't go well." Jennifer waited for a reaction. She received none. Judy just stared at her. "I need some time to think. Let me go grab a coffee."

"This isn't optional. There is no time to think. I need a decision now."

Jennifer shook her head. She took a long, deep breath. "I need to talk to Dave first."

"One of the conditions of the severance is that you not talk to Dave without appointment. And not at all today. It's in the agreement."

"This won't hold up."

"Sign it or leave with nothing."

"What else does it say?"

"There's a confidentiality clause that says you cannot bad mouth anyone in the company after you leave…"

"You can't make me agree to that."

"I can if you want a severance package."

"Then I want more severance."

"Not negotiable."

Jennifer said nothing. The HR director let the silence linger.

"What else? What else is in it?"

"It specifically restricts harassment of company executives. You forfeit the entire package if you call Dave today, for example."

"I can't even talk to him? That's bullshit."

"Take it or leave it. You can make an appointment with him through his assistant. You can call her next week."

"So he is behind this. That's why he's off today. He didn't have the guts to face me. I really overestimated him."

Judy continued, "There's an acknowledgment of the non-compete clause you signed when you joined the company. We've added a specific exemption should you return to the Aldrich. Then…"

An exception for the Aldrich. For the first time, it registered with Jennifer that Claire may have had a role in this. Maybe she was trying to force her hand. Or arrange for her to meet the same fate as Sheila. Sheila had crossed Claire and "lost her job." Jennifer did not want to cross Claire.

She signed the document.

CHAPTER 8

Street Outside Clement Home: Sunday after Thanksgiving
December 1, 4:17 p.m. Mountain Time

Jennifer turned off the engine. She pulled the black fleece blanket over her pale, freckled legs, carefully tucking it under her thighs to minimize the risk of any warmth escaping. The afternoon's freezing drizzle glistened icily on the black pavement outside as the streetlights flickered on.

It had been a long weekend and a long day. She had hung out on Walnut Street in Old Town Fort Collins for hours. She started early – couldn't sleep – with cinnamon toast and over easy eggs at the Silver Grille Café, followed by smoked earl grey tea at Happy Lucky Teahouse. After that she browsed the shelves at Old Firehouse Books in the same historic former firehouse structure as the teahouse, its original observation tower and brickwork carefully preserved. For a time, she stared almost catatonically at the brass firepole in the middle of the bookstore, wondering where the boarded over hole at the top went. The anxiety and rage built up in her, growing hour by hour as she worked up her nerve. She finally pulled on to the Clement's street just before three. She knocked on their door and waited several minutes, finally recognizing that the Clements were out. So she waited in the car, turning the engine over every now and then to run the heat. She turned the ignition off within a few minutes each time to keep her exhaust from attracting attention.

They can't stay out all day, she thought. They must have a lot of leftover turkey and dressing to eat at home. Pulling her oversized down jacket more tightly around her, she shifted in the driver's seat.

She sorted through the story. It had to be Dave. He never took a day off. Except for Friday. He did it to avoid facing her. Well, he was going to face her now. She needed to tell him that he could shove his severance package. Except that she needed the money. Without it, she almost had to risk going back to the Aldrich.

She reached over to the cup holder and picked up her travel mug. It was silver and made of thermos material, meant to stay hot in the coldest weather. She sipped. Even it was getting cold sitting out here all afternoon.

"We'll have our little showdown, Dave," she said out loud in the car. She pondered the script. He would say he could not re-hire her. She would tell him that he had no choice. He could not afford to risk losing his own job right now, not this close to getting the brass ring – the ring he now chose to deny her. No, that was not his big issue. The big issue would be a way to make his precious Liv well.

She tapped her fingertips together. Where the hell were they?

Dave glanced over his shoulder to Liv, careful to keep one eye on the slick road.

"And, Mom, Daddy," she gushed. "That was sooo funny when the Senator found Adam Sandler behind that statue in the Capitol. He's old but he's funny."

The parents laughed as they recalled the scene. Mel had maneuvered out from under her shoulder belt and leaned against Dave's shoulder. "It's been really nice having you back this weekend," she said, caressing his arm.

Dave had successfully managed to stay off voice mail and e-mail since his Friday morning run. And he had, with Ed Hepp's encouragement, even disabled his text messaging. As the weekend progressed, being out of touch became easier. When Nick's messages came in, he listened to them. They were too important. The temptation to call back for more detail pressed on him, but he resisted. He found that after an hour or so, the compulsion to dial eased considerably, especially since Nick provided nothing but good news. The yields had improved dramatically since Friday morning and he expected to get a message tonight that the entire Aldrich shipment was out the door.

"It's nice being back," he said. "Thanks for putting up with me, you guys."

"You mean this weekend, Daddy? Or all the time? All the time is the problem, not this weekend."

"Well, I'm going to have to just make sure that things are better all the time then." Dave reached back and they clasped hands.

Mel thought a small prayer of thanks.

Headlights suddenly flashed in Jennifer's eyes. She gulped a mouthful of coffee as she slipped lower into her seat. Peering along the bottom edge of the windshield, she saw a Volvo roll down the street and turn into the Clements' driveway.

Doubts flashed through her mind. What if they don't answer the door or what if he slams it on me? Too late to second guess. She was committed.

"Showtime," she said out loud. Without putting on her safety belt or even taking the time to get erect in her seat, she turned the engine over and drove the half block to the driveway. She jerked the car to a stop, flinging the door open a split second later. Ahead of her in the garage, she saw the red brake lights of the Volvo go off. Liv climbed out the back door and Mel exited the front. They unloaded packages while Dave climbed out the driver's side.

"Hey, you!" Jennifer yelled.

The entire family turned.

Jennifer churned up rage as she stumbled across the icy driveway in her smooth loafers. "I mean you!" she shouted, violently pointing her finger in the air as she wobbled on precarious footing.

Liv recognized her first. "Daddy, I think it's a woman from your office."

Peering out from the garage light into the darkness, Dave called, "Jennifer?"

"That's right, you sonuvabitch!" I really like that word, she thought just before her feet spun out of control, flipping her into the air.

"Watch out!" Mel exclaimed too late.

The three family members, all in hiking boots with good tread, hurried out to the fallen woman. Dave dropped down to one knee and reached under a shoulder to help her up. He and Liv started to pull her up by one arm each.

"Wait," Mel said, placing a hand on each of their shoulders. "She may be hurt." Mel placed her face in front of the fallen woman's. "Are you okay?"

Jennifer blinked her eyes. She had landed first on her butt, but then bounced back hard on to her upper back and head. Dizzy, she looked up at Mel, Dave and Liv. Her eyes drifted to Dave. She wanted to yell, but the fall had knocked the fire out of her. Getting hurt was not part of the script. Improvise, she thought.

"I'll sue you, you bastard," she whispered woozily.

Mel fixed a puzzled gaze on Dave. "Dave, what's going on?" she demanded.

Dave held up the palm of his free hand. "Not a clue," he said.

"He betrayed me, Mel," Jennifer grumbled. "You can't trust him."

Mel looked back and forth at her husband and Jennifer. "What's going on, Dave?"

Liv's eyes widened.

"I have no idea" he said. "Let's take her inside to the couch and get her an ice pack. It feels like she has a big goose egg on the back of her head…"

After getting Jennifer situated on the family room couch, Dave approached Mel in the kitchen.

"Mel, I swear I don't know what this is about."

"Is she sleeping?" Mel asked calmly.

"She's been acting a little strange at the office…"

"Is she sleeping, Dave?"

He folded his arms and bowed his head. "I think so," he said, and then looked back toward Jennifer, gesturing with his hands. "Yes. Yes. She's sleeping. See."

"Do you think that's such a good idea?"

"We can wake her up and send her home at any time."

"Not with a concussion," Mel said. She had always understood that it was dangerous to sleep right after a concussion.

Dave walked back to Jennifer. Shaking her, he said, "Jennifer. Jennifer. C'mon, Jennifer. Wake up."

Her eyes fluttered open.

"Jennifer, sit up. You have to stay awake."

"What for?"

As Dave held his hand over her eyes, Jennifer swatted at him.

"What are you up to?" she demanded in an unsteady voice.

He pulled his hand away from her eyes and then put it back again. He did this twice.

"Her pupils are dilating and closing," he said to Mel who was now over his shoulder. "Probably not a concussion."

Jennifer leaned back away from him and peered through squinty eyes that struggled to adjust to the house lights. "Why, Dave? Why'd you do it?"

"Do what?" Mel asked her husband.

"Don't play stupid, Mel. You probably put him up to it."

"Up to what?" Dave asked.

"Oh, my head," Jennifer moaned, leaning her forehead against his chest to Mel's dismay.

"Dave," she continued in a little girl voice. "Why did you fire me?"

He pulled back and gaped at her. "What are you talking about?"

She pulled away. Her eyes narrowed and she whispered through clenched teeth, "You're a damned coward. You take your first day off in aeons and have Judy Baines do your dirty work. Did you think I would just roll over because you were out? Why wouldn't you face me?"

Jennifer dropped back on to a pillow, her eyes closed in pain, the back of one hand pressed to her forehead.

Dave stood up and looked at Mel. "I have a bad feeling I know what's going on." Routinely, he walked over to the fireplace. He turned on the gas switch. With a soft poof, the fire surged around the artificial logs. Pieces quickly fell in place in his mind.

"I should never have taken Friday off," he said, rubbing a palm across his forehead. "My place is at the office."

In the kitchen, Liv's ears perked up. She slowly placed the potholder down on the counter. She had been so pleased that her Dad had finally taken a day off and spent it with the family. Now, he said he regretted it.

From across the room, Mel saw tears well up in her daughter's eyes. "What is it, Liv?"

She shrugged. "I don't know. Hormones probably. I'm just being silly. I probably should go wash my face."

Out the side of his eye, Dave saw an emotional Liv head for the foyer. "Honey, you all right?" he asked.

"I'm fine," she said without looking at him as she hurried down the hallway for the stairs. "Just very tired."

"It was a great weekend," he called to her.

"Me, too," she called. Then as she ran up the stairs, she mumbled in a stage whisper that everyone heard, "I hate that woman."

Mel came over and sat down on the edge of the couch. She put an icepack behind Jennifer's head. "Why did you think I put him up to it?"

"Jealous wife," Jennifer responded.

"What do I have to be jealous about?"

"Nothing, that's the problem."

Mel's eyes narrowed.

"He's very committed to you, Mel," Jennifer said, trying to recover through the pain. "I've just been grasping at straws all weekend trying to understand why he did this. He didn't even have the balls to do it himself."

"We were both set up," Dave said, leaning across a rigid Mel. "I didn't fire you, Jennifer."

"No, you didn't," she countered, wincing in pain. "Judy did. That was your plan."

"I swear I didn't know anything about it."

Mel placed a hand on Dave's leg. "Close your eyes, Jennifer."

Jennifer did as she was asked.

"I already checked her for a concussion," Dave said.

"I'm re-checking." Mel counted ten in her head. "Now open them," she said. Mel studied her. "Your pupils are reacting a little slowly. You might have a mild concussion. We should go to the hospital just to be safe."

"No. They'll just make me wait for hours and put me through expensive tests."

"Then you need to rest. Your head has to be killing you. We can sort out all this drama later. Lay here for now."

"Thank you."

"We'll wake you every little while just to be safe," Mel said. "Sounds like you've had a rough couple of days. A little rest might be just what you need."

"She's right," Dave echoed. "Get some sleep. I'll figure out a way to straighten this out."

Jennifer closed her eyes and drifted off quickly. Dave and Mel walked across the family room and sat in the kitchen.

"So what do you think happened?" Mel whispered.

"Claire McQuaid."

Forty-five minutes later, Jennifer awoke and stumbled over to the kitchen table where Dave and Mel sat in whispered conversation.

"I didn't want to tell you because I was still hoping to hear from Sheila," he said.

"So Jennifer is our new way in," Mel said. "Doubtful in light of how Ed and Claire have discarded her."

Mel saw Jennifer approaching. "You shouldn't be up," Mel said.

"Maybe not," Jennifer replied.

"How are you feeling?" Dave asked.

"Like I've been run over by a truck."

"How about an iced tea?" Mel offered. "It's decaf."

"Thank you."

Jennifer sat at the table while Mel got up to pour the tea. Dave looked at Jennifer and she looked away. There was only silence until Mel returned to the table with the tea.

Jennifer took the glass, and then peered at Mel between narrowed eyes, her lips tight.

"Have you put two and two together yet?" Mel asked.

"I think so. It doesn't make sense. If Dave was behind it, he wouldn't deny it. I know him well enough to know that's not his style."

"Honest to a fault," Mel said with a forced smile.

"I heard you talking," Jennifer said. "There is a vaccine, a vaccine that works in later stages of the disease. I didn't tell Dave everything before."

"How do you know that?" Mel asked.

Jennifer's fingers latched on to the edge of the table. Her head pulsed painfully; she felt like it had swollen to twice its normal size.

"You okay?" Mel asked, leaning forward and taking Jennifer's forearm to steady her.

"Just a little woozy. But I'm all right. Sheila, the lead researcher that Dave contacted, and I are very close."

"Then she really meant she had a cure?"

"She meant what she said. I've known her for years. We're close and we have a bond. She'd never mislead me. And she isn't somebody who exaggerates things."

"Why would Claire McQuaid keep it a secret?" Mel asked. "Why would she not want Liv, the daughter of her so-called partner, to have it?"

Jennifer shrugged.

"Maybe she thinks we could somehow cause competitive problems if I knew about it," Dave offered.

"No way," Jennifer said. "Do you realize how many companies and government bodies have tried to solve this riddle? Claire knows she's on solid ground."

"Well, she's protecting something for some reason. Hepp asked me to fire you a week ago. I told him no. He told me Claire wanted you out. I told him I wouldn't do it so he backed off."

Jennifer squinted astonishment through eyes narrowed to minimize the light inbound to her throbbing head. "Why would Claire want me fired?"

"You were hurting the relationship or something. I assumed it was about my conversation with her about the vaccine."

"You betrayed her trust," Mel said, her eyes focused with concern on Jennifer.

"No, it's not like that. She trusted my judgment and Prodeus has a confidentiality agreement with the Aldrich. Because Prodeus doesn't have a business need-to-know, it may be a little out of bounds, but it's more of a gray area than black and white."

Mel turned to Dave. "I'd say your job's not very secure either. When's McQuaid going to tell Hepp to fire you?"

"I'll be fine," he responded. "I think I just somehow touched a big nerve with this AIDS cure."

"Looks like it," Mel said. "You have to find out what's going on. Liv needs help sooner, not later. Why haven't we heard any more from Sheila?"

Jennifer looked away.

"It's pretty plain," Dave said. "Sheila's gone underground on all this. She's in the lab. She's seeing the paranoia first hand."

"You have to get me back in Prodeus, Dave. Claire's being ridiculous."

"And Ed's being a coward. I'll sit down with him tomorrow and see if I can get him to back off," Dave said.

"You can't tell him we talked," Jennifer said.

"Why not?"

"They made it a condition of my severance package that I not speak with you."

"Well, he's going to have to tell me. He knows I'm not going to be happy about this. I'll just insist that he reinstate you."

"He won't do it," Jennifer countered. "The man has too much at stake with Claire. Remember, they're the two that fundamentally put Prodeus in place. And she sits on your board. He cannot afford to undermine his relationship with her. For that matter, neither can you."

Dave sat back, digesting Jennifer's thoughts. "Well, if you're right, I'll help you find another job."

"That's the least of my worries."

"Seems big enough," Mel said. "What else are you dealing with?"

Jennifer, hands folded in her lap, bent her head over the edge of the table. "I think they're going to kill me," she said, looking Mel in the eye.

"They what?"

Jennifer lifted her head and said, "They're going to kill me. I think Claire is going to have me killed."

Mel's eyes flashed disbelief, but Dave studied Jennifer's unflinching eyes.

"That hit on the head must have knocked a few things out of whack," Mel said.

Jennifer placed a hand over her eyes. Tears began dribbling down the side of her face as her reserve melted away. She looked up. "What if I told you she's already had someone else killed?"

The couple exchanged glances. "You know this?" Mel asked.

"Know is a tricky word. I do know that someone is dead and I do know that the circumstances are very mysterious. And I know that Claire has not acknowledged the woman's death or disappearance to me, even though she knows we were close."

A jolt of alarm raced through Dave. "Woman?"

Jennifer looked at him through red-rimmed eyes.

Mel was the first to say it. "Sheila?"

"Sheila," Jennifer replied.

"What the hell?" Dave said.

"She pissed someone off big-time. She'd been pushing to get the AIDS vaccine into clinical trials. They gave her a lot of resistance."

"Oh come on," Mel said. "You don't think that - "

"It adds up," Dave interrupted." It explains the absence of contact. Even at Evan's memorial service, Sheila seemed committed to help and stay in touch."

Mel slipped back in her chair. "That poor woman."

"Do you know for certain that she's dead?" Dave asked.

"Pretty certain. Cop in Walden gave me a unique description of a woman found murdered in a motel up there."

"Why would Sheila be in a Walden motel?"

Jennifer shrugged and shook her head.

"Assuming it is Sheila, why do you think Claire is somehow involved?"

"AIDS cure is central to Claire's strategy and Sheila may have been getting ready to jeopardize it."

"By talking to me?"

"I'm not even sure Claire knows about that. What I do know is that Sheila confided accusations to me about the drug discovery effort. They would have done serious damage if they went public. Claire has been adamant that the mere existence of the AIDS cure be kept completely confidential."

"What kind of accusations?"

"It's complicated."

"Whatever they are, I don't see Claire as a killer."

"I don't know for certain, but if it's not her, it's her people, someone on her team at the lab. She has ex-IRA running security."

"Ex-IRA?" Dave said. "I didn't know that."

"Brought 'em in two years ago. I dated the chief for a while – ."

"Mike Farley?"

"Yes. Ironically, Sheila introduced us. We really liked each other, but he could be scary."

"I met him. He's the one that separated Sheila and I at the Conger service. Do you still see him?"

"No. Not in a long time."

"Wait," Mel interrupted, "Why wouldn't Claire want a cure out there?"

Jennifer shook her head as she spoke. "Sheila didn't get that at all. The only thing I could get from her was an analogy to Nazi Germany."

"Jews?" Dave quizzed.

"You're close. Holocaust. Genocide."

"How?" Dave said.

"Where?" added Mel.

"Not a clue," Jennifer said. "That's all she would tell me. I think she was trying to shield me until she knew more. She and I planned to meet to discuss the cure and how to make it available for people like your daughter. She probably would have told me more then. But she never showed up for the meeting."

"How do you know for sure it's Sheila they found?"

"Cop told me about a tattoo on the dead woman's inner thigh. Rocky 28714. That's Sheila's tattoo and I don't think anyone but she and I knew about it."

Dave wrote it down on a napkin and studied it.

"It's the phone number of an ex," Jennifer said. "Some twisted revenge thing after way too much to drink one night."

"Okay," Dave said at last. "Let's say this dead woman is actually Sheila. I still don't get the connection to Claire. She's about saving lives. Not taking them. Sheila is a protégé and a critical asset to the Aldrich team."

"I can't guarantee the connection to Claire, but I can pretty much warrant the link to the lab."

"How?"

"I know that Sheila was at her computer at 11 p.m. Thursday night - "

"How would you know that?" Mel interjected.

"She told me in her email that she was at her desk. She'd have no reason to lie to me about that. Unless the administrator screwed with the time stamp, she sent it at 11:03 p.m. And if they did mess with the time stamp, that raises further suspicions, right?"

"Right," Dave agreed. He remembered that the new and last cloud upload from Sheila took place the same night.

"The police found her body in Walden, thirty-five minutes from the lab, at eight in the morning. The coroner said she'd been dead for nine hours."

"Placing Sheila at the lab at the time of her death," Mel surmised. "They moved the body."

"Dear God," Dave whispered. He rubbed a hand on his forehead. "And what about you? If Claire really had Sheila killed, and she's conducting some kind of cover-up, what keeps her from coming after you? Especially if my conversation with her had anything to do with this."

"I don't know. I don't understand killing people."

"I...," he started to apologize, but decided that he had nothing constructive to say for the moment.

Mel inhaled deeply. She pondered Dave and then Jennifer. The silence lengthened. A part of her wanted to throw the intruder back outside. She did not want that threat in her house, not where it could spill over on to her family. Yet Jennifer's knowledge held out hope for Liv. She really seemed convinced that a cure existed. She could provide the map for finding it.

She placed a gentle hand on Jennifer's wrist. "Do you want to stay here tonight?"

"No, thank you," Jennifer said. "And you don't want me either."

"Look, I don't know what to make of what's going on with you yet, but if what you're saying is true, you don't want anyone to find you. Stay here tonight while we all sleep on this."

Jennifer's face softened. "You're sure that you're okay with this?"

"Positive," Mel said, suppressing the danger claxon ringing inside her. "And I'm sure you'll be willing to help us with Liv, too."

Jennifer nodded.

CHAPTER 9

Prodeus HQs
December 2, 10:45 a.m. Mountain Time

Dave held the black handle up until his mug filled within a quarter inch of the top. He looked at the cream and the sweeteners aligned in their containers beside the coffee machine. Not this morning. Only strong, black, unadulterated coffee would due. He looked at his watch. 10:45. Ed Hepp had not yet arrived, extending his Thanksgiving weekend by a few hours.

Sitting in his office had not helped Dave's anxiety. His staff meeting at 9 a.m. had been awkward. Middleton, Goodman, Stan Peters and the others all asked who would fill in for Jennifer's multiple functions, first and foremost as project manager for the PDNA launch, only weeks away. The conversation started spontaneously as Dave sat down.

"I'm not a fan of Jennifer's," Middleton said, "but your timing's terrible, Dave. We're right in the middle of the launch. The Aldrich, the World Health Organization and the press will need constant hand-holding through this. My team doesn't have the bandwidth for that."

"That's my job, Brian," Stan Peters offered. "I own post-sale support. Jennifer had delegated management of the sustaining issues to me."

"That's fine, but you don't have a relationship with McQuaid," Middleton continued. "You ask Dave if…" Middleton hesitated, catching a look of complete befuddlement on Dave's face. "What's wrong?" he asked his boss.

"You've both completely lost me," Dave said, hoping he had decent acting skills. "What's wrong with my timing? Where's Jennifer?"

"You fired her, or had her fired," Stan offered sarcastically. "Remember? Your vacation seems to have been overly long."

"Why would I fire Jennifer?"

Middleton perked up. "You really don't know about it?"

Dave pursed his lips and shook his head "no."

"Well she's gone, no matter who did it and it's all going to fall on my team." Nick Goodman looked very stressed as he spoke. "We pushed all that stuff out over the last week. There's bound to be some quality issues whenever you ramp that fast…"

"I thought you worked the yields on the line, Nick," Dave interrupted.

"We did, but that's not enough. I still think engineering should have conducted a more extensive DVT. We're relying on software routines from the Aldrich. I have no way of making sure they're right - "

"We did field betas," Middleton said."

"Right. For three weeks at the Aldrich and a remote in Lokoma. Brian, you know as well as I do that the sample is too small."

Dave held his palms up. "Hold on, guys. Just hold on a minute. There's no benefit in re-hashing old decisions. The horse is out of the barn, Nick. We're shipping and we need to make our customers happy."

"And Jennifer signed off on shipping this release. I notice she's not around."

"Evidently not and I intend to get to the bottom of it. Meanwhile, all of you need to be clear on one thing. Jennifer may have physically signed off on the release, but she did so with my direct involvement. If she had not signed, I would have. So if you have an issue, you have it with me."

The room grew silent for a moment.

"Just make sure I'm authorized to hire who I need," Nick finally said, almost below his breath.

"For now, Nick, you need to make do with what you have. We're early stage. We don't have big company luxuries. We just make things happen. Anyone who doesn't like that is welcome to join Jennifer at the unemployment office."

Now, as Dave sipped his coffee, it occurred to him that he had better walk through manufacturing and do an attitude check. If Nick was that frustrated, he might be sharing that with his troops. Heading for the back stairs, he ran into Ed Hepp.

"Hi, Dave," Ed panted as he reached the top stair. Overweight, altitude and Parkinson's did not mix well with exertion.

"Mornin', Ed. Got a minute?"

"I do. We need to talk."

The men made small talk about the weather and football during the short walk back to the office. Neither wanted the discussion about Jennifer heard by others. Once in Ed's office, Dave closed the door behind them.

"What the hell happened here on Friday?" Dave opened.

"With Jennifer?" Ed asked almost rhetorically as he leaned his hands on the desk.

"Yes."

"It had to be done, Dave."

"If you were going to override me, you could've at least told me. We had an understanding."

"None of that matters," Ed said. "She was hurting the team. Claire McQuaid wanted her out and I wanted her out. You should have done it yourself like I asked."

"That's it? What about the launch and all the customer hand-holding we're facing over the next couple of months?"

"You have all those stock options and get paid the big bucks. Make it happen."

Dave weighed the merits of protesting a fait accompli versus lobbying for resources. "I want to re-hire her," he finally said.

Ed sat down. "Not an option," he said.

"The company needs her. We can re-visit her future in a few months."

"Dave, it's a done deal. Accept it or you may be next out the door."

Walking over to the window, Dave leaned his hands on the sill. He spoke as he looked at the distant mountains.

"We can't let Claire or anyone else tell us how to run our business."

"We can when her company's the key to making our numbers."

Dave turned. "You realize what you've done to me? You caught me completely flat-footed. My staff already knows this happened without me. They…"

"How'd that happen?"

"How? That's easy. Jennifer didn't show up for my 9 o'clock meeting. Did you think I wouldn't miss her? Or that my team wouldn't say something. What the hell were you thinking, Ed?"

"I was thinking about keeping our top customer and partner happy, something you lost sight of."

"Did you ever think that my staff might now feel a need to go around me, to build job support elsewhere? Like with you?"

"Dave, look." Ed held out his trembling hands and nodded at them. "The medication isn't controlling the Parkinson's like it should. I won't be able to work full-time within six months. I'd like to have a rich retirement from our public offering. And I need you to run this when I'm home managing my new money. No one else understands the big picture as well as you. Anything I do for you is meant to help you succeed." He put his hands back on the desk.

Dave returned to a chair and put his head in his hands for a few seconds before looking up. "God bless you, Ed. I will do all in my power to get you that retirement. But I'm still concerned this move will undermine me."

"Which would hurt us all," Ed said. "So make something up about your supposed ignorance this morning. The truth stays between you and me."

"And Judy Baines."

"No, Judy thinks you were on board. I told her to give you a Thanksgiving present and do it for you while you were gone. Judy thought Jennifer's advances toward you made it a very difficult thing for you to do, lest they be misconstrued."

"I understand the thinking. I just don't agree with letting Claire have that kind of control of our internal business."

"It's done, Dave."

Dave got up to leave but quickly dropped back into his chair. "What about my daughter? Jennifer knew how to get her help."

Ed's eyes narrowed. "Dave, I feel badly about Liv. I understand the hunt for better medicine. I'm dealing with the same thing with my disease. But Jennifer would not have been able to help her. The woman was trying to impress you with half-truths."

"How do you know that?"

"Think about it. If the Aldrich had a cure for AIDS, it would be worth a heckuva lot more to them than a humanitarian investment in West Africa. Do you think they would let anything distract them from getting it out?"

Dave wondered if Ed might be right. Maybe Jennifer had filled him so full of her distorted point of view that he had lost sight of common sense. Maybe he was just so desperate to solve Liv's problem that he was willing to believe anything even slightly credible.

"I don't know, Ed. Those are good questions."

"Do yourself a favor. Back off Claire and this magic potion. You'll just piss her off more. And stay away from Jennifer. Don't answer her calls. Don't e-mail her. She can only bring harm to you and your family. The woman is unbalanced. Claire told me that much. And trust me. If we find that there is any indication of a cure coming out of the Aldrich, I'll be right at Claire's doorstep with you. Meanwhile, we have bigger fish to fry, the kind that could just give you the money to find a real cure."

Running a hand over his forehead, Dave nodded. He thought of Jennifer's negative fantasy about murder. She portrayed Claire as crazy, but Jennifer made all the advances on him, pushed for a relationship he did nothing to encourage. Jagged Edge. The old movie with Glenn Close and Michael Douglas, where the mistress came back to kill the family. Who really had a screw loose?

At a minimum, he thought, she could be a target herself. If they found her at his home, Mel and Liv could be loose ends to "clean up." When he returned to his office, he called home to make sure everyone was okay, as though his calling might provide some level of protection. Only after he dialed did he remember that Mel was at work and Liv at school. He hung up before the first ring and chided himself for paranoia.

CHAPTER 10

Clement Home
December 2, 11:15 a.m. Central Time

Jennifer lay on the Clements' family room couch with an ice pack on the back of her head and another on her right knee. Dave and Mel had left for work hours earlier and Liv would be at school until 4. She climbed the stairs to Liv's room right after they left. There, she removed and destroyed the pinhole "stalking" camera planted in Liv's closet by Aldrich security months ago. Though she was the only one that monitored it, she did not want to risk being discovered through it.

She tried to think through what Claire expected of her. She wanted her back at the Aldrich, but the place had turned dangerous. Claire, Sheila and Jennifer had been a team for years. Claire mentored them both as though they were all very close sisters. If Claire could have Sheila killed, all bets were off.

Jennifer rolled on to her side facing the back cushions of the couch. She felt safe here where Claire and her minions could not find her. She had not slept well in her apartment since her trip to Walden, every noise she heard and every headlight that passed through her window blinds throwing her into a state of high alert.

Dave and Mel had offered her temporary sanctuary here partly out of compassion, but primarily as a trade-off to access her knowledge of the AIDS cure. They did not know that Jennifer needed to get back to the Aldrich lab to make sure it worked. And she did not plan to go back until she knew Claire meant her no harm. Dave could help insure that if Jennifer successfully compromised him. When he did not bite on kickbacks from some of the vendors, Jennifer thought sure she could get him with her advances. But the man was a rock.

That left Claire's final Dave solution. Jennifer had been clear with Claire that she would not do it. Now she no longer felt so certain. Part of Jennifer rationalized that Dave would be a dead man if he did not play ball, especially now that she knew the Aldrich did, in fact, kill. But the final solution felt like a step too far. Fixing it after implementation would be up to her now that Sheila was gone – and Claire meant for it to be both implemented and fixed. She knew Claire believed that exchanging a handful of lives to save millions amounted to great humanitarian leadership. Jennifer and Sheila both believed that, too, as they developed their drugs over the years. Then Sheila developed misgivings and paid the ultimate price for them. Jennifer could not afford misgivings. If Claire asked her again about the final Dave solution, she would have to comply or die.

A heavy overcast passed over the family room windows, turning the room dark. Jennifer nodded off, one hand still holding the ice pack to her head. She felt a hand on her shoulder and tried to shrug it off to keep from waking up. The hand squeezed harder and shook her.

She opened an eye and turned her head slightly to see who it was. A jolt of fear rushed through her. Mike Farley tightened his grip.

CHAPTER 11

Madison, New Jersey: Irish Bar
December 2, 10:10 p.m. Eastern Time

The band approached the end of its set of old Irish tunes. Jim Reilly, in civilian clothes, nodded yes as the waitress offered him another pitcher.

He poured as the men harmonized to Lily the Pink above the pounding of drums and electric guitar fugues. The mandatory tambourine jangled in the hands of the lead singer.

"...'twas efficacious in every way..."

It had been years since he had heard any of these songs. They made him homesick for the good times of his childhood, but he knew they had been few. The most consistent memories involved staying up late, listening to gunfire and worrying that it might hit home somehow. He remembered an angry father and a frightened mother. He recalled far too many funerals and the beer-fueled vehemence of the older boys at the wakes.

Then one day, the British soldiers came and took his father away. Wrongfully, his mother insisted, right up until the day that the cancer finally took her. Jim always thought that a big part of his mother wanted to die. If Dad had been home, if she had had more hope, she might have seen the doctor sooner about the lump. Only in the end did she seem to understand what her dying did to her boys. When her eyes grew still in the final stare of death – "she's seein' the angels," Mike had said – their last decent anchor in life turned to dust.

Dad had not been allowed out of prison for her funeral, so paranoid were the Prods and the British. A fine old priest helped with the arrangements, but Mike would have nothing to do with making them.

"God took her, Father," he said. "I'll be at the ceremony, but I want nothin' to do with sendin' her away to Him."

While ten year old Jim, then known as Sean, went back and forth between home, the mortuary and the rectory making things right for his mother, Mike went off with friends and developed a fondness for Guinness, anger and scheming. He brought his boys to the wake, kids that had been on his football teams since age 4. Mike had been the best forward of the bunch and had been elected team captain each of the last three years. But when the soldiers killed one of the boys nine months earlier, the boys started to drift apart. Fear accounted for some of it. Some parents decided to keep their boys on a tighter leash. A few that could manage it moved out of the area. Another boy was sent away to school.

But in the days following his mother's passing, thirteen year old Mike rallied the boys still in the neighborhood and talked of "makin' things right."

Now, Jim/Sean pondered his Guinness in a dark booth at the back of a New Jersey bar. He wondered again how he could have stopped it all, how he might have brought Mike closer to God instead of perdition. He lifted the mug to his mouth and guzzled enough to make his head spin.

The knuckles of a big hand knocked once loudly on the varnished top in front of him. "Heard you were askin' questions." A young but enormous bodybuilder, not yet out of his twenties, stood over Jim. The man's accent was pure northern New Jersey.

"I'm lookin' for somebody," Jim said, trying to shake the beer fuzz from his brain.

"Why?"

"He's a friend."

"Who are you to him?"

"Tell him I made his mother's funeral arrangements. He'll know."

The man sat down and handed Jim a piece of paper and a pen. "Write down your contact information."

Jim did so. The bodybuilder stuffed the paper in his shirt pocket.

"If he wants to talk to you, you'll hear from him. Otherwise, I wouldn't be using his name without the proper respect. Understand me, Mick?"

They have to believe you're ready to return to the life, Fr. Adam had cautioned him. Convince them, he admonished.

Jim leaned forward, placed a hand on the man's shirt collar, pulled him closer. "Listen, Yank. We're not Micks and I don't want to hear it from your mouth again. Himself wouldn't like it either."

"Let go of me, old man. It won't be pretty if I have to pound on you."

Jim thought about it, started to ease his grip on the guy's shirt, and then said, "What the hell." He jerked the guy forward and let go. Challenged, the guy started across the table at Jim, but was met by a left-right combination that knocked him back into the corner of the booth. Though dazed, the guy started toward Jim again, this time met by a single right that knocked him back for the count.

"Make sure my message is delivered," Jim said. "And, next time, show a little more respect."

He downed the rest of his beer in a long swallow and walked out to find a cab. That should raise questions about my commitment to the priesthood, he thought.

CHAPTER 12

Fort Collins: Clement Home
December 3, 5:50 p.m. Mountain Time

Liv returned home full of enthusiasm from her first practice in two weeks.

"We look good, Mom. I can't believe how good we are. If we win our next two matches, district is ours."

Normally inclined to temper any of Liv's braggadocio, Mel hugged her instead. The moodiness that had plagued her since she passed out in the game seemed to be gone. Mel, with Dave's support, had insisted Liv rest more, including doing absolutely nothing but eating turkey and going to movies over the Thanksgiving holiday. Shopping on Black Friday, other than online, did not happen for the first time since Liv discovered clothes and shoes. Mel thought sure that the ongoing drug regimen with more rest had likely raised both Liv's CD4 count and ratio.

"I'm really proud of you," she said.

"And I didn't bleed or spit on anybody, Mom."

Mel stepped back, momentarily stunned. A mischievous smile raced across Liv's face.

"C'mon, Mom. We have to laugh about it. Life goes on."

"You're a sick person," Mel smiled, wagging an admonishing finger.

Liv scooted past her mother into the kitchen and straight for the refrigerator. She hovered at the door, intent on finding the right snack.

"We're going out to dinner with Daddy tonight," Mel hinted.

"Mother. I have homework. Lots of it. And finals in ten days."

Homework had become the standard excuse for getting out of activities with the family. "We'd like you to join us," Mel persisted.

"Why? It's a school night."

"Liv, we still have company."

Turning her back on the refrigerator, Liv said, "That's two days. How come? Doesn't she have her own place?"

"She may be in danger."

"From klutziness near as I can tell."

"There's something going on with the business and Daddy's trying to figure it out."

"Oh, great," she said putting her head back in the fridge. "Just what I want to do, spend the night listening to Daddy's business issues. Whether I go or not, I'm really hungry right now."

Mel evaluated her daughter's slim figure. She could handle the snack.

"You're right. Daddy will probably be late anyway."

"As usual," said Liv, pulling baked ham out of the meat crisper. She placed the ham, mustard, pickles, American cheese and whole wheat bread on the kitchen island. She rummaged through the utensils drawer. "Y'know, he works way too hard, Mom. We have to help him lighten up."

"Good luck."

"It's good to have him back home, though. Thanksgiving meant a lot more this year. It's easier to be thankful for things when you've learned what it's like not to have them. You don't think he really regrets missing work Friday? Because they fired our guest?"

"No, he just wishes that Hepp didn't take advantage of him like that. I'm certain he'd rather be with you more than anything in the whole world."

"For a lot of the weekend, I believed that. I still do a little. Maybe he's changing."

Mel stood at the kitchen table and pulled a calculator out of her briefcase. She opened the calculator's battery compartment. "Do we have any 'n' size batteries?" she asked.

Liv placed her sandwich on the table. Taking a dead battery from her mother's hand, she studied it. "I don't think so. These are hard to find. But I might have the same ones in my calculator. You can have them. I'll get some more tomorrow or maybe while we're out tonight."

"That's very considerate," Mel said, "I like you better rested. Please don't overdo it again." She reached out and hugged her.

"What's wrong?" Liv asked, seeing tears well up in Mel's eyes.

"I've just been worried about you."

Liv sat down at the counter. Biting into her sandwich, she looked pensively at the air in front of her. "Thanks," she finally said.

"Excuse me?"

"Thanks for caring. I'm not sure I could have cared as much for a kid with this kind of disease."

Mel sat beside her. "I love you, sweetie."

Liv took another bite of her sandwich. She finished chewing and swallowed before she answered. "You don't know where I got this, Mom."

"No. Does it really matter?"

"I think it does."

"Not to me."

"Maybe not now, but it will matter. When I start to get sick again, you're going to have to explain it. People are going to want to know how I got it. And they'll assume the worst."

Mel sighed before she spoke. "People are a lot more sophisticated about this than they were even a few years ago."

"But, mom, people will want to know how I got it. They're going to think I'm some kind of drug-using, lesbian nymphomaniac."

"No one's judging you, sweetie."

"Because only you guys and the doctors know."

Mel gently placed a hand on Liv's forearm. "There's someone else now. One of the reasons, we're taking care of Jennifer is because she thinks she can get access to some kind of cure or vaccine."

Liv pulled away. "She knows? You guys told her? Why would you do that?"

"Because she knows about HIV. She was on the research team on AIDS at the Aldrich."

"Omigod. I can't believe you didn't tell me this."

"I'm telling you now."

Liv bit her sandwich. "Ok," she said after a moment. "I get it. I'm a little freaked out that she knows, but this could be good." She looked her mother in the eye. "But you do need to know how I got it. Especially if we're going to start bringing other people into the conversation."

"Do you know?" Mel asked. Her breathing visibly slowed as she waited for an answer.

"I have some ideas."

"What kind of ideas?"

Eyes now closed, Liv folded her hands and pressed them to her forehead. "You'd tell Daddy."

"He should know. He worries about you."

"He judges me."

"No, he doesn't. He loves you no matter what. So do I."

"I'm sorry, Mom. I thought I was ready to deal with it. It's too soon and everything's really confusing."

Mel's face turned beet red.

"Please don't be mad," Liv said. She rose from the table and threw her arms around Mel.

"How can I help," Mel asked.

"Pray for me," she said, turning to leave. "And talk to Daddy for me. I really want off the hook tonight."

As she trudged up the stairs to her room, tears filled her eyes. She thought she had good reason to be upset, but she knew the medication made her moods vulnerable to chemistry. Her mood swings still yo-yo'd wildly on the medication, but she tried hard not to show her parents. She saw herself as living forever one minute and as a huge burden on everyone the next. At this moment, she wondered if things might be better for everyone if she just died. She wondered that a lot lately.

It's the drugs, she thought. "Keep believing," she mumbled aloud.

CHAPTER 13

Fort Collins: Clement garage
December 3, 7:25 p.m. Mountain Time

"I thought you stayed home because you had homework to do," Jennifer said.

"That's true," Liv said. "But this is important, too."

"Your parents are not going to be happy with me if you don't get your homework done."

"Jennifer, lighten up. You're not my babysitter. I'm almost 16 years old. I know what I'm saying and what I'm doing."

"So how long have you been climbing?" Jennifer asked, finally giving in.

"Couple years, off and on," Liv answered. "It gets my mind off things."

"You're too young to be... Sorry."

"That's fine," Liv replied, "Mom told me you knew about it. I don't feel like I'm dying. Probably won't, right? They can keep HIV under control forever now. At least with some people."

"The fact that you're so young and athletic has to be a big factor."

"I hope so," Liv said as she leapt up to the chin bar. "Count for me."

"Are you sure you should be doing this? Won't it hurt your immune system?"

"Nope. Makes me stronger. Just count, please."

Jennifer looked up and watched Liv's back muscles ripple as she pulled her chin over the top of the bar. It was unusual for a girl to have so much upper body strength.

"One...two... three...four... five... six... seven... eight... nine... ten... eleven..."

Liv finally stopped at sixteen.

"Wow," Jennifer said. "I don't think I've ever known a woman that could do that many pull-ups."

"I'm pretty light. That helps. I could barely do one a year ago, but I started bouldering --"

"What's that?"

"Where you traverse a huge rock going from side to side without ropes or any other support."

"Oh, I've seen that. That's incredibly difficult."

Liv reached over and set a Powerblock to 20 pounds. "I'll tell you what got me started. I was climbing with some friends up at Horsetooth Reservoir and got stuck under an overhang. Even with ropes, I couldn't pull myself along and over that thing."

"I know, but we're better than guys at the straight-up stuff."

Liv talked while she curled the Powerblock. "Because guys try to use their arms for everything. Climbing's mostly lower body and hips. Bouldering's more upper body."

"So have you been back to that overhang?"

"Of course. Now it's my bitch."

Both women laughed.

"How about you?" Liv asked, slightly winded, as she put the weight down. "Are you a climber?"

"In college, I used to go to the climbing gym all the time. I've only been outdoors on an Outward Bound vacation."

"That must have been fun."

"It was, but it was grueling."

"How do you stay in shape now?" Liv asked.

"Run every morning and go to the gym three times a week."

Liv nodded toward the chin bar.

"No, not me," said Jennifer. "I'm still sore from my acrobatics in the driveway the other night."

"C'mon, get up to ten and I'll take you climbing."

"In this weather? I'll pass."

"Don't be a wimp, Jennifer. After the first five minutes, you'll be toasty from the effort."

Jennifer looked up at the bar. She looked back to Liv and then again to the bar. Without another word, she jumped up and did three pull-ups. She struggled to do a fourth so Liv put her hand on her waist and gave her a slight boost to finish the rep. With that, Jennifer dropped to the floor, stumbling into Liv. The sharp end of Jennifer's bracelet cut into the teenager's arm as they fell to the concrete floor.

Liv laughed, standing up first. She reached a hand out to Jennifer.

"You need to work on your dismount," she said.

"I know… Liv, your arm."

Liv looked at the bicep on her left arm. Blood oozed from a short gash. "Oh, no," she said quietly.

"We need to stop that."

Liv backed away. "No, no. It'll be all right. Just stay away from me. You don't want any of this on you. You could catch it. This is so dangerous."

Jennifer held out her hands, palms down to reassure Liv. "It's okay. Remember I'm a scientist. I know a lot about HIV. We need to just find a way to stop the bleeding."

Liv hovered her right hand over the wound, but would not touch it. "Should we put a tourniquet on it?" she asked.

"I think I have something better in my bag. Wait right here."

Jennifer ran out of the garage, returning in two minutes. She peeled back the aluminum on a small packet.

"What is it?" Liv asked.

"It will stop the bleeding and help close that wound."

"Just be careful you don't get any blood on you."

Jennifer sprinkled a fine powder on the wound. It dissolved in the blood almost immediately. She then placed a large bandage over the wound.

"Thanks," Liv said.

"No, thank you for being concerned about me."

"Do you really know about a cure for this?"

"Yes, there's something in the works. It's not done, but it's close."

"How do I get it?"

"I'm working on that. You'll have to give me some time to figure it out."

"Secret drug company stuff. I know all about that from Dad."

"I imagine you do."

Liv studied her hands as she chalked them to get a better grip on the pull-up bar. "So you must think I'm a real slut," she said without looking up from her hands.

Jennifer's face dropped. "I don't think that at all. I understand HIV. There are other ways to get this."

"I know. A blood transfusion. I never had one."

"There are even more ways."

"Saint Mel and Saint Dave didn't give it to me when I was conceived. I can just about guarantee that."

"You shouldn't do this to yourself, Liv. I can't tell you how I know, but there are ways to get HIV that most doctors don't know about. No way you got it through sex. I'll have your back on that if anyone wants to debate it."

Liv looked straight at Jennifer. "What other ways?"

"You'll find out soon enough. I can't say anything because of confidentiality agreements with my last job."

"But I did have sex. With another girl."

"Really?"

Liv nodded, looking Jennifer straight in the eye now.

"I thought you were straight," Jennifer said.

"I am."

"Oh. Junior high sleepover, I'll bet?"

"Yes."

"Experimentation perfectly normal at that age. That's not really sex. I strongly doubt that you caught it that way. You have to lay off the guilt."

Liv put the chalk back in its tray. She slapped her hands together to get the excess off. She turned back to her companion. "I trust you, Jennifer. I think you're the real deal."

Jennifer impulsively hugged Liv. As though she had startled herself, she backed away quickly. "Anyway, how sick can you really be?" she said. "You just did sixteen pull-ups."

"Work with me and you'll be at ten in two weeks," Liv said. "A little holiday climbing up at the reservoir, what do you think?"

Jennifer looked back to the chin bar before answering. "What the heck? I don't have anything else to do. It should be diverting."

CHAPTER 14

Fort Collins: Saigon 17 Restaurant
December 3, 7:55 p.m. Mountain Time

The frigid wind cut through the Clements as they climbed the short flight of stairs and entered the foyer of the Vietnamese restaurant. Few people were out in downtown Fort Collins on this weekday night. They were seated immediately.

The restaurant occupied a century old building. The current owners had renovated its hardwood floors and plaster walls. In the back, table service was provided in a fenced in courtyard, but the evening's chill made that undesirable.

Dave and Mel quickly glanced at the leather bound menus and placed them back on the white tablecloth. They had been here often enough that decision-making had become a very abbreviated process. A young girl, probably no more than a few years older than Liv, took their order of spring rolls, lemon-grass chicken and hot tea.

"I don't know what to make of it," Dave said, continuing the conversation they had begun in the car.

"What if Ed's right that Jennifer is dangerous?" Mel said. "For all we know, she could be the one who killed Sheila."

Dave ran his fingers along the base of the candleholder on the table. "Then we'd better get in the car right now. I don't want our daughter home alone with a killer."

Mel sipped her water. The possibility that Jennifer might be dangerous in a physical way had not crossed her mind until now. She suspected the girl had a thing for Dave, but she could control that. The possibility of murder presented a completely different set of risks. "Dave, why didn't you say something before? I can't believe we left her there if you were having these doubts."

"I don't really think she's like that at all," he said. "I'm just… I don't know. This is all new turf. I don't know what to make of it." He picked up his mobile phone and dialed. Liv's phone rang four times before voicemail clicked on. "No answer," he said.

"Let's go home," Mel said. "Keeping Jennifer hidden in the house to keep Claire's people from finding her is the point of all this. If they're not home, then something is wrong."

She turned to look for the waitress. Dave's mobile chimed. It was Liv.

Dave answered, "Hi, honey…No problem. We were just calling to check on you and tell you we were at Saigon 17… Uh huh… Everything's okay, then? … That's good, sweetheart. Call me if you need anything… Bye-bye."

"What are they doing?"

"Working out in the garage. That's why they couldn't pick up the phone faster. Liv sounds like she's having a good time."

"Overdoing it again."

"Hopefully she's learned her lesson and knows when to stop."

The tea arrived and Dave poured it for both of them.

"Which is it with Jennifer, then?" Mel asked. "Is she a threat to Liv or is she her potential savior with this AIDS cure?"

Dave put the edge of the teacup to his lips, but it was still too hot to drink and he put it down. "Hepp asked a good question today. If there really were an AIDS cure, why would the Aldrich not make it priority one? Aldrich is a business. An AIDS cure would be worth billions over time. Humanitarian activity in West Africa is likely to do very little for the company financially."

Mel stirred sweetener into her tea as she spoke. "Either there really is no AIDS cure or they're going to make more money in Africa than you think."

"Oh, they'll make money on it," he said. "Primarily through aid agencies. UNICEF, the Global Alliance for Vaccines, outfits like that. It just won't be the huge home run that an AIDS cure would be."

"On the other hand, why would Jennifer risk her career, her credibility with Claire, to tell you there was a cure?"

"I don't know. Miscalculation?"

"To what end? There's more to this, Dave. My gut tells me not to trust any of them."

Dave smiled. "Well, maybe we should go with your gut. The data sure isn't helping."

"But someone did kill Sheila."

"That's the other question. There's nothing more in the papers about the woman they found. I called the Walden police and they wouldn't discuss it."

"One way or the other we may be in danger just by association no matter who did it."

"No, we're okay," he said. "My bet is that if it is Sheila, she had some kind of secret life and that something went wrong. Claire's running a business, not the Mafia."

The spring rolls arrived. They each placed one in the middle of a piece of lettuce, sprinkled sprouts and cucumber in it and rolled up the mix. They dipped them in a clear, slightly sweet sauce and then bit in. As Mel finished chewing her first bite, she asked, "'Do you think the tests could come back positive?"

Dave shrugged his shoulders and swallowed before responding. "The whole thing about testing us is a CYA thing that Doc Resnick's doing for us. It protects us against well-meaning snoops."

"He's making sure you're not a deviant," she said.

"I'm fine with that."

Mel took his hand. "Today, she started to tell me where she thought she may have caught it, but she backed off."

"So Liv has a promiscuous secret and we're supposed to ignore it?"

"She's not promiscuous. If anything like that happened, it was a one-time deal. And the HIV defied the odds."

"That's hard for me to believe. And I'm her father. How are other people going to feel when the word gets out?"

"That's why we need to be there for her."

"What about Jennifer?" he asked.

"The truth?"

He nodded.

"She's a conniving bitch. And I don't trust her with you. I'm worried about what might have happened while you were living at the motel..."

"Nothing, Mel, I swear. She..."

She placed a finger on his lips. "Don't," she said. "Let me finish."

He dropped his shoulders and sat back, eyes focused on his wife.

"Our daughter is more important to me than anything in this world. I'd consider a bargain with the devil himself to save her. So we ride it out with the bitch from the office. We keep an eye on her, but we ride it out. We need that cure."

"If it exists." Dave picked up his mobile phone and dialed Liv. Mel looked at him through narrowed eyes.

"Just checking one more time," he said.

She reached out and eased the phone from his hand. "You're cut off," she said.

CHAPTER 15

Morristown, New Jersey: Mother Egan's Pub
December 4, 3:10 p.m. Eastern Time

Jim Reilly stood at the urinal in the single stall men's room at the rear of the small pub. He had ordered shepherd's pie, something completely unavailable in Rome and Sierra Leone. The blend of mashed potatoes, peas, carrots and seasoned ground lamb had been delicious. He had passed on the Guinness this time, instead choosing to drink iced tea to insure he remained very alert. As he emptied his bladder, he read the headlines on the USA Today front page posted behind glass on the wall in front of him. The FBI had arrested several college kids for seditious comments on e-mail. This surprised Jim. He always thought Americans could say or do anything they wanted as long as they did not hurt anyone else. He guessed the world had changed in the years since the war on terror had started.

The caller back at the motel told Jim to expect contact here between 1:30 and 3. For some reason, they had chosen to leave him a large time window to hang out in the restaurant. Probably wanted to check his motel room to see what they could find out about him. They also probably wanted a good bit of time to see if anyone either followed or accompanied him.

To make good use of the time, Jim reviewed the back-story Monsignor Zabinski gave him in the briefing. Francesca Vitello. The woman in Rome who took his picture and ran off. Turned out she wasn't Irish at all, but a set-up to provide a rationale for why he was leaving the priesthood. Pictures had been taken of their spat at the café and their other encounters that evening.

He loved Francesca, the story went, but she refused to continue to sacrifice her youth to a priest. He had come to believe in the causes she championed including the allegations that the Vatican had serious corruption issues. More than anything, he believed in their love. She had insisted they were through, but he hoped that he could reconcile with her once she knew how committed he was to leaving the priesthood.

What a crock, thought Jim, but he only needed his brother to believe it.

Returning to his booth, he noticed that the pub had emptied out. Though he had only been gone a few minutes, no other diners were present and the bartender and waiters were not to be seen. The shades had been pulled on the front windows as well. Then he saw him, sitting in Jim's booth, sampling the leftover shepherd's pie. The dark-headed man, now gray at the temples, looked up at Jim and grinned.

"Good to see ya, boy-o," he said and then stood to hug his younger brother.

"I never thought I'd see ya again," Jim said.

Not even slightly tentative, the men hugged for a long moment, patting one another heartily on the back every few seconds. When they finally separated, Mike grabbed Jim by the shoulders.

"Let me look at ya," he said, the full accent of his youth brought out by the presence of his baby brother. "Great saints, you're taller 'n I am. But still not nearly as strong."

"Aye, Mike. Sure, I can smell it."

Mike laughed, his eyes sparkling with genuine delight.

"It's grand seein' you, too," Jim said as they sat down in the booth. "I prayed for your crazy ass day in and out these last few decades."

"Did ya think I'd die?" Mike asked. "I wasn't the one runnin' around machete-wieldin' gangs with no weapon but a prayer book."

Jim started to form the words that defended prayer, but stopped himself. He needed to stick to his role as disillusioned ex-priest..

"Damn near got me killed, too," Jim answered. "But we're both here, amazin'ly. Ya never were very good with bombs. Thought sure ya'd have blown yourself to bits by now."

Mike looked at his brother solemnly. "Sean, that landlord was the last bombin' I did - "

"Careful. It's Jim now. Sean's gone."

"Jim it is. You were right about that bombin'. It wasn't surgical enough. Killin' his family was a damn stupid thing to do. I don't have much in the way o' regret, war bein' what it is, but that affair hasn't sat well in my belly over the years."

The past raced up on Jim as though time had never moved.

CHAPTER 16

Belfast, Northern Ireland
April 7, 1982, 11:12 a.m. Greenwich Mean Time

Seething from the stormy Irish Sea, churning clouds of cold gray mist curled around soot stained buildings. Fingers of fog floated through narrow streets polishing cobblestones into a slippery gauntlet. The drab gloom transformed living things into illusory silhouettes, their borders shaped by gentle shifts of the icy breeze.

Between pockmarked brick walls in an alley the length of a coffin, a boy stood lookout. Two weeks' worth of peach fuzz no more succeeded in its mission to hide his swollen acne than it disguised the determined set of his protruding jaw. Through murky drizzle, he watched his younger brother gather his nerve beneath a leaky shop awning across the road that ran perpendicular to the alley.

Under the shredded black awning, Sean Farley, short and skinny even for eleven, sucked in deep anxious breaths. He tasted wet air that smelled vaguely of stale cigarettes and of the muddy earth in the sidewalk cracks from which worms crawled as the rain nudged them out.

He glanced furtively toward his big brother for a reprieve. Three years older, Mike acted as both mother and father since Mum's passing nine months earlier. With an intense glare, he lip-synched for Sean to "get movin'." Though he could barely make out the details of Mike's face in the fog, Sean read clearly the familiar body language of his older brother's displeasure.

One hand latched to his umbrella, the other squeezing his yellow slicker closed, he trudged forward on the sidewalk's crumbling concrete. Ahead, three boys leaned against a wall, wet cigarettes dangling from their mouths, the orange ends of the Samsons glowing in the mist. As Sean emerged from the murk under the awning, the hoodlums crossed his path toward a dark green Mercedes parked on the curb. The eyes of two large men posted near the rear of the vehicle followed the teenagers.

Shoulders hunched, Sean wedged himself between the boys and the right front fender of the Mercedes. Suddenly, the small gang collided with him, pummeling his midsection with their fists. He tumbled sideways into the gutter, one shoulder slamming into the curb, the other against the *undercarriage. As the boys kicked him, Sean scrambled to position the canopy of the umbrella as a shield against the flurry of booted toes.*

"C'mon, ya bloody Prod, on your feet and take your beatin' like a man," one taunted.

Hidden by the umbrella, Sean slithered beneath the car. Overhead, the bodyguards shouted at the rowdies. Sean had only seconds to do what he had practiced repeatedly. He pulled his tools from his slicker.

"Leave 'im alone, ya Taig bastards," one of the men shouted.

The boys threw back anti-Protestant epithets and the men were on them, pulling the punks away from Sean and the car. In the distance, a policeman's whistle shrieked. Frantically, Sean fumbled with a very thin wire. He ran it from the base of the doorframe to a small packet of putty-like Semtek. With duct tape, he affixed the explosive to the exhaust pipe. His brother had assured him that the blast would be very confined, hurting no one but the car's occupants.

Pushing the umbrella ahead of him, Sean crawled back out. The other boys still struggled with the men. The policeman approached in time to see Sean brushing away tears of fright.

"Ya all right, son?" he asked.

"It's them that did it. They wanted me brelly."

Sean pointed at the boys. The policeman joined the bodyguards in quelling their youthful exuberance. Heaving a deep breath, Sean sprang from his toes, dashing around the nearest corner. As he ran, he shed his yellow slicker for a black one that had been tightly folded and stuffed in his pants. Jumping fences and racing between brick walls, he worked his way round to the alley where Mike waited. They watched as the policeman and the bodyguards finally chased off the Catholic rowdies. The three lads would be rewarded later for a job well done.

Within moments, a large black taxi pulled up. A woman and two girls stepped out, one barely a teenager, the other no more than two. The youngest, clinging to her mother's elegant hand, toddled in a frilly white dress.

"My Lord," whispered Sean as he watched from the alley, "It's his wife and kids. We gotta stop it!"

Mike grabbed his arm, his fingertips digging in painfully.

"It's too late, Sean. Besides, they'll probably not go off with him."

"Who ya kiddin'? Look at the hour. They've come for lunch."

"Maybe they'll walk."

The woman and the girls climbed the five concrete stairs leading into the building, the toddler awkwardly negotiating steps half her own height.

Sean watched the seemingly flawless face of the teenage girl turn to the bodyguard holding the door. He could make out "thank you, sir" on the full, red lips curled around her smile. He felt an unfamiliar tug, a warm, confusing flush that swiftly intensified into panic.

Sean jerked free of Mike, dashing into the street. He held no thought of danger to himself, only the well-being of the girls and their mother. But Mike anticipated his move. The older boy clipped Sean behind the ear with a heavy black cudgel.

He stumbled onto the wet cobblestones, his head spinning from the blow. His brother dragged him back into the alley and they waited. A few moments later, the woman and her children left the building. The husband, dressed impeccably in a suit with white shirt and orange tie, held one arm around his wife's waist. In his other arm, he carried his two year old whose frail pink arms tightly enfolded her father's neck.

Beside them walked the teenage girl, her angelic image filling Sean's head, her slightly freckled alabaster complexion ethereal under a wreath of auburn hair. She cuddled close to her dad, cooing up at her sister – and then she smiled across the street at Sean. Their eyes met and he froze under her gentle gaze. Her emerald eyes seemed to cut straight through to his soul. Then she looked back to her family. Sean had been told the father was a Protestant bastard, a slum landlord who overcharged his Catholic tenants. Now, he just looked like a good, caring man – like Sean's father before the troubles. There must be another way to fix the rents, thought Sean.

Still in a twilight state from the earlier blow, Sean surged back toward the street, but Mike knocked him down again, slamming the cudgel against his neck. He tried to crawl forward, the stones of the street cutting into the palms of his hands. A meter into the street, a warning shout formed in his throat, but a rough hand seized him by the mouth and jerked his head back.

"Ya done good, little brother," Mike whispered in his ear as he tightened his grip. "Now just watch your work in action."

A bodyguard held the back door open. Mother and children crawled in. The teenager, her silhouette shimmering in the mist, looked toward the prone Sean just before she ducked into the car. Her mouth twitched into a quizzical smile; later, his memory would struggle to separate fact from illusion, feeling the flash of her glowing emerald eyes seek out his soul in that split second, pulling him into her.

Frantic, he squirmed to break his brother's determined hold.

The father and the second bodyguard walked behind the car to enter the front from the passenger side. The first bodyguard finished getting the mom and the girls in the back.

Sean bit down on his brother's hand. "No" erupted from his mouth.

The bodyguard opened the driver's door.

Fire and metal suddenly mushroomed into the air, the flash blinding, scorching heat instantly drying the damp pavement. The deafening shock wave dissolved Sean's warning cry, turning all sound into a ringing hum. In the disorienting silence that followed, he saw the father and the second bodyguard, not yet to the car door at detonation, flung across the street. His older brother, his mouth flapping orders without sound, rushed Sean down the alley.

The boy pulled away, drawn to the carnage. Silhouetted by flames, roasting forms shriveled in the back seat, their humanity already barely discernible. A piece of white dress, one edge aflame, lay on the cobblestones steps from Sean. Gasping, his ears popped.

"...bloody idiot!"

His brother's epithets, now audible, landed without acknowledgment.

Above the din, the father's anguished wails pierced the nightmare. Bleeding, one pant leg dragging and misshapen, he crawled close to the flames and twisted metal. Repelled by the heat, he latched on to a tiny white shoe blown into the cobblestones. He hugged it, gazing desperately at the withering shapes in the car, longing to feel the softness of his wife and daughters, to feel their warm breath as they nuzzled his neck.

Instead their warmth had become fire, their breath the curl of black smoke in the mist.

CHAPTER 17

Morristown, New Jersey: Mother Egan's Pub
December 4, 3:34 p.m. Eastern Time

In the dark shadows of the empty pub, Jim blinked away his past, the time before a kind Catholic priest gave Sean Farley sanctuary, a new name and new hope in life. He studied his brother's black eyes. He grabbed his water glass, squeezing it until he thought he would shatter it.

"Whatever happened to the father?" Jim asked.

"Paisley finally died about twenty years ago. We put 'im in a wheelchair, ya knew that?"

"That was pretty much the last I knew."

"They say he was a bitter man, but he spent much of his fortune tryin' to help the poor get out of the damn ghettoes. He set up an enormous scholarship fund that put four needy boys a year through prep school, two Catholics and two Protestants. He thought it would plant the seeds to change people's hearts, make 'em stop killin' each other."

"Not such a bad man."

"All of us have at least a little redemption in us."

Jim sipped his water and put the glass down, finally letting it go. "Does the scholarship still exist?"

"No. Three of his boys died in a gun battle with police. He stopped fundin' the scholarships after that. Disillusioned him once and for all, I figure. By then, he was pretty sick with the cancer that killed him. Turned the runnin' of his estate over to the survivin' daughter, but she didn't want anything to do with the tenements -"

"Mike, wait," Jim interrupted. He placed a hand on his older brother's wrist and continued. "I never knew one survived. The baby?"

"No. Joanne. The teenager. Pretty badly burned, but they saved her."

Jim remembered young Joanne's emerald eyes, seconds before he destroyed her life. "Ya never told me."

"Ya never asked. You were too busy runnin' from me and the life."

"What became of her?"

"She sold all the properties after her Dad died. We knew she wanted to study to be a doctor, but she disappeared completely. She must have used some of her inheritance to erase herself."

"Where could she hide for so long? Jim asked.

Mike laughed. "Probably livin' high with a husband and three brats in Surrey for all I know. She's certainly changed her name. Unless she's dead.."

"Was she pretty or did we scar her?"

"There were no marks on her face. But I have no idea what she looked like other than that. My information is all second-hand. I've tried to forget about the whole thing."

Jim sipped the bottom of his iced tea. He noticed that Mike had a beer that he must have poured for himself when he arrived.

"But you're still killin'?"

"It's different. It's more like assassination. We're not about terror anymore. Any killin' is for very specific purpose with very specific targets."

"Not sure Mother would be please with us in any event," Jim said.

"She died from cancer with no husband beside her. We were just boys. We couldn't even afford an aspirin to calm her pain."

"Da was in prison."

"Caught up in the interment by the British army. He wasn't a criminal, Sean. He wasn't even IRA. Buy you were too young to know or remember. Da was a victim. He died of a broken heart in a jail cell when Mother passed, never found guilty of a thing."

Jim struggled to suppress the rage that had once boiled so hot in him. It only surprised him a little that Mike's words excavated the ancient heartache.

Mike looked at him, a knowing glance. He changed the subject. "I hear ya left the priesthood, ya damn fool."

"Ya heard right."

"Why would ya do such a stupid thing?"

Jim shook his glass, trying to spin the withered ice cubes in the bottom of it. He recalled the details Christus had shared about the raid on the Karanjas' village. The pain was real.

"Because I can't make a difference anymore. Because by converting them, I may have killed more of my parishioners than I ever would have if I'd stayed with you and the boys. And because I probably finally know exactly who I am." He leaned forward. "I wanted to kill my enemies in West Africa, Mike. Literally. I wanted to have a gun and just kill them. There would have been no remorse. Like ya said, it's different when your target's very specific."

Mike nodded, licking foam from the beer off his upper lip. "So ya want to come back?"

"I do."

"The other boys are goin' to doubt ya."

"I know that."

"We have to fix that lest one of 'em cut ya in your sleep."

"How do we do it?"

Mike leaned back in the booth. He looked his brother over, contemplated his eyes. "Ya have to take this on faith, little brother. We're assigned to protect a very important research facility that could help put an end to disease as we know it."

"So you've become a humanitarian yourself."

"Sure. Ya knew I would. And I have a humanitarian mission for you."

Jim leaned in to listen.

"There's a young woman named Jennifer Winter who is trying to undermine the research. She's in league with people who thrive on other people's suffering. She's very dangerous. She's already killed one of the lead research scientists. And now she's disappeared herself."

"So call the police."

"We can't involve the authorities because very sensitive research could be disclosed in the investigation, making the research vulnerable to outside interference."

"So ya want me to find her?" Jim asked.

"Exactly. And then pay the price of admission to get back into the IRA."

"How?"

"Kill her."

Monastery, Georgia
September 1988

The wet, warm humidity of a September in Georgia curled over him. It penetrated his pores like thousands of tiny, stinging needles. And his clothes, wet only by the rain in Belfast, seemed to stay wet here.

Six years earlier, Fr. Fogarty, the same priest who buried his mother, found him hiding in St. Brigid's in Belfast. The priest listened to him, hugged him and forgave him, though the boy seemed incapable of forgiving himself. In his daily prayers for the rest of his life, Sean Farley, who would become Jim Reilly, asked the Lord's forgiveness and promised to never again hurt anyone. During the remaining weeks in Ireland, an underground network of priests moved him from location to location, hiding him from both the IRA and the police. In those years, the IRA did not tolerate its members leaving the fold, particularly one who had inside information about an event like the bombing of the landlord's family. After Sean made his initial confession to Fr Fogarty, all the priests insisted Sean not talk to them about what happened. They carefully protected him from seeing newspapers, hearing the radio, or viewing TV. An apology to the family of the victims was out of the question.

Instead, Sean voraciously consumed books, mostly books about the saints as well as the New Testament. He latched on to Chapter 4, verses 6-7 of Paul's letter to the Philippians: "Be anxious for nothing, but in everything by prayer and supplication, with thanksgiving, let your requests be made known to God and the peace of God, which surpasses all understanding, will guard your heart and mind through Christ Jesus." After his ordination as Fr Jim Reilly, Sean would give his very first sermon about the comfort he received from that verse throughout his youth.

At the very end of his time in Northern Ireland, Sean returned to Fr Fogarty. The priest presented him with a baptismal certificate that matched the name on the birth certificate of a boy who died just days after Sean's birth 12 years earlier. Then, Fr. Fogarty took him to Derry, walked him to a plane to the United States and said goodbye.

In Dublin, a young nun dressed in jeans and a turtleneck met him and joined him on his connection to the States. She stayed with him all the way to Atlanta. They had little to say of substance. He could talk to Fr. Fogarty. The priest knew his confession. But Sean knew not to talk with the nun about any of that. So he had nothing to say. Thoughts of his dearly departed mother and the bombing, the estrangement from his brother, the image of the beautiful teenager he killed — these were all that filled his head. Nothing else had yet found a place.

A man in shorts and a golf shirt met them at baggage in Atlanta. "Adam," he said as he introduced himself. He showed them to an SUV that smelled of cigarette smoke and running shoes. He dropped the nun at a parish in Stone Mountain before continuing the journey to the monastery in the rolling green hills halfway to Augusta. It surprised Sean to see the unpretentious man in the shorts command so much respect as they walked into the central stone building of the facility. "Fr. Adam," they called him.

For six years, the priest and brothers trained Sean under Adam's paternal eye, building his character and his mind, teaching him to move forward committed to Jesus as the path to overcome the sin that haunted him. Sean thrived in the monastery until an anonymous donor rewarded his self-absorbed commitment to studies with a college scholarship six years later. Fr. Adam became the second and last man to know his secrets, to earn his complete confidence, rooted in the seal of the confessional.

When he left for the seminary that September morning, the boy no longer known as Sean never looked back, never returned to those who knew him best. With a duffel bag carrying all that was his, he high-stepped through the tall grass outside the monastery, headed toward the bus. With each step, he stomped out one more painful memory, until he could put them out of his mind - all except the captivating emerald eyes of the landlord's teenaged daughter, a young girl who caught his gaze seconds before she died at his hand.

CHAPTER 18

Fort Collins: Inner Strength Rock Gym
December 4, 4:20 p.m. Mountain Time

Liv's toes, outlining the sticky rubber sole of the rock shoe, gripped the edge of the plastic hold. The fingers of both hands, white with chalk to help keep her grip dry, crimped on hand holds, both good-sized sturdy ones known as "jugs" in climbing vernacular. Her thin, taut body splayed starfish-like on the overhang of the gym's climbing wall. Twenty feet below herwas a floor covered in closed cell padding atop a thick layer of open cell foam, designed to cushion the blow should she fall.

Glancing downward, her old fear of heights surged inside her. The muscles in her arms and legs tightened. The thing to do now was to look straight into the wall and take slow, deep breaths. When she tried it, she realized how shallow and fast her breathing had become.

Okay, she thought, shift your position. Relieve at least one leg before getting too pumped and cramping. Don't want to cramp up on an overhang, or any rock face for that matter, not when you're so dependent on your own strength to survive.

Cautiously, she peered between her shoulder and the wall. A small foothold welcomed her eyes near her knee. She looked up and right. A large handhold, the climbing wall's version of a small rock fissure, was just above her head on the outside edge of the overhang.

If she could get her left hand on that jug, then she could move her left leg to the new foothold. Then she could lean into the ledge with her left side and be able to shake out both right limbs. Then, with one good push, she could be on top of the ledge. Tightening her grip with her right hand and re-steadying her feet, she quickly swung her left hand to the large handhold. Crimping her fingers, she firmed both grips. Taking a deep breath and mentally blessing herself, she now eased her left foot along the simulated rock to the new foothold. Testing her position by pressing with her left foot and pulling with her left hand, Liv assured herself she could now shake out her right side.

Dangling her right arm and right leg in the air, she shook them, but not so hard as to loosen the tight grip of her left limbs. Again concentrating on taking deep breaths, she felt her right side relax. But as it did, the fingers of her sweaty left hand began to slip off their hold. She was going to fall. Desperately swinging her right arm around, her free hand struggled for a hold. It slid past its former hold, the momentum of her slippery left hand throwing her body outward. Even the rubber of her rock shoe was not sticky enough to resist the pull of her full body weight. Shouting "falling!", she plunged into the air, the floor suddenly racing up at her.

She bounced hard with a teeth-jarring jerk as the harness tied around her waist and hips quickly reached the end of its tether, catching her before she traveled more than a few feet, the weight of her body now completely supported by her mid-section.

As she made like a four-pronged pendulum, hands and feet reaching downward as they swung in small circles, she thanked God for "protection", the obvious and well-named climbing term for safety hardware. The belayer, holding the rope in a braked position below, smiled up at her. She nodded and the unshaven young gym employee slowly let the rope out, lowering her to the ground.

"Thanks," she said with a smile. She walked off to a seat to catch her breath and let her frightened heart slow down.

"No problem," he said as he followed her. "You're doing great. You have a lot of strength. You'll beat that overhang, but next time you need to stay in tune and listen for me. You had some slack in your rope caught by your knee and I couldn't pull it out. That's why you fell three or four feet. Without the slack, you would've gone nowhere. I kept calling to you, but you either didn't hear me or you ignored me."

There had been many things Liv had not heard lately. "I'm sorry. I need to remember to pay attention."

"No harm done. Want to try again."

Her muscles trembling, Liv opted to pass.

She sat on the bench and worked her fingers, trying to undo some of the tightness in the little muscles and tendons that ran up and down through them. She looked up to the spot where she had fallen.

I can deal with death, she thought. Like that. But not a wasting away. She had taken notice of every picture of an AIDS victim that she had seen over the last several months. She did not remember noticing many at all before then. Now they seemed to be everywhere. Their faces were always sallow, often peppered with sores. Their eyes often seemed disproportionate to their sockets, almost like cartoon characters - except that Liv found nothing funny in their misfortune.

It troubled Liv that the only white people in the pictures happened to be gay men. All the women and children, some of them little babies, were black and not American. She could not remember seeing one of a teenager. It felt very lonely and very wrong.

She needed someone to confide in, someone other than her mother. She loved her mom, but with kids, it was different.

She smelled the dusty, dry chalk as she wrung her hands. Mortality was new to her. She had read about it. People had told her about it. A great aunt had died when Liv was 12. But, in the insular world of affluent 21st century America, Liv never thought death would apply to her. Somehow she thought she could be the first to break the barrier and live forever.

Now, she often re-read the story of the Assumption of Mary. She had heard about it since she was very small. Only recently, it had provided her comfort. The Catholic Church taught that Mary had died, but only briefly. After the disciples laid her in her tomb, the angels had come and raised her body and soul to heaven. True immortality.

Of course, Liv thought, Jesus' resurrection offered the same hope of immortality. But I'm not God, she reminded herself. God would not do some of the things she did. And God would not look at tanned and toned male legs and feel tingling downstairs.

Her friends thought only deviants got HIV. Even if Liv managed to forget her... shame... no... yes, shame... every menstrual period poked at her again, reminding her of what she was. She hated the smell and the mess.

She remembered how a pregnant girl in the other ninth grade class had been unwelcome at school last year. The whispers around town had been intense. She remembered the usually very outgoing and warm Mr. Higgins being very sheepish at a Christmas party. People were nice to him, but he enjoyed no comfortable conversations. Mrs. Higgins, on the other hand, grew very loud and assertive, complaining about gang problems, how law enforcement and liberals were letting everyone down. She acted very self-righteous, way out of character for what had always been a very controlled, kind woman. They left very early, their two youngest children in tow, their pregnant daughter a no-show from the outset.

Liv looked down and saw white streaks and handprints on her otherwise pink thighs. Unconsciously, she had rubbed her chalked hands up and down them in anxiety. Breathing deeply, she slapped her hands on the top of her thighs, kicking up a small storm of white dust. She liked the hardness of her legs, the strength that she was building in her body. Might not be able to keep that up for long, she thought. Let's have another go, she thought as she stood up. She could prove her courage, her worthiness, right here on the plastic rocks.

No, she did not fear death so much as other things. Hanging alone on plastic rocks, master of the jugs, beating that darn overhang, actually seemed a very safe aspiration to her. In that, for now, she found peace.

CHAPTER 19

Freetown: Refugee Camp
December 5, 7:15 a.m. Greenwich Mean Time

Steam swirled from scattered puddles in the early dawn overcast as a dissonant chorus of waking birds celebrated surviving nocturnal predators for one more night. Hamara and Mariama navigated the tents and garbage barrels to the concrete block barracks that acted as the infirmary. Heavy dew dripping from the corrugated tin roof created a miniature moat in the red mud surrounding the building. At the door, both Karanjas kicked their sandals against a log, placed there for just this purpose, knocking off the excess mud. As she kicked, Mariama gripped the doorjamb with one hand for balance while holding tightly to a small white plastic bag with the other.

Hamara slipped on the wet surface of the smooth gray cement floor just inside the entrance. Mariama quickly thrust her upper body under his shoulder, keeping him from going down. They walked the familiar route to the ward where Sara stayed among thirty-two other children crammed into a combination of small twin beds, sleeping bags and air mattresses. These children had been classified as not contagious, bad news in the end for little Sara.

Sara's hair had grown long since coming to the camp, but it lacked the sheen it once had. It readily broke off when combed or brushed. While her hair grew, her body remained small, the result of malnutrition.

Not that Sara lacked food at all, but the small ration allotted her generally consisted of rice mixed with variant combinations of soupy sauces with a portion of fish or chicken thrown in once a day. Vegetables or fruit rarely showed up on anyone's plate in the camp because of logistics. Humanitarian agencies did not have the resources to assure rapid enough distribution from distant places to get the food there before it spoiled. Canned food did not present a reliable option because it proved too expensive. Moreover, locally grown food or good imported product landed in the hands of the black market and local Freetowners who knew the system, never in the hands of refugees.

Learning of Sara's full blown AIDS diagnosis late last evening, the Karanjas chose not to tell her. They knew it was a death sentence -- unless you were wealthy and could buy the medicine. Few in Sierra Leone were that wealthy.

Sara would not comprehend the disease or the details about it anyway. She would only understand that she was dying. Even though death had become more and more familiar to her through the passing of several other children in the ward, there seemed to be no purpose in doing more to aggravate her own anxiety.

Lying on her stomach, she saw her parents arrive. She rarely slept past dawn as the sun, peeking through the coastal overcast, poured directly through the window across from her bed. The Karanjas had not complained since windows inside the long, concrete walls were at a premium. Kept open round the clock, even in the rains, the window allowed an occasional breeze and the cooler nighttime air to ease the swelter of the building.

Rolling on to her side, Sara smiled and pushed herself up and on to the floor, landing her tiny ear in her father's waistband as she hugged him. Reaching out, she pulled Mariama into the circle. Her energy always seemed to start out high in the morning. It normally faded well before lunchtime.

"Papa! Mama!" she squealed delightedly, "You're so early! Can you have breakfast with me?"

Mariama reached into the plastic bag and pulled out a Sara-sized purple caftan.

"We don't like infirmary food, Sara, dear," she said. "Why don't you come with us and we'll cook some breakfast at our new home?"

Sara's eyes widened, the glimmer back in them for a moment.

"I can leave?" she asked.

"It's been too long," Hamara said. "It's time you came back to us, don't you think? There's no sense in hanging around here when Emma needs a big sister."

Sara began jumping in place, her frizzy black curls bouncing off her back and shoulders and swirling around her smiling face.

"I can't believe it! I can't believe it!"

A few minutes later, after Mariama had put the caftan on Sara and while Hamara did paperwork at the administrative office, Sara asked, "Does this mean I'm all better, Mama?"

"It means that…"

"Because I don't feel all better, Mama."

Sara stepped back from her mother and gave her a sincere look with knitted brows. Mariama studied her, her heart breaking. She looked at the legs she once thought lithe with youthful muscle, now merely fragile and bony appendages that recalled the long legs of a newborn fawn for Mariama.

"You won't be all better, my sweet girl. The malaria's worn you down. It can keep bothering you."

"How will it bother me?" Sara asked, "I don't want to be sick anymore."

Mariama squatted to bring herself face to face with her daughter.

"Have the nuns taught you about Jesus here?"

"Yes."

"He didn't promise that our bodies would always feel good, did he?"

"No," she responded, a puzzled look on her face.

"He promised that if we trusted him our spirits would feel good…"

Sara filled in the blanks. "And that's the most important," she said, "Because our spirits stay with us forever, even after we die."

Mariama pulled Sara close to her in a full hug, hoping she would not see the tears as they started to drip down her face. Quickly, regaining her composure, she pulled back, a hand on each of Sara's shoulders.

"You're a very, very good girl, Sara Karanja."

Sara grinned, her full upper lip folding back far enough to reveal the gums above her teeth. Growing solemn, she placed a hand on the side of her mother's cheek.

"Am I going to die, Mama?" she asked.

Her dark eyes, now ringed with yellow instead of white, blazed a path of sincerity across the short distance between them.

Except for her own eyes, Mariama did not move. She glanced at Sara's hand, little more than an inch from her left eye. She looked at her face, the mouth firm in anticipation, the eyes focused. How could she lie? Why had she not known Sara would ask this question?

"No, Sara," Hamara replied, re-appearing behind his daughter. "You're not going to die." He gently massaged the child's shoulders. "Instead, you're going to show us all how to live."

After settling Sara in the family's tin and cardboard home, Hamara joined other chiefs and elders on the front deck of a small coffee shop just a few blocks from the camp's front entrance. Wet rot and greenish-black mold riddled the deck's wide wooden slats, slats ripped off war-ravaged homes from the surrounding neighborhood. The slats perched on four short pillars of concrete blocks above the cracked and pitted asphalt of the street. A weak sea breeze cooled the men's sweat, making the muggy heat more bearable.

"You look good, Musa," Karanja said to his formerly bloated elder. "Camp life agrees with you."

Musa, one of the few benefiting from the sparse diet, enjoyed a much svelter figure than when they had left the village. He laughed softly, but said nothing. He had shared his complaints with Hamara more than once before. He told him that he missed the village and had yet to find his moorings in Freetown. He had never heartily endorsed the village conversion to Catholicism, but rather than blame Hamara, he chastised himself for not being stronger spiritually when the priest wove his spell. Now it was too late. The spirits had avenged themselves on the Lokoma people.

"Has everyone lost enough sleep over this little incident at the front gate last week?" one of the chiefs from an area near the Ghana border asked.

"We need to do more than arm a constabulary," responded another. "We have men for an army. We should fight."

"Who will we be fighting?" Hamara asked. "We don't know who the enemy is. There appear to be many rebel groups that…"

"Don't do this, Chief Karanja," Issa, the border area chief, challenged. "We can understand if you don't want to fight your son?"

Hamara's face darkened as his neck swelled. Musa put a calming hand on his shoulder. Hamara took a deep breath before speaking.

"Jacob has not joined the rebels."

"Your own elders say he has."

Hamara looked at Musa who shrugged his shoulders. "No one knows where my son is. He disappeared at the time the rebels kidnapped his mother."

Issa, keeping his arms in his lap, leaned across the table. He spoke gently. "Hamara, we have not known each other long, but I respect you and consider you a friend. What's happened with your son is hurtful, but a chief cannot let his personal feelings interfere with decisions."

The table shook as Hamara's fist slammed down. His nostrils flared as he glared at Issa. "My son is ten years old. For all I know, he may be dead. If he does fight for the rebels, he does so at the point of a gun. And how many other children are with him? Would you have us go into the jungle and kill our children and our brothers?"

"If the spirits have turned them against us," Issa said evenly, "they no longer are the same people. If they are crawling into huts chopping up innocents, the spirits we knew no longer reside in them. For us, they are indeed dead."

"I cannot accept that. They're not spirits. They're our flesh and blood."

"I understand how you feel, Hamara, but your honor will win out in the end. You're too good a man and too good a chief."

Hamara did not respond. He picked up the chipped mug that held his very strong coffee. As if on cue, the others did the same. Issa lifted his arms from his lap and pressed the stumps at the end of his wrists against the sides of the warm mug before lifting it to his lips. He had long sleeves. When the rebels overran his village, teenagers held him down on the ground in the midst of the smoking huts and gave him an option.

"Long sleeves or short sleeves, old man?" they had demanded.

He stared wide-eyed at them, frightened and uncomprehending.

"Answer or we'll take off your head!"

He only wanted to get free of them and help his wife. They held her on the ground five yards away. She screamed as they ripped her clothes from her and used her. Issa knew her best chance now would be if he kept his mouth shut. He had watched as boys cut off the lips of one of his elders because the man had begged them to leave his wife alone. They made the man's wife eat them as they raped her.

So, to his lasting shame, Issa said nothing.

"What is it? We don't have all day!" they demanded.

"Long sleeves," Issa blurted.

And his hands were immediately chopped off at the wrists, his arms now gushers of blood. Short sleeves would have cost him his arms at the elbows.

"Your president said your fate is in your hands," a young man consumed with drugs declared. "What will you do now that you have no hands?"

The boys around him guffawed.

Hamara knew this background. He knew Issa struggled between compulsions for revenge and his responsibilities as a chief.

"What do we lose by fighting?" Issa asked. "What kind of life is this here? We'll never return to our villages. In the end, they may kill us here if we don't stop them first."

"Who is 'they'?" Hamara challenged. "Rebels? Or bandits? Whatever we call them, they're all around us. Here in Freetown I'm told that rebels exist among the citizens, ready to rise up whenever told. But you can't tell one of them from the rest of us…"

"So what do we do? Just await our fate? My God, man, you're watching your daughter die here because there is no medicine for us. In America, she would have medicine and she would live a normal life."

Hamara closed his eyes to keep control of himself. "Issa," he said, "You seem obsessed with my children today."

"Because we should all be obsessed with the children. They are the future."

"But you seem to think they have no future."

Issa had no answer. Hamara thought he had struck a nerve. No real hope existed in the camp.

"There can be a future," Musa broke the silence.

"How?" Hamara asked.

"We go where we can get all the medicine we need. We go where everyone has a home. Where Sara can get medicine. A place where people don't live in tents and cardboard huts. You've seen America on the television. It's heaven on earth."

Hamara smiled at Musa like the elder was a mad man.

"Musa, that won't happen."

"Why not?"

"Because this is our home."

"A home where our children die far too young, a place where our wives are treated like cattle. Can you really call this home?"

Issa spoke, "There is a way out."

"Would you have us fight our way across an ocean?" Hamara challenged. "There are no armies there, just lots of salt water. Or perhaps we can hijack an airplane. Except we could never get everyone on one plane. And if we did, the Americans would shoot us down when we got there."

Issa held Hamara's gaze. "I'm very serious," Issa said. "There is a way. A number of us have already started to put a plan in place. You can join us. Perhaps you'll be in America before Christmas."

Hamara had already lost Ketta, Ani and Jacob. If he could do anything to keep what was left of his family alive and well, he would do it. But exposing them to more danger was not an option. Musa picked up a banana he had purchased and began to peel it. As he did, he glanced at Issa who returned the glance. Hamara caught the exchange.

"What is it with you two?" Hamara asked. "Has my elder joined another tribe?"

Musa nodded at Issa who then spoke.

"Chief Karanja, Musa respects you as do all your people, but he has approached us to, ah, understand options."

"Which are?"

"One finds favor with a number of us," Issa said. "We have already done our homework on this option. We see only one major obstacle."

"What is that?"

"You, Pa," Musa said matter-of-factly.

Hamara studied Musa. He had always been outspoken, but never dangerous. Hamara had always been able to control him. Things had changed. Hamara no longer was the single ultimate authority. In this environment, he shared power with other chiefs. A simple declaration from him no longer sufficed. Musa knew that. He seemed a natural politician, right down to his recent change in appearance. He even seemed to groom better.

"So, my old friend," Hamara said, "How am I an obstacle?"

"Because you seem ready to wait out the government. You seem to think we will be able to return to our land."

"We will because we'll fight for it when the time comes."

"No, Pa. We won't. We don't have the funds, the weapons or the lawyers to deal with our government and the global powers backing it. Our government doesn't care about our rural tribes. Peoples that lost their lands ten years ago still don't have them back. And they've scattered to the winds to earn a living - most with no hope. The same will happen to us."

Hamara knew that to be right. He knew, too, that he needed to return the Lokoma to their hereditary land. And to keep them together. "So what options do you propose?" Hamara asked..

"Well," Issa said, "We can form a new rebel group and try to overthrow the government. One more rebel group should keep the bloodshed going."

The men smiled and nodded. No discussion was necessary. They would not even begin to take such a course seriously.

"Then there's the Parliament," Musa suggested. "If we have enough money, we could perhaps buy the votes to get our land back."

The men, except Hamara, laughed at the absurdity of their remarks. Hamara remained solemn, anger just below the surface of his firm face. The parliament had been powerless and corrupt for well over a decade. The Leoneans had been subject to a string of corrupt leaders, none well meaning. Contention for control of the nation's leadership and its spoils lie at the heart of the civil war.

"You see, Hamara," Musa said after the laughter died down. "They've taken away our options. Even if we should be so fortunate as to return to our villages, we will not be allowed to live as we wish. We will have no way to support our families or ourselves because the bauxite industry won't return, and all the other jobs are being concentrated in the cities."

Hamara peered at the grounds in the bottom of his now empty coffee cup. He gently shook the cup to see if they would move, but they were wet and stuck to the bottom. He spoke without looking up. "The rebels and the ambitious in our government, or should I say governments, have soaked our material well-being out of us. Now, we sit at the very bottom, the dregs, of this new order of things. Clearly, we cannot readily rise again within it." He looked up and showed the bottom of the cup to the others.

"We are stuck here just like these useless coffee grinds. Like them, I suppose, we can be put back into the ground as fertilizer for their new order, but more than likely, we will just be washed away in the new times."

The others nodded.

"So where do we turn, gentlemen? I think perhaps God is the only place left to us. And not the spirits of the rainforest, but the God of the priest. I know more clearly now why Jesus insisted his kingdom was not of this world. He knew we could never find ultimate peace in it. He knew that men who sought material things would ultimately come to something like this sad, bloody war that has destroyed our lives and taken our children."

Musa drummed his fingers on the table as Hamara spoke. He watched the eyes of Issa, a faithful Muslim and enemy of fanaticism. Musa finally exploded in exasperation. "Do you hear yourself, Chief Karanja? The priest is dead. The rebels killed him, just like the Romans killed his God. Maybe there is a heaven, but I'm not ready to go there yet. Our children live here now and so do we. If they seek peace in the Bible, they may find themselves executed if certain extremist factions consolidate power. Open your eyes, man! We need to act, not pray."

Hamara rose from the table and walked inside the little coffee shop. Its screen door squeaked as he opened it. It slammed shut when he let go.

Issa turned to Musa. "Is he finished with us?"

Musa shook his head. "Give him a minute. He'll refill his cup and return with an open mind. The priest also taught us that his God helps those who help themselves."

"Allah and his God are one and the same," Issa said.

Musa's forecast proved accurate. Hamara returned in a moment with a full cup. "So, Musa," he said as he resumed his seat, "You and Issa clearly have something up your sleeve. Tell me about it."

CHAPTER 20

Fort Collins: Clement's kitchen
December 5, 8:47 a.m. Mountain Time

Dressed in black slacks, low heels and a pink cashmere sweater, Mel rushed into the kitchen and reached into the cabinet for the green can of protein powder. Dave and Liv had been gone for over an hour; Jennifer still slept soundly in the basement guest room.

Mel shoveled a scoopful of the powder into a drinking glass and swung open the refrigerator door, pushing aside 2% milk and a carton of orange juice to find the soy milk. Flipping open the top of the box, she poured the vanilla flavored soy over the protein powder. Kicking the refrigerator door shut as she turned, she stirred the concoction. Glancing at the digital clock on the microwave, she saw she had just twelve minutes to get to her office ten minutes across town. Tilting the drink back, she drank quickly, chewing the lumps remaining before swallowing them. As she put the glass into the sink, she tossed her head back in frustration. Protein powder had spilled on her sweater. She reached for a dry towel on the counter to wipe the white mess off. As she did, a pill rolled out from underneath the towel.

Brushing her front with one hand, she picked up the pill with the other. She squeezed her face in discouragement.

A few minutes later, Mel spoke into the headset attached to her mobile phone as she raced through a yellow light at College Avenue and Harmony Road. "Dave, this isn't going to work. It's the second time she's skipped a dose in three weeks."

On the other end of the phone, Dave tried to find a bright spot. "She took two of the pills, anyway."

"Paul Resnick told us that all three are needed. Otherwise, the virus builds resistance faster."

Dave, in the midst of reviewing a report when Mel called, responded in frustration, "What do you want me to do about it, Mel?"

"You know what, Dave. Not a damned thing. You keep living in your little make-believe world of business. You haven't changed a damn bit. I'll get the pill over to her after my meeting. But please don't try to help. Please don't push Claire to tell you about the cure. You wouldn't want to screw up your politics with Ed."

"It's not that simple."

"He's not going to fire you. He needs you too badly and he knows it. Plus you know this business now. Where's he going to find someone to replace you fast enough? If he really wants to go public, he's not going to risk losing you."

"I wish I could be that confident."

Dave could hear her seething on the other end, her breaths long and heavy.

"No problem, Dave. You keep being wimpy. You and your lazy sidekick sleeping in the guest room. I'll take care of everything at home. Just like always."

"Mel, wait a minute…"

"Bye, Dave. Thanks for listening."

"Wait, Mel. It's…"

But the line was dead.

CHAPTER 21

Loveland, Colorado: Prodeus Headquarters
December 5, 8:56 a.m. Mountain Time

Sitting behind his desk, Dave put the handset back in its cradle. He slumped back into his thickly pillowed leather chair. Gripping the armrest with one tense hand, he squeezed his temples between the thumb and fingers of the other, letting the fingers slide across his eyelids before rubbing his forehead.

"Dammit," he mumbled. What would it hurt to call Claire one more time? Now that she thought Jennifer was out of the picture, maybe Claire would be more receptive. He could read her reactions and back off if she seemed to get squirrelly about it.

He picked the phone back up and dialed Claire's direct line. To his surprise, she picked up immediately.

"Hi, Dave," came the cheerful voice on the other end before Dave could say anything.

Caller ID, thought Dave. "Hi, Claire," he said.

"Your timing's perfect," she said. "I'm just looking at the first reports from Sierra Leone. The PDNA's doing just what it's supposed to do."

The good news distracted Dave from his main mission. "Fantastic," he said. "How many tests have been done?"

"323. That's yesterday alone. Our first day in. We've only deployed two of the devices. By the end of the week, everything you shipped over the weekend should be through quality control here and on planes to Freetown. If Adrian Guerra has the resources lined up that he claims, we'll roll through over 6,000 people a day. Maybe more."

"What's your objective?"

"We want to be through with most of the Freetown refugee camps before Christmas. The UN thinks that's about 120,000 of 'em."

"Refugees?"

"Right."

"How about Lokoma? Did we get the PDNA operating up there?"

"I'm sorry, Dave. The village is abandoned. Adrian said they moved into a refugee camp after a rebel raid. They're being inoculated there."

Dave remembered the kids and the animals milling about the village center. He remembered Sara, tiny and fragile, curled up in her father's arms.

"How bad? How many killed?"

"We don't know. The chief lost some family members, including his son."

"Jacob?"

"I don't know his name."

"He's his only son." Dave shook his head. His problems seemed smaller than they were a few minutes earlier.

"What's the yield on the 323 tested?" he asked, shifting back to business.

Dave heard a keyboard clicking as Claire searched through the on-line report.

"Sixty-one percent. Roughly 197 if my quick math is right. That's 197 getting the malaria vaccine."

"Is that about what you expected?"

"No, it's a little light. We thought about seventy-five percent would be genetically enabled to respond to it, but this first round's not a statistically sound sample yet because of the selection. I'd bet that if we dug down a little bit into the data, we'd find most of 'em are from the same tribe."

Dave did his own quick calculation. "So that would mean 90,000 doses of malaria vaccine by Christmas?"

"At seventy-five percent. Right."

"That'll put a dent in their healthcare problem."

"You don't know the half of it," she said.

"What's the rest?"

Claire hesitated. "Claire?"

"I'm still here. You know I have to maintain some corporate secrets."

"I learned that lesson," Dave responded, seeing an opportunity.

"How's that? Oh. The thing with Jennifer."

"Right. I'm sorry for stepping out of bounds on that."

"I understand. You love your daughter. I'd probably do the same thing."

"And if you were me, you'd keep asking, wouldn't you?"

"Don't, Dave."

But Dave already had stepped through the gate. "Claire, look what we've done for you already. You have a success story well on the way. We've been a good partner."

"There is no AIDS cure."

"And that's all I would tell anyone else. I don't know what your strategy is, but I respect your desire to keep it under wraps. At the same time, you can help my little girl."

No sound came from the other end. Dave hoped Claire was pondering how to help him.

"Dave, don't screw up this business relationship over your kid's indiscretions. You know why Jennifer went down and I feel no compunction about leaning on Hepp to do the same thing with you."

Confirmation. Dave's hand tightened around the receiver. "Don't threaten me, Claire."

"It's not just a threat."

Dave could barely suppress his rage. "Listen, Claire. I don't know what the hell you're up to, but don't lose sight of the fact that you need me just as much as I need you."

He waited for an emotional response. Instead, Claire spoke in a measured cadence. "For the moment, you may be right, Dave. From a business standpoint. But things change. When they do, you stand to lose a lot more than a job. You need the Prodeus IPO and the money from it. It will help you buy the leading edge medical help and drugs to keep your daughter alive until there really is a cure. Oh, and should I come up with a cure here, it's awfully unwise to make me angry. Wouldn't you agree?"

Dave put the handset down for a moment, rubbing his eyes, trying to squeeze out the stress. He knew she was right. It pissed him off even more. Charging straight ahead like a bull in a china shop did not help at all. This was chess, not football. He picked up the phone, feeling the energy, the power, sapped from him. "Yes, I agree, Claire. I'm acting out of control. Please forgive my indiscretion. I'm not dealing well with the AIDS thing."

"Clearly," Claire responded, offering no quarter. "It's time you changed your tactics. Before it's too late."

The phone hung up before Dave could say anything else.

CHAPTER 22

Fort Collins: Inner Strength Rock Gym
December 5, 5:07 p.m. Mountain Time

Jennifer pulled in the rope slack as Liv traversed the overhang 20 feet above, the rope pulling on the ledge. Liv dug the rubber of her rock shoe into the same foothold that had been her last before falling yesterday. Now she pulled upward with her arms, thrusting with her hips.

Liv's hips rolled on to the ledge, trapping her right hand beneath her. On the floor below, Jennifer whooped, but it was premature. As Liv extricated her arm, she slipped to the edge of the overhang with no holds to grab. She tumbled head first into the air. Below Jennifer struggled to hold the rope as it went tense with the teenager's weight.

"Rats!" echoed through the gym. Liv's cussword substitute for the week.

"You want to try again?" Jennifer called.

Instead of answering, Liv swung into the wall and attempted to pull up on a large handhold. Her shoulders screamed with exhaustion.

"I'm done," she called and Jennifer started slowly letting out rope as Liv climbed back down hold by hold.

"Coconut water?" Jennifer asked when Liv stepped back on to the ground.

Liv blew out and leaned against the wall. "In a minute. I'm whipped."

"Well, you've been going at this pretty hard the last few days." Jennifer wound in the rope and wrapped it up as she spoke.

"I don't think so," Liv said, a deep rasp in her throat, her breathing almost a pant. "This isn't normal for me."

"You think it's the, ah…" Jennifer looked around. No one could hear them, but she decided to be cautious anyway. "…the sickness you've been dealing with?"

Liv nodded affirmation, her chest rising and falling in hard pulses as she fought for breath.

Jennifer cinched an end of the rope as she spoke, "Probably just the medicine. That stuff will take it out of you."

"So you don't think it's my CD4s?"

"Probably not. You're way too early in this process. It's just the drugs. They're very strong. Now step out of that harness and let's get something to drink."

A few minutes later, the two sat at a small table next to the gym's snack bar. Liv's breathing remained slightly labored.

"Have you told anyone at school?" Jennifer asked.

"Oh, no. That would not be a very smart thing to do."

"Not even your best friend?"

"Chelsea? Thought about it. But no. We're in kind of a fight anyway."

"About what?"

"We like the same boy. We're civil, but not close like we were."

"Guys get between girls," Jennifer said, "No matter what, you need someone to talk to, someone your own age."

Liv shook her head no and sipped through her straw. She looked away when she finished.

"How do you feel now?" Jennifer asked, trying to stimulate conversation.

"Tired," Liv answered, dropping back in her chair.

"We can go," Jennifer offered. "Maybe we can stop at Old Firehouse Books on the way home and find something to read. No one will recognize me in a bookstore."

"Not worth the risk. Plus I'm really worn out."

"Let's just go then."

Liv shook her head from side to side and then looked down. Jennifer sipped her drink from the bottle.

"You almost had that traverse. If you…"

"Do you think," Liv started, turning away from Jennifer and looking across the gym, "that… that my friends will stay my friends when they find out?"

Jennifer tilted her head with curiosity. "Why would they find out?"

"Either I go away when the time comes or the disease will be very visible. Plus you're right. I need to be able to confide in people. But if I do, then no boy will ever date me. I'll die a lonely miserable death."

Jennifer scrutinized the teenager briefly before smiling. "You're kidding, right? You don't seem like the type to feel sorry for yourself."

Liv turned her eyes back on Jennifer. "No, but sometimes I get very afraid. Not so much of dying, but of being alone. Sometimes, I just want to cry."

"Do you?"

"Cry? Yes, a lot when I'm alone. Particularly at night. Maybe it's just the drugs."

Jennifer took another sip of her drink and leaned across the table. "Have you told your parents about your fear?"

Liv rolled her eyes. "No way. Their lives are hard enough. If they think I'm not good with this, the pressure will be unbearable for them. I mean, they just got back together."

"They love you. You need to trust them with that. You're the one thing that will always unite them, not separate them."

"Do you trust your parents?"

Jennifer did not respond. Instead, she played with her drink bottle, slowly turning it with her fingers.

"I'm sorry," Liv said. "It's none of my business."

Jennifer let go of the drink and dropped her hands to her lap. "No, that's all right. We're sharing things. My mother. I trust my mother. Dad's with his third wife in Oregon. He's his community's good hippie, a drop-out Ph.D. Lovable in the community; totally useless to the family he abandoned in Texas."

"Men can be very selfish."

"Yep. If you ever find a good one, latch on."

"I think I have one."

"Oh? What's his name?"

"Michael Winston."

"Michael Winston?" Jennifer said, smiling through narrowed eyes. "Hmm. Who's Michael Winston?"

Liv's cheeks reddened as her eyes lit up. She pulled her knees up to her chest, wrapping them in a hug. "I don't know. I just made the name up."

"You are so lying, Liv Clement."

"Yes, I am," Liv grinned.

"Well?" Jennifer persisted, now leaning across the table.

"He's a very sweet boy."

"Sweet?"

"Okay. Seriously cute."

"Are you going out?"

Liv's face darkened. "We don't even talk anymore. I've been such a bitch at school. He probably hates me."

"Has he stopped saying hello or anything?"

"No."

"That doesn't sound like he hates you. Have you hinted that you'd like to go out with him or anything?"

"No. At least not in a while."

"That's a great way to get a guy," Jennifer said rolling her eyes.

Liv dropped her legs to the floor and laid back slightly spread-eagled in the chair. "I know," she said. "I know."

"Why don't you give the guy a break and talk to him?"

"Because if he doesn't hate me now, he will eventually."

"How can you say that?"

Liv looked firmly at Jennifer now. "Duh, Jennifer. Because I'm sick. When he finds out, I'll be the last girl he or any other guy wants to date."

"You're being really hard on yourself. If this guy's as cool as you seem to think, he won't let it get in the way. Romance is a very compelling thing."

"Really?"

"Trust me. Plus any guy with eyes is going to overlook a whole lot of things to get close to you. You're a very cute girl with a really good body."

"You're not gay, are you?" Liv asked, leaning away in her chair, her face screwed up.

"Hardly. I just remember what it's like to be in high school, not knowing where you stand. None of us know we're pretty at your age. But you're very pretty. And in really buff shape, just like your Dad."

Liv eyebrows furled. "That's really disgusting, Jennifer. He's my dad. I do not want to think about him that way. Anyway, he has a belly on him."

"He's a very attractive man."

"This is very weird. My parents love each other. You shouldn't be thinking of him like that."

"It's not like... I thought you'd be flattered that younger women would find your Dad attractive."

"You're definitely grossing me out."

"I'm sorry," Jennifer said. "I'd never come between your parents."

"Dad wouldn't let you."

"Believe me, I know that."

Liv's eyes widened. "How are you so certain?"

Jennifer dropped her head, rubbing a hand on her brow. "It's just that I can read these things," she said. "It's the way he carries himself. He doesn't have a for sale sign out. His sign says no vacancy – ever."

"Good," Liv said, her lips pursed and her eyes intent on Jennifer.

Jennifer returned to slowly spinning her drink bottle with her fingers. She glanced at Liv, but said nothing for more than 30 seconds. "Think it's my turn to try that traverse," Jennifer finally said, standing up.

Liv did not move.

"You promised to belay me. Are you coming?"

Liv straightened in her chair and sighed. She took a sip of her drink and then looked at Jennifer. "Sure," she said.

CHAPTER 23

Clements' Home
December 5, 6:38 p.m. Mountain Time

Dinner that night did not turn up the volume on normal. Dave, for once home from work at a reasonable hour, added nothing constructive to Liv's peace of mind.

After the blessing over the food, he remained silent, preoccupied as he often was upon coming home from work. He had conversations in his head, sometimes working himself into a lather. Almost like a last gasp to blow the day out of his system. Tonight, though his family did not know it, he wrestled with managing the workload abandoned with Jennifer's termination. Usually, he compartmentalized things in neat little boxes and lined them up in a row to be checked off in sequence; however, when he mentally got to the point he arrived at this evening, he found himself looking at all the problems at once. It overwhelmed him. That even made him more anxious because he needed to think he could handle any situation. And in the un-tested conversations in his head, he started to blame Jennifer.

Without warning, he turned pleasant chit-chat into tension between bites of string beans and hamburger steak. "Why are you still here?" he asked Jennifer with a chew of hamburger still visible in the back of his cheek.

Dropping her fork, Jennifer slouched down in her chair. "What do you mean?" she said, trying to act stoic, but the hurt quickly manifested in her body language and wide eyes.

"I mean how long are you going to keep up this charade? You come into this house giving me hell, firing off negative fantasies about some kind of conspiracy, and taking advantage of our situation with your stories about a cure that doesn't exist."

Jennifer sucked her cheeks in. She stabbed her fork at a piece of burger, but did not pick it up to her mouth. Instead, she twisted the fork around slowly in the beef. Liv stared at her father in disbelief. Mel, too, seemed stunned by Dave's harshness.

"Bad day at the office, Dave?" Mel asked, a sharp edge in her tone.

"There have been a lot of bad days lately," he answered with his eyes still fixed on Jennifer.

"What are you saying?" Jennifer said. "Are you accusing me of lying? After all we've been through in that business for nearly two years, are you saying you don't trust me?"

"It doesn't add up," Dave responded. "Why would the Aldrich not put out a vaccine that could make it a fortune? Why would Claire or her people kill one of their top researchers? And right at the time of implementation in

Sierra Leone. And then why would you be in fear of your life over some relatively minor indiscretion? It makes no sense."

"You're calling me a liar."

Dave's eyes quickly reconnoitered the table. Mel sat poised to rip into him. Jennifer seemed to be on the edge between hurt and rage. And Liv had a confused look, suffused with a combination of fear and hurt.

He closed his eyes and expelled an explosion of air. "I don't know what I'm doing," he said in a much quieter and calmer tone, realizing negative fantasies had seized his thoughts.

"Getting out of control," Mel offered.

Dave wiped his napkin across his lips and got up from the table. "Just figure out how to get that cure," he said as he walked away.

"Butthead," Liv mumbled as soon as Dave exited the kitchen.

Mel glared at Liv.

Jennifer started clearing dishes from the table. "I'm not lying, guys," she said.

"I don't think you are," Liv said.

Mel nodded a weak assurance.

"He's not so attractive now, is he?" Liv added.

Jennifer's eyes widened.

"What's that about?" Mel asked, her antenna sprouting.

"Jennifer said he's attractive."

"I was talking about your family," Jennifer rejoined.

Mel's mouth formed a narrow, straight line as she spoke. "Right now, you can have him," Mel said.

"I don't want him."

"Who would?" Liv piped in.

Mel and Jennifer laughed uneasily. Then they busied themselves with cleaning up. Silence ensued for a few moments until Mel spoke off-handedly while loading the dishwasher. Liv had taken a short bathroom break.

"Do you have a thing for him?"

"No, no, I don't," Jennifer responded while she kept rinsing.

"Did you ever?"

"No," she said. "It was just business. You know Dave. It's always just business with him."

"I didn't ask about Dave," Mel said. "I'm talking about you."

Scraping a plate into the disposal, Jennifer answered, "I look up to him. He's been a mentor and I admire him. Nothing more than that. When I said that to Liv, I was trying to help her own self-image, telling her she comes from attractive parents."

"Parents or father?"

"Both."

Mel put the last dish in the dishwasher and slid the drawer in. "If you want to help my daughter, figure out how to get to that cure."

"Liv's really a sweet girl. I'll do anything I can."

Mel closed the dishwasher door and twisted the knob to start it. "How can I help?" Mel asked.

"I don't know. We have to get Claire to open up, but this whole thing is way out of hand. I don't know if she had anything directly to do with killing Sheila, but there's reason to believe she might have. Sheila was my way in."

"Is there anyone else you know inside?"

"Not that will help. And if Claire or her security people heard I was trying to get to somebody, I could end up like Sheila."

"I don't want you risking your life. You want a de-caf?"

"Thanks."

Mel pulled a bag of ground coffee out of the cabinet and spooned it into the coffeemaker. "Do you think the cure is in Boulder?"

"No, it's where Sheila worked. At the lab in Cameron Pass."

"How do we get in there?"

"With an army. The place is heavily guarded. They'd see us on camera as soon as we were within 50 yards of the gate."

Mel began filling the coffee pot with water. "Do you still know anyone working at Cameron Pass?" she asked.

"No one I can trust," Jennifer said, folding the same dishtowel for the third time.

"Why would they keep the cure a secret? Does it make sense to you?"

"No, none of it makes any sense, but that's from my perspective. Claire McQuaid is very brilliant. She probably has very sound reasons, at least from her worldview."

Mel poured the water into the coffeemaker and flipped it on. "Too bad you didn't take her offer to go back to work. You could work this from the inside."

"Or be killed," Jennifer said contemplatively.

"If you're not just being paranoid."

"I wish I knew that answer."

Mel nodded as the coffeemaker started to gurgle.

CHAPTER 24

Sierra Leone: Mountain Road
December 6, 3:22 p.m. Greenwich Mean Time

From the cover of the jungle, Jacob and the boys, their cheeks gaunt from hunger and their strenuous hike, pondered the roadblock at the foot of the bridge. Hundreds of refugees queued up on the pitted dirt road, consulting their companions and preparing to offer the bribe that would cause the tee-shirted criminals at the makeshift obstacle to let them pass.

For three days, the boys fought among themselves in the jungle. They had alternated between high agitation and extreme weariness, but their withdrawal from the crack cocaine their leaders had administered already had begun to temper. The fire had gone from their eyes, replaced now by fearfulness and depression.

Automatic fire exploded in the air. A body bounced down the embankment beside the road, the man dead almost instantly as the sickening thud of bullets ripped his torso.

A family approached the guards with trepidation. A series of questions and answers were exchanged. The father, a man with only one arm, handed one of the gunmen a parcel his toddler daughter had been carrying; the family walked on. Whispers carrying the right answers passed down the line of refugees. All knew they could be killed if they said they came from the wrong village or if the teenage gunmen did not like their look. They knew they could be kidnapped, too, particularly if they were coveted for either their bodies in the case of the women and girls, or for their potential as soldiers or laborers in the case of the boys and men.

"They'll kill us for sure," one of the boys commented to Jacob.

"We're on the same side," one of the others said.

"Until we killed our commanders," Jacob said.

"You think the word is out?"

"This jungle doesn't keep secrets very well," Jacob responded

"What do we do?"

The roadblock sat at the foot of a bridge that spanned an otherwise un-fordable white water section of river. They might be able to ford the river miles upstream, but large bandit elements controlled most of the land along the route. Jacob feared that word of their mutiny outside the refugee camp had spread. He feared they had pictures of at least him if not the other boys. The other side of the bridge had been government-held territory earlier in the week. Maybe it still was.

The boys watched as four rebels wrestled a boy about their age and a man who must have been his father, pulling them from near the head of the line of refugees. The four pushed them at gunpoint toward the center of the bridge, jabbing them with the butts of their rifles, kicking them and shoving them when they tried not to move. The boy clung to the man and he held him close. They could hear the boy crying, begging. Several pops sounded; father and son fell into the water, small trails of blood tracing their fall.

"We attack," said Jacob.

"Are you crazy? They'll come after us."

"After they're dead, grab their packs," Jacob continued. "They'll have food and extra ammo in them."

"It's suicide."

"We have no choice."

One of the boys dropped to the ground whimpering. "I just want to go home," he said.

Jacob kicked him in the side and threatened the butt of the gun against his head. The boy rose.

"You can hit us if you want, chief boy," another challenged, "but we don't want to die today. Who else stands with me?"

Two other boys walked over to join the protestor.

"They will have jambaa and crack in those packs," Jacob said, referring to the marijuana and cocaine the boys still craved.

"Are you certain?"

"What does it matter?" another asked. "If there's even a chance they have any… Let's get them."

The boys voiced unanimity at the prospect of getting drugs.

"All right, here it is," Jacob said. "This bridge is the best chance we have to get away from the rebels and find our way back to our homes. Let's have one last good fight. Then we can be done with all this."

He used leaves and lines in the dirt to show the boys his plan.

A few moments later, one of Jacob's boys raced from the jungle and toward the head of the refugee line. He took a basket off a woman's head and began to run among the queuing refugees. Two of the teenage bandits gave chase. As they did, Jacob and five of the eight remaining boys emerged from the greenery firing a deadly hail of bullets at the remaining five thugs. Two went down immediately, but a group of terrified women and children ran forward into the line of fire.

"Stop shooting," Jacob yelled and his boys relaxed their trigger fingers.

It did not stop the bandit gunmen. Using the women as shields, they turned the fire back on Jacob's boys. One dropped on each side of Jacob, including the one who had begged to go home.

"Get them!" Jacob yelled, instinctively running at the human shields so that the gunmen could not see him. The two surviving members of his band followed his example and the boys quickly forced hand-to-hand combat with their bigger opponents.

Further down the line, three more of Jacob's boys appeared inside the queue stepping between the fleeing thief and his pursuers. The pursuers were cut down rapidly. The three boys and the fourth who had set up the diversion with his theft ran back toward the front.

There they discovered four of their comrades dead. Only Jacob had so far survived the hand-to-hand combat. Unarmed, he scrambled away from a pursuer to recover his gun. The rebel aimed his rifle at Jacob, but a bullet cut him down before he could fire. More gunfire followed and the rest of the bandits fell.

The five surviving boys did not stop to mourn their friends. The sound of the gunfire would draw other gangsters out of the jungle within minutes. Jacob recovered his rifle and the thief returned the basket to the woman. They all quickly scavenged their victims' packs and pockets for drugs, ammo and food, but found nothing but a few candy bars. These dead teens had little more going for them than Jacob's boys.

Throwing the rocks and wire that blocked the bridge into the river, the boys paused to count bandit bodies.

"I count seven," Jacob said, "There were eight."

"No, I think there were only seven."

"I counted eight," Jacob reiterated. "One of them has escaped."

Another boy spoke up, "I remember seeing eight, too."

"Then let's spread out into the woods and find him," another boy encouraged.

"We can't," Jacob cautioned. "We made enough racket that they'll find us in a few minutes. We have to run."

"They killed our friends. We have to avenge them. Rambo would."

"They died so that we could get across the bridge," Jacob argued.

"They'll find us anyway if that man gets away," another boy said.

"I'm going to cross that bridge," Jacob insisted. "You can come with me or you can stay."

"It's not enough to cross the bridge, Jacob. We have to do more."

"If you cross, you cross alone."

"I saw the man, captain chief. He grabbed a pack and ran with it as soon as we started firing. He must have the drugs."

"There are no drugs on the other side of that bridge, not with the government troops," another said.

Jacob looked at the bodies of his fallen friends, saw their eyes wide open in the shock of death, their mouths agape in surprise. He had seen far too much of this. He wanted to just run away, but paramount chiefs did not run. He felt the small welt on his temple where the rebels cut him and put in the cocaine that enslaved him. It made him feel strong, like a chief.

While the boys debated, the refugees began pouring past them, not stopping to say thank you, not even understanding what had happened.

Nothing abnormal had occurred for them. The random violence had simply turned temporarily in their favor.

"Do all of you want to find the missing man?"

"We want his crack and jambaa," declared one of the boys.

The remaining boys said yes in unison, a couple of them pounding the butts of their awkwardly large rifles on the ground.

"Then let's go," Jacob said, leading his followers away from the bridge they captured at such a high price. A part of the bony, ten year old gave up at that moment. The cycle of violence would not stop. For every death, more would need to die in an ever-expanding circle of carnage.

CHAPTER 25

Fort Collins: Clements' Kitchen
December 7, 9:10 a.m. Mountain Time

On Saturday morning, Jennifer, dressed in a green Colorado State sweatshirt and blue jeans, found Liv curled up on the family room couch watching cartoons. Liv caught her arrival in her peripheral vision.

"I'll change it if you want," Liv said.

"No, this is great. I love cartoons."

"Aren't you a little old for that?"

"Aren't you?"

The two laughed.

"It's always fun to be a kid," Jennifer said.

"Mostly," Liv replied without taking her eyes off the screen.

"Your folks up?"

"They're on the back porch having coffee."

"I probably should say good morning."

"I'll save your seat," Liv said.

Jennifer pushed the sliding glass door open and walked out to the patio. Mel and Dave sat bundled in sweat jackets, sipping coffee in the forty-degree temperature. The sun hung low in the southeastern sky causing the shadows of the leafless aspens and the full-bodied Ponderosa pines to expand to twice their actual length across the golden expanse of winter grass in the backyard.

"Aren't you guys cold?" she opened.

"Sun's warm," Mel said. "There's more coffee inside."

"I'll get it in a minute. We need to talk."

"Be my guest," said Dave.

"Something's been bothering me. I don't know if I should even raise it. I'm sure it's already a big enough effort to believe me as it is."

"It's not about believing you," Dave said. "But I am concerned that you have a very convoluted understanding of reality."

Jennifer pressed her palms on her thighs, blowing out. "I'd better get a coffee before I tell you any more then."

She returned a moment later with the coffee pot. She refilled Dave's cup and Mel's before filling her own. She put the pot down and sat on the porch step, starting to shiver slightly. She pulled her knees up to her chest and tucked her coffee mug into her bosom for warmth.

"Sheila told me something that I completely discounted as paranoia at the time, but in light of everything, it's worth putting this in the mix."

Mel nodded.

"Go ahead," Dave said.

"Sheila said the presence of IRA as security really troubled her. It caused her to do a little probing. She apparently got cozy with a few of the IRA boys and they would run their mouths as they got more and more comfortable with her. They told her that a splinter IRA group had infiltrated the lab."

"An IRA group within an IRA group?"

"I don't know. And Sheila didn't. She only had pieces of the puzzle. It caused her to conclude that this element somehow had links with the Vatican. She surmised that their objective had something to do with sabotaging the malaria vaccine to demonstrate the dangers of westernization in Sierra Leone."

Dave choked on a sip of coffee. "Really?"

"Yes."

"Your friend was truly paranoid. Maybe she killed herself."

"Dave," Mel said. "That's way out of line."

"Was. Not is. I saw the body, Dave. It was no suicide. And she wasn't paranoid."

"Look, Jennifer," Mel said. "This is all pretty incredible to us. We've spent our lives working in middle class America, earning a regular living and being pretty average. What you've described to us since you showed up on our doorstep amounts to a parallel dimension."

"It's hard for me, too," Jennifer replied. "I grew up in a small shotgun house in Lockhart, Texas. My mother managed a small barbecue joint. We didn't see any of this stuff either."

"So do you believe it?"

"I'm probably like the two of you. I don't know what to believe."

Dave shifted uneasily in his chair. "A Vatican conspiracy's a little over the top."

"You have every right to be skeptical. All of this is bizarre. But I'm looking at the world a lot differently since I figured out that Claire had Sheila killed."

"How about going to the police or the FBI?" Mel asked.

"She can't do that," Dave responded for Jennifer. "The Aldrich is up to its ears in Federal contacts. Every President in the last 20 years, if not longer, has some ties to Thatcher Ripley. Going to the FBI is going to just let them know where she is."

"And let them know you're involved," Jennifer continued. "I don't think there is a place to turn."

"Well, you can't hide here the rest of your life," Mel said.

"If we could get some hard evidence, we could get the press involved," Dave said. "The press could force the Aldrich's backers to be extremely careful and make you untouchable."

"I agree," Jennifer said. "That might be my best hope."

"How do you get evidence?" Mel inquired.

"That's the rub," Jennifer said.

"Well, you two work on ideas," Dave said, getting up. "I need to get down to the office for a few hours."

"Can't you just stay home one Saturday?" Mel said.

"I did that over Thanksgiving weekend, Mel. All we got for that was a house guest."

Dave looked past Jennifer. He bent over and kissed Mel. "Later," he said.

Liv heard her father call good-bye and walk through the foyer to the garage. Other Colorado families went skiing on December weekends or Christmas tree shopping, she thought. Not hers. They sat around and waited for their workaholic father to come home. But he's doing it for us, she reminded herself. At least, he thinks so.

She reflected on the pills she had not yet taken that morning. They can wait, she thought.

CHAPTER 26

Aldrich Mountain Lab, Cameron Pass
December 9, 11:05 a.m. Mountain Time

Eldridge Perry moved his mouse over the pad, bringing the screen to life with teeming organisms. With a few clicks, the simulation zoomed Eldridge and Claire deep into the heart of a DNA strand.

"This is the chromosome to which Epstein Barr is linked. Watch this." Eldridge changed the view again. "See the broken chain. That's why malaria cuts these people down so readily."

"Fascinating," Claire said, squeezing Eldridge's arm.

Eldridge's rock hard upper arm, the result of lifelong habits and frequent trips to the lab's fitness center, provided the only succor to Claire's long-since eroded stereotype. Beyond that, Eldridge bore no resemblance to his namesake's super masculine menial descriptor for African American men. Perry's parents, black activist lawyers in Chicago, had both read Eldridge Cleaver's Soul on Ice while Mrs. Perry was pregnant with what proved to be their only child. Finding Cleaver's seminal work explicatory of much of what they had experienced in mid-twentieth century America, they memorialized him in their son. The Perry's had only been slightly disappointed when their son demonstrated a clear preference for science over social activism.

"Our Mal-D protein shores up that chain, providing immunity to known mutations of malaria," Eldridge continued.

It had taken Claire to plumb the depths of the man and kindle the latent flame of activism his parents could not see from perspectives rooted in litigation, a process that often bore no consequential fruit. Their son's path, however, would bear fruit that would change history on a grand scale.

Claire credited him as the backbone of the lab's successful research. Both brilliant scientist and able administrator, Eldridge ran the day-to-day research operations of the mountain lab, carefully compartmentalizing the work into small teams of people who had little or no knowledge of the work of their peers elsewhere in the facility. Sometimes, only an individual handled a certain piece of the project so important was it for that person and others not to see how the activity connected to anything else.

As a result, only a handful knew what the total end product would look like. If anyone uninvited entered that circle, both Eldridge and Claire considered it a security breach of the highest order requiring expeditious dispatch.

"Mal-D's action leads to shoring up the DNA linkages attributed to Epstein Barr Virus or EBV," Eldridge said, reiterating what they both already knew as he practiced his presentation. "Gives us a cure for EBV, a very viable commercial product in the US."

"Which lets us be the good guys in the third world while we make money at home on the same product," Claire added. "We can't emphasize that enough."

"Right. And through another protein, we get what we're after on the HIV/AIDS front."

"Problem is we don't have CEM15-D finished."

"We'll get it."

"We need it," Claire said. "We're not going to get away with this charade for too long if we don't deliver. Maybe we need to force Jennifer back in now. She'll know how to drive this project home."

Eldridge's eyes blazed. "I don't know why you keep going back to that. I can do anything Jennifer can do."

"There's only one of you, Eldridge."

"I have a team."

"And we lost its best member because you got careless. You blew the compartmentalization. She should never have known enough to be nervous."

Eldridge breathed hard through his nose, almost a snort.

"It's not that you can't do it," Claire added. "It's a bandwidth issue. If Jennifer were here, she would have had more time to monitor Sheila's activities."

"Whatever you say," he snapped. "Right now, I don't see Jennifer back here. And she can be very dangerous to us on the street. You're being too damned sentimental, Claire."

Claire pondered him through narrowed eyes for a moment. "You know better, Eldridge. I had a soft spot for Sheila, too, but I followed the recommendation of you and Mike Farley. I don't let sentiment get in the way of business."

Eldridge tapped his fingers on the side of the keyboard. Thirty seconds passed.

"Why don't you show me the rest of what you have," Claire said, rolling her chair back a bit. It annoyed her that she felt qualms of regret about Sheila. Maybe that did, in fact, cloud her judgment about Jennifer.

"Fine," Eldridge said. "Let's just move on."

He clicked twice more. A white blood cell and an HIV infected cell appeared on the screen. In a time-lapse sequence, a Vif-D protein, manufactured by the Aldrich, moved away from the HIV host and attacked the healthy cell's wall. A CEM15 gene moved to stop it, but immediately collapsed, a result that would not have happened so readily with natural Vif. Natural Vif would ultimately lose the battle but it often took years, not moments as in this case.

On the monitor, the HIV quickly penetrated to the center of the cell. Suddenly, it replicated rapidly and the replicants nearly exploded from the cell.

"That's what I've done for this effort," he said.

"So it's working perfectly."

"Like a Swiss watch."

"And no one will be able to detect the introduction of the Vif-D with the malaria vaccine?"

"Exactly," Eldridge said, relaxing as he re-focused on the technology. "The PDNA test, done before administration of the vaccine, shows that the patient is a good candidate for the malaria vaccine. If they have HIV, the report shows they have a pre-existing, but hitherto unknown, mutation of the virus. Of course, the reality is that they did not have our new, more aggressive HIV sub-type until after they received the vaccine, but our hack of the PDNA will show the subjects had it all along."

"And no one will ever be the wiser because there has never been enough research in Sierra Leone to identify the prevalent strain of HIV there," Claire said

She sat back in her chair and crossed her legs, careful to pull a wrinkle out of the inner thigh of her blue jeans as she did so.

"We can thank Evan Conger and Dave Clement for this," she said. "Adrian Guerra did a masterful job of getting them to move the malaria vaccine effort to Sierra Leone."

Eldridge smiled now. "If they had stuck with Nigeria, we'd be dead in the water," he enthused. "The mutation there, HIV-1 clade G, is so well-researched that our little mutation would have jumped out and caused suspicion from the outset. But not in a country where the carnage has kept even Doctors Without Borders on the sidelines. No one knows what's there. Our mutation, clade – which one are we up to?"

"I believe it will be L," McQuaid answered.

"Clade L then. It's like it's been there all along. No one has any way of knowing otherwise. And the PDNA proves it. If anyone needs to do primary research on HIV-1 Clade L, they won't need to go back and take fresh blood samples. We'll have provided everything they need with the PDNA's data. It's just incredible that we've pulled this off."

"And only we'll know that anything ever existed there other than the mutation," Claire added calmly, her eyes glazing over as her mind wandered to Sierra Leone.

"It's foolproof as long as no one cracks the code or talks. Sheila wrote it so that risk is minimal."

Eldridge clicked to the PDNA page and studied the analysis. The PDNA had completely re-written the history of each subject's virus. Amazing, he thought. He spun his chair around.

"Your team at Prodeus did a great job with this technology, too," he offered. "You really did a good job of picking them. And they still don't know the difference, right?"

"That's right," Claire said, nodding. "Thanks to Jennifer. Don't forget that."

"I suppose the employees there are the only ones outside of our control who could really figure this out."

Claire responded, smiling, "As long as their top dogs are motivated to see things our way, any suspicions from their troops will be stopped dead in their tracks."

"And I suppose that's been a big part of what Jennifer's done."

"Might never have pulled it off without her."

"When you told me to give her up two years ago, I thought you were out of your mind. She was my key informatics person, but you were right."

"And playing both sides of the fence as kind of a double agent is very stressful," Claire said. "The pressure never came off her."

"I can't deny any of that," he said. "But it doesn't make her any less of a security threat now."

Claire did not respond. She lifted her eyebrows as if to say, "Anything else?"

"No matter what," he said, changing the subject, "we will soon announce the coincidence of our timely discovery of a new HIV mutation, clade L, as a result of our malaria vaccine implementation. A marvelous and serendipitous event."

"A mutation that kills in months instead of a decade," Claire added, grim satisfaction in her voice.

"We're changing the face of a continent," Eldridge said, almost dreamily. "We're allowing the countries of sub-Saharan Africa to get back on their feet, to build sound economies without the twin burdens of malaria and HIV. Billions and billions of dollars can be routed productively instead of prolonging lives already lost."

Claire said nothing right away. She steepled her fingers and studied her top man. "All the killing doesn't bother you?" she finally asked.

Eldridge looked at her quizzically. "You're the one that taught me to measure this from the perspective of two generations into the future. These people are going to die anyway. Maybe some would linger but they would only be parasitic. No, I have no qualms about this."

Claire moved her head up and down slowly, her green eyes now burning into Eldridge's. "Never waiver, Eldridge. Never."

Claire rose from her chair very carefully. Like an old woman, Eldridge thought.

Moving between the gray shadows of the specialized lighting for computer viewing, her frail frame appeared ghost-like as she shuffled from the room without saying another word.

CHAPTER 27

Prodeus Offices
December 10, 9:55 a.m. Mountain Time

Ed sat, hands folded on the conference table. Dorfmann jabbered at high speed at the opposite end of the table. Between them, Dave sat puzzled.

"Thatcher Ripley's the best house on Wall Street," Dan said. "Why should we be bothered? In fact, I think we should be complimented..."

Ed interrupted Dorfmann's monolog. "Dan, hold on. With Centerview and Leerink not bidding, Thatcher Ripley's got us over a barrel. That does not feel comfortable at all. If we can't generate any more interest than this, we'll end up undervalued when we go out."

"How much of a problem would that be?" asked Dave.

Dorfmann spoke, "It's still a big number, but without other underwriters bidding, we may have no choice."

"Cuts into our ability to assert some independence with the Aldrich," Ed added. "It will be tough to afford to get FDA approval for the PDNA in the US on our own if we don't have that cash increment."

"Maybe we can cut back somewhere else," Dave suggested.

"Where?" Dorfmann said, throwing his hands up.

Dave shrugged. He knew that Prodeus already operated on a shoestring. Getting more working capital for new hires was one of the key missions of the IPO. Many Prodeus employees put in average weeks in excess of 55 hours just to keep up with current requirements, an unsustainable average over the long run. Moreover, field deployment required better internal systems and a larger support team.

"I could almost understand it if Leerink or Centerview had come back to us with caveats, but to just bow out of bidding...," Ed mused.

"These things happen all the time in public offerings," Dorfmann said, "The others probably don't realize Thatcher's in so hard. Remember, this is what I know best."

Dave shook his head. He pondered arguing with Dorfmann's logic, but he knew Ed completely trusted the CFO on financial matters. The image of Liv lying on the gym floor popped into his head. He again heard her soft crying the night they first found out about the HIV. He thought of the pills in the medicine cabinet. The pills and the bills – and the bills yet to come for therapies that insurance might not cover. Plus all the uncertainty created by Sheila's disappearance – and murder if Jennifer were to be believed. No, Dave already had rattled Hepp's confidence by not firing Jennifer. Wading in against Dorfmann could do real damage. Whether the IPO brought in $5 less per share or not, Dave looked to have more money than he ever imagined, enough to take care of his family indefinitely.

Looking to Dorfmann, he offered a supportive grin. "You're the finance guy, Dan. Just tell me what I need to make happen on the ops end."

Ed rested his elbows on the conference table and steepled his finger. "Four months ago, before we started shopping this deal, underwriters called us daily," he said. "The interest bowled me over. Nothing about our story has changed since. The IPO market for our space is even hotter. It's almost like someone called off the other underwriters."

"Who would do that?" Dave asked.

"Thatcher Ripley," Hepp suggested. "They have the weight to do something like that."

"But why?" Dorfmann asked. "There's nothing for them to gain in that. Plus it's illegal as hell."

"Right," Ed mumbled, squeezing his hands together tightly on the table, "What if we went back to other underwriters? At least we could line up some boutiques as co's."

Dorfmann drummed his fingers on his notepad. "I've done that," he said. "They'll co-underwrite, but it's crystal clear. TR is the lead. They're not going to buck that. And they said that they won't work with any other lead."

Ed eyes widened. "That's walking away from an easy fee. I don't get it."

Dorfmann shrugged.

Dave thought about the conversation much of the remainder of the day. Another conspiracy theory in the works, this time involving Thatcher Ripley. He remembered that Pamela Thatcher sat on the Aldrich board, with her family trust in effective control of the business. Did the cross-interests affect the course of things here? Had Jennifer or Sheila worried Thatcher and Claire with some kind of forbidden knowledge?

Dave wished that Conger still lived. He might offer enlightened insight into all this. The plane crash had… Sabotage. The word flashed in Dave's brain. Maybe Sheila had not been the first victim of this "plot."

Dave pulled out a Celestial Seasons Tension Tamer tea bag. He walked down the hall to the hot water tap. As he poured the scalding water into a mug, he chastised himself for succumbing to paranoia. Too much Jennifer Winters in the house, he thought. No conspiracy, he concluded. Just the ongoing ebb and flow of life's fortunes. And if there were a conspiracy, he could not do anything about it in any event. The players he speculated about had far more effective resources than he could ever muster.

He put the mug to his mouth, carefully sipping the hot liquid. The aroma of the tea wafted to his nose on a cloud of steam. Already, he felt more at ease.

Better get back to problems he could do something about, he thought as the doubts burrowed deeper into his sub-conscious.

CHAPTER 28

Fort Collins: Interstate 25
December 10, 5:15 pm. Mountain Time

Dave left the office before six that night without a business reason. He just wanted to get out. As he sped up I-25, paranoid fantasies persisted. TR and the Aldrich -- they knew about Jennifer's hideout. Or suspected it. But he had no reason to think they did. Except for paranoia. Anyway, what would that have to do with an IPO?

Emptiness pervaded him, the kind that accompanies fear when you cannot find a place inside to latch on. He found his hands could not get comfortable on the steering wheel as he opened and closed his fists.

What about the HIV vaccine? he wondered. What about Claire's complete denial of a program Dave believed must exist in some form? Did the murder have something to do with the AIDS vaccine? Every time he brought it up to her, Claire, normally completely under control, got extremely edgy.

And the whole Vatican conspiracy thing that Jennifer laid out. That, Dave thought, amounted to the ultimate in ridiculous.

Pulling into the driveway, he cut the ignition and leaned his head against the neck rest of the driver's seat.

"You're imagining problems," he whispered to himself. "Relax. Jennifer's stories have you worked up."

He watched the flutter of light snow flurries softly reflect the dim, orange light from the lamp that peered from behind the drapes in the living room window. Peaceful and quiet. Snow calmed him. Even better than Tension Tamer, he thought.

He knew his peace would be short-lived. In a few moments, he would be inside getting updated on Liv's life. He could not even begin to imagine how it felt to be in her skin every day. He thanked God that the other kids knew nothing about it.

He remembered that Jennifer would be inside, too. He hoped she would have something constructive to report. Then again, how could she? She had not done anything to help. What had happened to her? For two years she had been at his side in the business, trusted by him. He had confided in her. Then, in a matter of weeks, it had all gone away. She made advances on him, made him very uncomfortable and risked compromising him in the office. And the whole HIV cure thing. It appeared she had lost her job over that. Plus it seemed to diminish his personal capital with both Claire and Ed Hepp. Now, she hid in his house, running from some kind of hit man.

Dave thought that it still made no sense. Why would Claire risk relationship with Prodeus over his understandable indiscretion about the HIV vaccine? He thought that she wouldn't. Moreover, Jennifer had been her eyes and ears at Prodeus. When engineering tried to de-compile the code from the Aldrich, Jennifer had stepped in and made sure it stopped. And Jennifer brokered the joint development agreement. Dave believed that without her, PDNAs would probably not have been deployed in Sierra Leone so quickly. Middleton swore she was some kind of spy. She...

Dave felt the hairs on the back of his neck rise. What if she still was a spy? he thought. What if she was, in fact, right in the middle of Sheila's murder? What if she was setting up Dave and his family somehow? She and Claire had manipulated Hepp to get her fired at Prodeus, setting up the whole charade that put her inside the Clement household.

But why? Could the HIV vaccine be a complete sham? Something to draw his whole family in. But Claire and Jennifer could not have anticipated Liv getting HIV. Without Liv's HIV, Dave would never have approached Claire about the vaccine. That argued there was no plot involving both Claire and Jennifer. Unless...

Dave pondered the inconceivable. What if Jennifer and McQuaid had somehow arranged for her to contract HIV? No, they wouldn't do that, he argued with himself. What would be the point? Then he wondered why he expected obvious logic to step in now? Whatever was going on had logic that completely eluded him. Dave felt anxiety re-building inside him, his throat tightening and his pulse pounding.

"Stop it," he demanded out loud. "You're driving yourself crazy. None of this is true."

He sucked in a deep breath and then grabbed his safety belt to unlatch it. He laughed as a bizarre thought raced through his head. When he was a kid and somebody had cooties, you could protect yourself by grabbing your belt and yelling safety belt.

"Safety belt," he whispered as he unbuckled and got out of the car.

When he entered the house, its darkness chilled him. Only a small bulb under the stovetop provided any light in the blackness. Dave quickly turned on the foyer light and called for Mel and Liv.

Getting no answer, he moved from room to room flipping lights on. In the kitchen, he checked the answering machine. No messages there and none on his mobile. After checking the bedrooms, he went down to the basement looking for Jennifer in the guest room. He felt a small surge of fear through his midsection each time he turned a corner, but no one jumped out to greet or attack him. No bad guys. No Jennifer.

Looking in the garage, he saw that Mel's car was gone. Returning to the kitchen, he called Mel on her mobile and found her having margaritas and eating dinner at the Rio Grande restaurant with two of the women with whom she worked. She said she had thought he would be out until at least eight-thirty or nine as had become his custom. Liv and Jennifer, she said, had gone back to the rock gym on South Mason after Liv finished volleyball practice. She expected that they probably wouldn't be home until almost nine.

"Do you want me to come home and make you dinner?" Mel asked.

"No, you stay with your friends," he said, feeling a strange sense of pride in Mel's attempt to revert to the independent woman he married. "It's been a long time since you broke away by yourself at night."

"I can't," she replied. "I feel guilty."

"Are you having fun? Or were you before I called?"

"We were having some laughs."

"Then have another margarita. You've been taking all the heat around here."

Dave felt an urge to invite himself to join them for a margarita of his own, but he knew that would completely spoil the effect, giving into the addiction, not the cure.

"If I have another drink, I won't be home 'til after 9."

"Then make it one of those big ones. I think I might just head up to bed early and catch a sitcom. I could use a little brainless entertainment."

"You deserve it," she said. "There's leftover hamburger hash in the fridge. Put it in the microwave for three minutes."

"Thanks, Mel. Have a good time."

Dave poured himself a decaffeinated iced tea, squeezed in a big wedge of lemon. After re-heating the hamburger hash, he took the tea and the leftovers to bed with him. By 9 o'clock, he slept soundly, the bedside light on low, the TV's volume down and a book in the bed just out of reach of the hand from which it fell. His dinner dish, not a morsel left on it, and his tea glass, its ice melted around the lemon wedge into a quarter cup of water, remained on the nightstand.

By the time Mel found him an hour later, a circle of drool the size of a silver dollar dampened the pillow just below his open mouth. She gently dabbed a tissue on his chin and righted his head before fluffing his pillow. She kissed him on the forehead. Ten minutes later, she turned off the light and TV, crawling into bed beside him.

Dave rolled onto his side, his eyes flapping open in the dark.

"Mel?"

"Yes, sweetheart."

"You just get home?"

"Mm-hmmm. Go back to sleep. I love you."

A few minutes later, Dave had curled up behind her and showed signs of getting frisky for the first time in weeks. He must really be relaxed, Mel thought. At first, she entertained welcoming his interest. Then she heard the faint sound of voices from the television in the basement two stories below the master bedroom.

"We can't, Dave."

"Too many margaritas?" he whispered.

"That wouldn't be a problem. Jennifer's right underneath us. I don't think I want to share any more of our private life with her."

"Maybe we could be real quiet," he suggested.

She rolled over, seeing in his eye a glint of light from the street lamp outside their window.

"I don't know if you can do that," she whispered and then kissed him softly on the mouth.

"I'll try my best," he replied between kisses.

CHAPTER 29

Sierra Leone: Rebel Camp
December 11, 7:34 p.m. Greenwich Mean Time

Ani whispered a prayer to her son, careful not to be heard by her captors.

"If I only knew where this was, but I don't know the bush around here. You are all that keeps me going, Jacob. I pray every minute of every day for you to be well. I pray to all the gods I know, even your father's Jesus. He is the most comfortable one for me now because he always seems so kind. I miss kindness."

An eleven year old girl approached, interrupting her prayer. "I want to run," she said, "But he said he will kill me if I run. Will he really kill me?"

"If he catches you," Ani said, trying to smile, struggling to find a way to provide some comfort to the girl.

"Will he catch me?"

She was so skinny, so frail, her breasts no more than small buds. Ani felt certain the girl had yet to have her period. "I don't know," she answered, now adjusting her position on the fallen log she chose for a chair.

"But you're his wife. You must know."

"He made me his wife just as he made you his wife."

"Why?" the child asked.

Ani looked down at the ground thoughtfully. "For money, for power. They steal the wives and children of others because they think it will make them more powerful, that their spirits will become unbeatable. They chose my village because one of their leaders wants the bauxite deposits under our ancestral land. He is the chief of the Abo, a neighboring tribe." Ani's eyes watered. "They took my son. They took my home, my parents, everything I loved. To die is not a bad thing. It is something we all must do one day. My village has died. My God changed shape even before the bandits. My family is gone. To outlive everything you hold sacred is not a good thing."

"Should I want to die then?" the little girl asked, a warm hand on Ani's bare shoulder.

Ani sighed. "Oh, no, child, no. There is goodness yet in this life. I have seen it. I see it in you. But hold on to something."

The girl turned and faced into the jungle. She and Ani both sat on the edge of the log silently for a moment.

Ani looked down at the girl's head. She studied her braids, as disproportionate to her small head as her wide brown eyes.

"You have beautiful braids. Who plaited them?"

"My mama."

"Have you seen them?"

The girl looked puzzled.

"With a mirror?" Ani clarified.

"Yes. My mama always let me look in her mirror at my hair."

"Then you know how beautiful they are."

"Mama told me they were, but I thought mothers just said those things because they were supposed to."

"They say it because it's true and because they love their children. Like your mother loved you."

The girl put her arms around Ani, burying her face in the woman's shoulder, tears quietly flowing from her eyes. After a moment, the girl pulled back. Ani remembered when the rebels found her a week earlier. They took her and two other girls into an abandoned house one at a time. Four of the bastards made them undress and lay naked on a piece of brown cloth. She screamed and cried as they dragged her in.

"I don't know man business! I don't know man business! Please! Please!"

From inside the house, Ani could hear the girl pleading for her life. Then she heard her chant, "Father, save me from these men. Return me to my home. Father, save me from these men. Return me to my home. Father, save…"

The girl flopped down in the dirt beside her. Ani looked at her own hands. Her dirty nails had deep cracks in them, the blue and yellow of bruises coloring them instead of polish. Cuts, burns and bruises riddled her skin, products of the work her self-appointed husband made her do.

"Are you Jacob's mother?" the girl asked.

"I am. How did you know?"

"I heard them talk about Jacob Karja -"

"Karanja?"

"Yes, that's it. They say they are going to kill him."

Ani's breath caught. Hearing this, her nightmare, come from this child's mouth seemed to give it added credence. But the bandits threatened nearly everyone. There really was no news here.

"I know they would like to," she said evenly.

"No, he is very important to them. They say he is killing rebels, that he's a traitor."

Ani grew rigid. "They're not rebels, "she said. "They're just thugs whose only cause is their own gratification." She looked down the length of her leg to where her right foot had once been. He told her he had cut it off to make sure she never ran from him. He kept it in a canvas bag he made her carry, a bag filled with other hands and feet, his prizes, his power.

"When did you hear this?" Ani asked.

"When I served dinner. They have a picture of him on their phones."

Ani pushed herself up on to her good leg. She stood erect with a slight tilt to the right. It still hurt - a lot - but she had learned to hobble on the stump. She would hobble very far tonight.

CHAPTER 30

Sierra Leone: In the Rainforest
December 12, 1:05 p.m. Greenwich Mean Time

Jacob applied the wet rag to the boy's head.

"I'm cold, Jacob."

The sweltering sun on Jacob's back left him no doubt that this boy and two of the others had some terrible illness. Jacob and the two boys left standing had been ministering to them since the middle of the night.

"Malaria," Jacob whispered to Moise, one of the healthy boys.

"I don't think so," Moise said.

"What else could it be?"

"Brown-brown," the boy said using the name the bandits gave heroin because of the color of the powder they secured from the Liberians.

"Brown-brown makes you feel good," Jacob said, although his own personal experience had not gone beyond the crack they stuffed into slits they cut in his skin, that and the fragrant jambaa the rebels smoked to ward off disease.

"I've seen this. It gets bad if you don't have the drug for a few days. Then you get over it."

"It's been five days since they had any. They should be better."

"They got some from the rebels we killed."

"We found nothing."

Moise played with the rag in his hands.

"Moise?"

"They said they would kill me if I told you. I caught them night before last."

"Did you have it?"

"No, they said there was no more. Anyway, I was never given any in the first place. That's a poison I don't want."

Jacob looked down the hill to the boys lying against tree trunks. If he had been given the brown-brown, he might be with them. God had spared him from the brown-brown.

"Will they get better?" Jacob asked.

"I don't know what happens to them."

"Maybe we should leave them."

"I can't. One of them is from my village. He, Etan and I grew up together."

Etan was the remaining healthy boy.

"Too bad we did not find the other bandit," Moise said. "He might have had enough brown-brown to keep them going."

"He's joined up with others by now," Jacob said, and then, hearing something. "Get Etan and the guns!"

Moise ran up to Etan who was ministering to one of the boys in withdrawal. In less than a minute, the three healthy boys deployed themselves on the perimeter of their small encampment. The three sick boys lay off the trail where they would not readily be detected.

Through giant ferns, Jacob, Moise and Etan watched as two men approached on the trail below.

"Let's take them," Etan said.

"No, not yet," Jacob ordered.

Jacob knew the gangs often used a small point contingent to smoke out foes. A larger contingent likely trailed another forty yards behind these two.

Firing exploded not more than thirty feet away from the boys. The three sick boys emerged from the woods, AK-47s smoking. The bandits died instantly. The three, resembling hyenas, tore open the packs of the dead men and scavenged their pockets for drugs.

Etan and Moise started to get up to join them. Jacob yanked both boys to the ground.

"Dammit, no!" Jacob said.

He yelled across to the others.

"Get off the trail! Now!"

Two of the boys ignored Jacob. The third one gave him the finger. One of the boys came up with a small plastic bag. The boys quickly tore their shirts off. They pulled knives and cut into swollen, red welts on their chests, shaking small portions of the brown powder into the bloody gashes.

"They will be better now," Moise said. "Let's go. Maybe they have some jambaa and food in those packs."

"Stay down," Jacob demanded between gritted teeth but he could feel his resolve slipping as the perception of danger started to subside.

Etan and Moise pushed the brush out of the way and headed down the hill.

"No, don't!" Jacob tried again. "There could be more."

"We'll drag them into the trees," Etan called back.

Giving up and questioning his own judgment, Jacob started to get up when he heard underbrush rustling down the trail, then metallic clicking.

Standing up, he yelled, "Get in the trees! Now!"

Already on the trail, Moise turned toward Jacob, a smile on his face, ready to tell Jacob to relax. Before the words formed, his forehead exploded. Etan began to pull his weapon up to fire, but fell before it reached his waist.

Jacob raised his weapon, but it jammed after two rounds. He huddled close to the ground and pounded the gun, struggling to make it work.

Two of the brown-brown boys scampered for cover, but five teenagers surrounded them, beating them to the ground with their rifle butts.

The third brown-brown boy had time to pick up his AK-47 and took down two of the thugs before his body began bouncing along the trail as the gangsters emptied their guns in rage.

Jacob loaded and unloaded his weapon, but to no avail. It remained jammed. The acrid smell of burnt gunpowder, suggestive of hot metal and the tip of a burnt match, filled his nose as the smoke from the firefight drifted up to his position. His eyes stung and began to water.

The captured boy, the last of Jacob's boys, begged for his life with his hands in the air pleading. One of the bandits swung a machete down and the boy screamed as his hand flew off his left arm.

Jacob shrunk deeper into his hiding place as the boy's screaming filled the jungle. The teenager who had swung the machete picked the hand up and stuffed it dripping blood into a souvenir bag on his waist. Another one stuck a machete in the waist band of the boy's shorts and sliced through their seat, causing them to drop to the ground. One of them put a hammerlock on the boy while another played with his testicles. Jacob watched in horror as the bandit stuck a knife into the testicle bag and sliced it off as the boy kicked and screamed maniacally. They picked the testicles up from the ground and stuffed them in the boy's open mouth. Jacob jerked his head away as the gangsters forced the boy to chew.

The boy dropped into the muck of his own fluids, moaning like a wounded dog. As he began vomiting, a bandit opened fire on his head with the boy's own AK-47. Jacob vomited and swallowed, desperate not to be heard.

Flattening himself on the ground, Jacob prayed the attackers did not find him. "Save me, Jesus. Please save me. Make me invisible. God, please make me invisible."

He watched in horror as the gang members sliced open the arms of the other victims and began sucking the warm blood from the lifeless bodies. He wanted to run, but the fear of being caught proved bigger than his revulsion at the scene below.

It would be another half hour before the thugs finished with their victory party. By then, a shivering Jacob, curled up like a fetus, would sink into a puddle of his own sweat and urine, his prayer for protection now a whispered mantra. He would not get up to bury his friends for hours.

CHAPTER 31

Fort Collins High School
December 12, 5:10 p.m. Mountain Time

Chelsea and Liv exchanged awkward smiles in the locker room.. They had been distant with each other since the discussion about Michael Winston. Tonight, Chelsea walked over to Liv's locker.

"Are we not friends anymore?" she asked.

"We're friends."

"You never told me what I did to you."

"Nothing, Chelsea."

"There's something. You're definitely not yourself."

"What's that supposed to mean?"

"Like what the hell, Liv. Give me a chance here. I'm trying to talk to you."

Liv finished zipping her jeans and reached for her gym bag. "We should probably talk, Chels. I know I'm not being fair to you. We have a half hour before the activity bus leaves. You want a soda?"

The two girls headed to the cafeteria where they poured drinks from the soda dispenser. Guided by Liv, they selected a table far away the after school crowd. Liv sipped her soda and then pondered Chelsea. She placed her hands on the edge of the table and sat up straight.

"I need your solemn promise that what I'm about to say goes nowhere," she said.

Chelsea raised her right hand in the air. "Oath. What's said between us stays between us."

Liv had rehearsed a dozen different ways to broach the subject. She did not know which one would come out of her mouth. "I don't know any other way to say this than to say it," she said. "I have a sickness. And you might have it, too."

"What kind of sickness?"

"Do you remember a couple years ago when we, ah, touched each other?"

"Touched? It was more than that."

"We shouldn't have done it."

"I still have no problem with it. I liked it and I thought you did. It doesn't make us lesbians. I still like guys."

"I exclusively like boys, but that's beside the point, Chels. We might have given each other something. "

"You mean like an STD? No way. You were my first. If anyone gave anyone anything, it was you."

"C'mon. You know that I still don't do that kind of thing. I've never even been kissed by a guy. And what about Aidan Vale in 7th grade?"

"Forgot about that. We didn't do it, though."

"You told me you touched and licked things."

Chelsea laughed. "That was so awkward."

"So maybe he gave you something."

"Aidan? He had zero experience. Trust me. And if he did, wouldn't he or I be sick?"

"You might not know it."

"What are we talking about, Liv?"

"HIV."

The smile dropped from Chelsea's face. "Tell me that's not what we're talking about. That's a death sentence."

Liv looked away.

"Omigod, Liv. I swear that you didn't get it from me. Like I mean, we'd know, wouldn't we?"

"You should be tested."

"No. I'm clean. You have to think about where else you might have gotten this."

"I don't know where else."

"It's not me. At least, then it wasn't me. Now you're making me nervous about what I've done since."

"Well you should be."

"Don't judge me."

"Sorry."

Chelsea dropped back in her seat. She grabbed her soda cup and brought the straw to her mouth, but she didn't sip. She put the cup back on the table. "So what do you do for this?" she asked.

"Drugs. Lots of drugs."

"Do they make you better?"

Liv laughed a slight laugh. "A little. Mostly they keep me from getting worse."

"So that's what's been wrong with you this whole time. When did you find out?"

"July. I had a low grade fever that wouldn't go away. And I felt miserable. Mom thought it was hormones. I wish it was."

"I haven't had any of that. How else could you get it?"

"Transfusions."

"So that must be it. Unless you have a love life that you keep incredibly secret."

Liv started to tell Chelsea that she had never had a transfusion, but chose not to. "No secret love life. You should still be checked. Just to be safe."

"What am I supposed to do? Tell mom I need an HIV test because I'm not the good little virgin she thinks I am. I don't think that works."

"Doctors have to keep it confidential. You can go to a clinic and they'll test you."

"For free?"

"I don't know."

"Is that what you did?"

"Would have been nice. No. My mom and dad knew as soon as I did because I had no clue what was going on. I didn't think I had anything to hide."

"How have they been?"

"Good. Most of the time. I think they both suspect I've had sex."

"They know about the transfusions, right?"

"Sure," Liv lied. "But I still think they wonder."

"The Liv I know is more likely to be the school's last standing virgin. I'll tell them if you want."

"That's not necessary. I'm not even sure I want them to know you know. The fewer people involved the better. And I may want to be a virgin, but it doesn't mean I don't want a love life."

"Does that love life have a name?"

"That's the other thing we have to talk about. Michael Winston."

"No way. I staked that claim weeks ago."

"You didn't ask me. Michael and I had already been talking."

"You little bitch," Chelsea said, but now she was smiling. "He's the hottest guy in our class. How do you rate?"

"Because I'm cute. Plus he heard about my HIV and thinks I'm easy."

"Very funny, Clement."

CHAPTER 32

Sierra Leone, Peninsula Mountains
December 13, 6:25 p.m. Greenwich Meantime

Jacob felt wet. His sweaty shirt stuck to his back; the top of his khaki shorts kept clinging to his thighs. The dry harmattan winds from the Sahara came less and less frequently now. Instead, the weather all seemed to come from the sea. Jacob could taste the salt in the air as he looked over 30 miles out to sea from a perch high atop the hills southeast of Freetown. In the distance, he could see deflected orange rays of the sun as it prepared to set behind cloud cover on the horizon. He had stowed away in the back of a truck full of sheep, the smell choking him. When he recognized the rutted road that went to his family's village, he jumped off, inhaling completely for the first time in hours.

After swatting away a mosquito, he brushed at a tickle on the hairline at the top of his forehead, imagining another pest invading there. He scratched the tight black curls on his head and stomped his feet. The itching never seemed to stop lately. His head, his ankles, his nose, in his pants.

Shrugging away the last of the irritation, he quickly slipped into the jungle beside the rutted road. Two months ago, bandits filled the air with the sounds and smell of gunfire, with the boisterous condemnation of everything Jacob ever knew.

On the morning of the attack, one of the villagers had seen Jacob running toward him from the direction of the village. The man, Ussam, had gone out in search of his own son who had disappeared during the night. He feared the boy had died. Encountering Jacob, he asked him if had seen Disa.

"No, sir," Jacob asked, paralyzed by the man's open anxiety and grief.

Ussam looked hard at Jacob. "Where were you?"

"I thought I heard something during the night and went into the jungle to see what it was."

"Were you alone?"

"Yes, sir."

"Why weren't you with your father in Freetown?" Ussam probed, his eyes narrowing.

"I wanted to stay with my mother."

The man hunched down and put his face close to Jacob, studying him for sincerity. "You've been through a lot with this Catholic religion, haven't you, boy?"

Jacob sighed. "I'm okay," he said."

"And your mother?"

Jacob had overheard Hamara say that Ussam had coveted Ani as a young man. Now Ussam's anger struggled for boundaries since Hamara had first spoiled her and then discarded her, leaving her good for no man.

"It hasn't been fair for her."

"Or any of us. Your mother is still a very pretty woman."

"They've taken her."

Ussam's shoulders rolled forward and up toward his ears, his eyes widening with rage. He threw a fist into the air, pacing.

"Do you think Hamara brought this on us by turning his back on the spirits of our ancestors?" Ussam demanded.

"What?"

"The attack. The murder of your grandparents and the others. Maybe my son."

Jacob turned away. "No, no," he insisted, "The priest said his God is the only one. There are no other spirits."

The man, seeing the further pain he had brought to the boy, leaned forward and put a hand on Jacob's shoulder. "Do you believe that?"

The vision of his grandparents, of the puddles of blood on the village grounds, all of it overwhelmed the young boy.

"Sometimes," Jacob conceded, "But these men are not spirits. They're an enemy who walks like us."

Ussam nodded and straightened up. "You're a good boy, Jacob," he said. "And loyal. Someday you will make a good chief. Now, come with me. You need someone to watch out for you. Maybe you can help me find my son."

So Jacob trudged beside the man back toward the village until, within a mile of it, a handful of bandits approached, shooting their guns into the air. The group could well have had no coordination with the group that had attacked the village, so anarchic were their ranks.

"Don't look at them," Ussam whispered. "They'll go away."

But Ussam was wrong.

"What you got there, old man?" demanded one of the teenage invaders.

Jacob's guardian looked up. "This?" he asked, pulling up the small pack hanging on his waist.

"No, mister. Your son."

Jacob spoke, "I'm not…"

But Ussam pulled Jacob toward himself and shut him up. "He's a little boy," said Ussam.

"He's a strong boy. He comes with us."

"I'm not going with you," Jacob protested. "I'm not…"

Ussam yanked Jacob's arm up behind his back.

"Owww!" Jacob squealed.

Bending over, Ussam whispered in the boy's ear. "They will surely take the chief's son prisoner. Keep your mouth shut."

Jacob's eyes widened and he nodded.

The rebels surrounded the pair and pulled Jacob away from the man.

"You leave him be."

"He's ours, mister."

They began to walk Jacob away.

"Wait!" Ussam called, not willing to lose another boy today, "You can't take him. We can trade."

Jacob looked up to watch the response of his captors. He saw a mean grin on one teenager and listened to others laugh.

One of the boys, still smiling, turned toward the guardian.

"Say good-bye to your father, boy," the bandit said to Jacob as he and his friends opened fire, surprise and shock being the last sensations Ussam felt.

Jacob ran toward the fallen man, but bandit hands scooped him up and carried him away.

Days later, the bandit leaders, claiming to be rebels on the side of good, came to Jacob showing him pictures of Hamara and himself. He suddenly received much more attention from his captors. They told him they thought that his royal blood could protect them from the evil spirits roaming the jungle at night.

Since then, Jacob had returned once to the village as a rebel recruit, confused and filled with the so-called rebels' tales of his father's betrayal. Now, Jacob re-traced the tracks of the morning of the attack, alone and uncertain of who to blame for the collapse of his life. This time, he stayed off the road. He did not want to die like Ussam. He wanted to die fighting for something. He grabbed the clip on the weapon hanging over his shoulder, pulling it up like boys in other places might pull on a baseball glove.

Near the edge of the village, Jacob heard voices. Cautiously, he climbed a rise and looked out on an excavation. In the twilight, men and boys, some under guard, dug into the wet ground and then sifted what they pulled out. Fifty yards beyond the workers, big yellow earth-moving machines rumbled and rattled over the plateau that provided much of the village's food over the centuries. The small plateau provided one of the best planting areas in the region; it had kept generations of Karanjas from going hungry.

Now, the earthmovers' huge tracks ground the village's plantings into the soil, creating a giant flat, dusty area where once there had been green.

Jacob held his weapon up and talked to it. "It's our land. They're digging up our land." He thought of the morning of the attack. He remembered again that Hamara had not been there. He had left them all to die. Of course, he needed to help Sara, but he could have been back that night. If he had been there, he would have stopped the attack. Either that or he, too, would have been killed.

Jacob would be chief now. He would not abandon the village.

He shifted into a prone position and picked out one of the guards in his sight. He started to squeeze when he saw the man had on a regular army uniform. Jacob moved the sight around the work camp. He stopped on another man. He knew that man. He definitely worked with the rebels. Jacob lay the weapon down. He could not understand who these people were. Some he knew as enemies. Others as friends. He recalled the Rambo movie they showed repeatedly in the rebel camp. Rambo would have killed all of them.

"But he would have been smart about it," Jacob said to his weapon.

He saw that the shadows of the hills now covered the workers below. The sun had only a short time left today.

"We need to go to the village and see what they've done there first."

To Jacob's surprise, the village buildings still stood. And all were empty. As twilight turned to dusk, Jacob grew edgy. He listened for sounds, but heard only the chirping of insects and the distant sound of the workers going back to wherever they slept. No evidence existed that the village served any purpose to them. Jacob thought that perhaps they feared the spirits of the village, especially since they had claimed the land surrounding it.

He pushed back the hanging beads that acted as the door to his grandparents' hut. He half-expected to see Nona and Noni, but only dark silence greeted him. When a small animal scampered past, surprising him, he jumped to the side and started to pull his weapon up.

Stopping himself before he attracted attention from whatever lurked in the jungle, he caught his breath and listened for other things inside. He reached into his pack, pulled out a small flashlight. Passing it over the dirt floor, he saw that his grandparents' blankets lay folded carefully in a corner. Two low benches with inch-thick foam pads had acted as their beds. His flashlight scanned deeper inside and found the futon that had acted as the bed for he and his mother after the marriage to Hamara had been annulled. It smelled good in here, the aroma of small cooking fires in the tiny clay oven still predominating. He thought he could smell his mother and his grandparents, too. He inhaled deeply. For the first time in weeks, he felt peaceful.

Going to the corner farthest from the entrance, he curled up on the ground with his weapon. Tears trickled slowly down his cheeks as he drifted to sleep in only a few moments.

CHAPTER 33

College Avenue, Fort Collins
December 13, 4:22 p.m. Mountain Time

The trill of the mobile phone startled Mel from her focused navigation of the icy patches on Fort Collins' main thoroughfare. The sun had not been out for two days, an unusual event on this stretch of Colorado's Front Range. The temperature had risen above freezing for several hours causing last evening's snow to melt back into the streets. Now, as five o'clock approached, darkness accelerated its advance from the eastern plains, causing temperatures to quickly dip back into the 20s. The reassuring splash of tires spinning through watery roads had turned into the almost silent hum of tires rolling precariously over packed snow and ice.

Mel pressed the talk button of the steering wheel. In the interest of safety, she did not glance down to read the caller ID. "Hello?"

Dave's voice greeted her on the other end, resounding from the Expedition's speakers. "Hi, sweetheart. I'm in Salt Lake City waiting for my connection. Everything's about two hours behind schedule, but I should make it home by a little after seven."

"How was San Diego?"

"Perfect. Makes you wonder why we live in the cold and the mess."

"You forget summer and wide open spaces."

"Not hard to do tonight. Do you want to go out when I get home?"

"Liv has a Christmas party so we're completely at liberty."

"She can't drive in the snow."

"It's at the Wheelers. She can walk over on the bike trail in ten minutes."

The bleep of an incoming call interrupted the conversation.

"I probably should get that," Mel said. "Call if there's any problem with your connection."

"Love you."

"You, too," Mel said just before pressing the talk button again. "Hello?"

"Mel, this is Paul Resnick. I just received the results of the blood work we did a few days ago."

The large black SUV approached a red light. Mel down-shifted and gently applied pressure to the brakes. The Expedition started to slowly slide on the ice.

"Hold on, Paul," she said as she released the pressure from the brakes and then slowly re-applied it.

The big Ford jerked back into its lane as it found traction. Dave and she thought twice about getting such a big vehicle but it had proven invaluable in transporting the volleyball team around to away games. Plus it made Mel feel far more secure on roads like this.

"Sorry," Mel said. "You caught me driving on a black ice."

"Should I call back?"

"No, this is a good moment. I'm sitting at a long red light."

"I spoke with Dr. Ellis. We both think it's time to try something else. Her CD4+ count is 291. That's 84 points below last month, 234 below the prior month. What's most concerning is that the CD4 ratio is down to 19%, a huge drop from 29% last time."

Mel's vision blurred and she did not see the light change. Horns blew behind her. She gently pressed the gas, looking for a place to pull over. "How close, Paul?"

"AIDS is diagnosed at 14%. We don't want to get there."

Mel unconsciously tightened her grip on the steering wheel. Lisa Ellis was the best infectious disease doc in northern Colorado and Resnick had cared for Liv since she was an infant. Mel knew the two of them would not set off alarm bells unless necessary.

"What do we do?" Mel asked, feeling numb.

"Is she taking her medications on schedule, Mel? Is she missing doses?"

"I've caught her twice, but that's it."

"Doesn't explain this drop, then. Look, she may yet rebound and end up doing fine with the current medication, but I think we should consider a more aggressive course of treatment."

Mel drove the SUV over a curb into a grocery store lot. She braked and put the vehicle in park. "What are the options?" she asked, struggling to remain matter of fact.

"I'd like to prescribe Fuzeon. Added to her current meds, it should help."

"This is the one with the big side effects."

"Right. She may run fever and have some vomiting at first."

"That sounds like chemotherapy."

"It is. Basically."

"How about her emotions?."

"You'll need to keep an eye on her. It can both depress her and cost her sleep until she gets used to it."

"More of the same."

"Yes, but it could be exaggerated at first."

"Not very conducive to competing for the state volleyball championship."

"Not much choice, Mel."

"I know. So she takes it daily?"

"Twice daily."

Mel thought about how she would need to monitor Liv to make sure she followed the full regimen precisely.

"There may be a bigger challenge, too," Resnick added. "It has to be injected directly into the bloodstream. It can't be absorbed through the stomach because its molecules are too large."

"Oh," Mel said, pausing to absorb the information. "She hates needles. My guess is that I'll have to give it to her. That won't be fun."

"Fuzeon uses something called the Biojector 2000 instead of a traditional hypodermic needle," Resnick said. "It injects without a needle. You just have to be careful to rotate locations to avoid nerve damage."

"Got it," Mel said. "So how about volleyball?"

"See how she feels. Volleyball's good medicine for Liv's spirits. Might help her avoid slipping into depression. Or minimize it. She just may not be physically up to the exertion. She needs to get her rest."

"She's already having trouble sleeping. And Ambien gives her hallucinations."

"I wish I had easier answers."

"Maybe I shouldn't tell her about this. It will only get her down. We could just tell her you found a better drug option."

"Keeping her in the dark could come back to haunt you. This really isn't bad news. Understanding what works and what doesn't is just part of beating this thing. We'll get it on the run with Fuzeon."

"It just seems like we're one step closer to even worse news," Mel said as the windshield began to fog up. She quickly flipped on the defroster. The loud whir of the fan made it harder to hear Resnick.

"Mel, you're being a pessimist. That's not like you. Look, Liv hasn't even tried most of the existing AIDS treatments and new ones are coming.. We're just going through trial and error. We'll get this under control."

After Paul hung up, Mel told herself not to panic. Normally, she handled things very calmly, but this... She had a bad feeling about this.

CHAPTER 34

Wheelers Christmas Party, Fort Collins
December 14, 10:10 p.m. Mountain Time

Chelsea splashed the Chivas over the ice in the juice glass. One of the two boys standing at the family room bar leaned close to her ear and whispered. She curled her neck like a cat and giggled. Pushing the glass at the boy, he swallowed a gulp and immediately grew red-faced. He coughed, made a big fuss about the strength of the drink, and then chugged the rest. Chelsea filled two more glasses, nearly emptying the bottle.

Liv walked over to Chelsea. She reeked of marijuana and alcohol. "Chels, what are you doing? You're going to hurt yourself. And you're going to get Marci in trouble with her parents."

"I'm just relaxing, L-I-V. After our little talk the other day about you-know-what and Michael, I think I deserve to relax."

"Let's go, Chels," Liv tried to take Chelsea by the arm. Chelsea immediately pulled away and shoved Liv in the chest. "Go away, L-I-V."

Liv put her hands in front of her, palms forward to show she did not want a physical confrontation. "Why are you spelling my name?" she asked.

"Because I can. Just between us friends."

Liv shook her head and walked back across the room. She observed Marci Wheeler standing over her iPhone speaker station putting on more music, this time oldies from the late nineties much to Liv's chagrin. As the music queued, Marci studied the activity at the bar. When Marci's eyes registered the nearly empty bottle of her father's Chivas, her face turned white.

Michael Winston walked over and said something to Marci. Her animated expression betrayed anxiety as she responded. Michael moved toward the threesome at the bar. He opened the conversation with a smile, but in a moment Chelsea's face turned beet red. She began arguing vehemently. Michael's face set hard as rock. He said nothing, but Chelsea soon shut up and moved away from the bar. One of the boys pulled Michael by the shoulder causing him to face him head on. Michael glared at the boy. Quickly sizing up the odds, the drunken boy extended a hand. Michael shook it and the bar area was cleared.

Liv walked over. She picked up the nearly empty Chivas bottle and looked under the bar. Coming up with a bottle of J&B, she smiled at Michael. "Should we keep Marci out of trouble with her Dad?" she asked.

He looked at her curiously. "What are you doing? I just got these other guys out of this area?"

"Trust me. I'm looking out for Marci."

"Either too curious or too stunned, Michael said nothing as Liv opened the Chivas and poured 4 jiggers of J&B into it. She shook the mixture.

"Bet her dad never knows the difference," she said. "And with that dark green bottle, he probably doesn't even know how much is in the J&B."

Michael straightened and sized her up. "You're pretty clever."

Clever? She had wanted Michael to notice her for a long time, but "clever" had not been her first objective.

"Thank you," she said quietly, surprised that her voice wimped out.

Michael took her quiet tone to be questioning. "No, no. I mean it. Most kids would just shove it back in the bar and let Marci deal with the consequences."

Liv began to relax. "It's marketing. My dad taught me that perception is sometimes 90% of the value, particularly when it comes to soft drinks, liquor brands and cigarettes."

"I've tried them all, but I'm afraid soft drinks are the only thing I've stuck with," Michael said. "You sound like you know way too much about them."

Liv laughed a little. "Haha. Don't worry. I'm mostly talk. Second hand smoke's the nearest I'll ever be to a cigarette, but my parents let me taste booze since I was little. It made me realize that it was no big deal. A glass of wine with dinner on a special occasion's cool."

Two comments about parents so far, she thought. What am I doing?

But Michael stayed interested. "I'm not that under control," he said. "I got into this almost biker thing for a while where I thought smoking made me cool."

Liv did not respond immediately. Michael nervously filled in the silence. "But I was young. Seventh grade. That was a long time ago. I wouldn't touch a cigarette today."

Liv laughed. "You're cute," she said, "I didn't know you were cute."

"Thanks... I think."

"No, you know," she scrambled. "I thought you were just really good looking. But you've got more going on."

Unconsciously, Michael's chest swelled, his shoulders rolling back. Blushing, he nodded. "How's that?" he asked.

Liv felt her own breathing become very shallow. Her neck and ears suddenly felt hot. "You handled this problem here really well. Makes me feel..."

Michael's eyes focused completely on her as she sought the right word.

"... Protected. I guess. No, I mean, yes. Safe."

"Marci needed friends and they..." He nodded toward Chelsea. "... seemed like they weren't quite up to it tonight."

"Chelsea's a good friend, just a little out of hand right now."

As the conversation progressed, the distance between them closed. Liv felt an urgency she had never known before. She wanted to kiss him.

"I've wanted to get together with you since September." Michael's voice quavered as he spoke.

"Why didn't you call or something?" She felt her voice shaking, like the rest of her, her breathing shallow. Like his.

"I didn't think you'd want me to."

"Why?" Liv instinctively licked her lips and they glistened in the indirect lighting of the dark bar area.

"When I saw you at school you seemed, I don't know, almost mad at me."

She felt her heart melting as his little boy face fought a pout. "It isn't you, Michael. There's a lot going on in my life. I've just been preoccupied."

Silence. The unspoken stood between them like a giant wall. Neither wanted that wall up. The subtle sweet fragrance of her perfume filled his head, her warm breath now close enough to warm his neck. Her face glowed pink in contrast with the white and golden highlights in her blonde hair. In the steady gaze of her blue eyes, the reflection of the room's soft lights became for him the twinkling of a clear night sky. "I don't want to go where I don't belong, but I think about you a lot," he said. "And I worry about you. Like when you passed out at the volleyball game."

Liv's mouth went completely dry as her face burned crimson.

He continued clumsily, "I worry that you're sick, Liv. There's talk in school that something serious may be wrong with you."

Her antennae straightened. "Like what?"

"Nobody knows. You've missed a lot of time. And you passed out in a game. Some people say it's not dehydration. That worries me because I don't want anything bad to happen to you."

She wanted to throw her arms around him and say, "Yes, yes, I'm sick and I need you so much." But she did not. Instead, she cast her eyes downward and measured out a careful answer before speaking.

"I don't want to lie to you," she said. "But I can't answer right now. Not completely, anyway."

"It doesn't matter," he said. "I'd still like to be with you. If you are sick, I just want to be there to support you."

Liv wanted his arms around her. She wanted to nuzzle into his chest. She wanted to trust him, turn it all over. She had been waiting for exactly this boy for her entire life.

"This has to be our secret," she said, putting her lips next to his ear. "No one knows except my parents and a couple other adults."

He leaned away. "Wait, Liv. You don't have to tell me. It doesn't matter."

"What if I'm carrying some deadly disease?"

"That's not very likely. It wouldn't matter anyway."

"It might," she said softly. She felt his finger lightly caress her neck. Then, he gently lifted her chin upward.

"May I kiss you," he whispered in her ear, his breath caressing it.

Feeling tears rush up, she pressed her forehead against his shoulder. She nodded her head "yes." He pressed her closer and nuzzled his face into her hair. He closed his eyes.

"God. You smell good," he said as he gently pulled her tighter.

She wanted to kiss him. Her first kiss that mattered. A big step. She could make him sick. No, her research said you couldn't get it from kissing. What if the research was wrong? She felt so much for him. She did not want to hurt him.

He again picked up her face, this time drawing her mouth close to his. She closed her eyes and did not resist.

"Omigod!"

Marci's cry startled Liv and Michael. Thinking the cry directed at them, they jerked away from each other.

"Chelsea's undressing in my parents' bedroom!" Marci called to anyone who would listen. "And she's not alone."

"Oh no," Liv gasped. She and Michael looked at each other in shock and embarrassment. Liv touched his cheek and nodded toward the bedroom.

When they reached the room, Chelsea had nothing on but her unbuttoned blouse and a thong. The boys were hurriedly dropping their pants to the floor.

"No, Chelsea, stop," Liv called as she flew into the room. "You'll regret this. It isn't what you want."

The two boys turned toward the door, stunned to see Liv there. "Get out of here, bitch!" one of them demanded.

"I can have what I want," Chelsea slurred as she reached for one of the boys.

Liv stood at the foot of the bed, pulling the boys away. "Tell them to go, Chelsea."

Chelsea chugged from the bottle of beer staining the wood of the nightstand. She held it out to Liv.

"Lighten up, L-I-V," Chelsea said, slurring her words and again spelling Liv's name. "Drink up and get in here with me."

Liv's face turned crimson. She grabbed Chelsea's skirt off the floor and tried to slide it up her friend's legs in an effort to dress her.

Michael stood in the doorway, his eyes wide in astonishment. He stood behind Liv and she could not see him. Chelsea could, however, and she lashed out.

"I've had it before," she said, pointing the neck of the bottle at Liv's midsection. "It belongs to me, not Michael Winston or anyone else."

The two very flustered boys, now inhibited by the crowd gathering at the door to the room, hurriedly secured their zippers and belt buckles, pulling away from the scene.

Liv, her face crimson with embarrassment and anger, felt heat rising through her neck to her face as the boys stared at her in apparent fascination. "Get out of here, pervs!" she said to them.

"They like it," Chelsea said. "And it's true."

"Once, Chelsea, once. I didn't know what I was doing. That's hardly a relationship."

"Should have been more than once," Chelsea argued. "Especially since you think I gave you something."

"Shut up, Chelsea!"

She forced the skirt up to the drunken girl's hips.

"Experimentation? I don't know if I would call it that. You don't get sick from experiments."

"Chelsea!" Liv yelled. "You're drunk."

"Truth hurts."

Liv grabbed Chelsea by the shoulders and leaned close to her ear, trying not to be heard by others. "We were in middle school. We didn't know anything. I didn't want it. Any of it. Not then. Not now. Do you not get it!?"

Chelsea yanked Liv by the hair, pulling her face close to hers. "Don't you think it's funny that your name and HIV are spelled almost the same way. L-I-V. But don't worry. I won't tell a soul."

"You're drunk, way too drunk. Stop it now."

Chelsea squirmed away and moved her eyes over Liv's shoulder to Michael who was trying to figure out how he could help.

"What would you say, Michael? You and L-I-V here could be a couple soon."

Liv turned and saw the confused look on Michael's face, his mouth slightly open, not knowing what to say.

"Oh, Michael, no!" she exclaimed, feeling her heart and her hopes cave in.

Mortified, Liv raced from the room, one hand blocking her face as she burst into tears. She dashed into the guest bedroom and dug through the pile of coats until she found hers. In a desperate search for the front door, she bumped her way through the crowd with her coat half on. She finally got her arms in both sleeves as she hit the frozen bike trail beside the house.

Her cheeks stinging from the wind and the wet rush of snow, she trudged home through the accumulating powder on the dark trail that ran behind the houses. Tears poured from her eyes. They had almost kissed. It had felt so good, so warm, so exciting. She could still feel the breathless sensation. One more instant. Just an instant.

Chelsea is such a bitch.

She worried that Michael might have figured out what Chelsea was talking about. She worried he thought she was a lesbian with HIV. Or a big slut at a minimum. Objectively, she did not think that he would have figured the HIV part out from Chelsea's drunk comments, but emotionally, she feared what he might be thinking. She would fix it. She would make Chelsea tell Michael the truth. She could go to her house and make her call him. But what if she refused? She could get a gun, make her do it. And what if he asked why HIV had come up in the conversation?

No, no, Liv, this is too crazy now.

What if she just showed Michael the lesbian thing was not true. She could make out with him, showing him just how good a girlfriend she could be. Only problem: she had zero useful experience.

And no confidence. But she would be giving it up for the right reason. The thought of kissing Michael made her stomach contract and her throat go dry. She tingled and sucked the frigid air in between her clenched teeth.

As she entered the house, she greeted her parents cheerfully, the tears of discouragement she had shed on the hike home momentarily gone, replaced by the recollection of that intimate moment with Michael. Maybe her Mom or even Jennifer could give her some advice.

No way, she thought. She could not risk Mom finding out about this one. Way too embarrassing. Mom would think that the AIDS came from Chelsea. Maybe it did. But Chelsea showed no signs of being sick.

Within moments, however, the evening turned from confusion, discouragement and anticipation into a full-blown slow motion nightmare, worse than it had already been. Her parents encouraged her to sit in the family room, the fire light bouncing off her now red eyes. Her parents spoke. She heard all, but focused on pieces.

"...weren't going to tell you... Dad and I decided you would want to know...some bad news...may not be working... drug resistance... not a big deal... new injection..."

They did not say it straight out at first. They made the point, but did not get it in so many words. Disbelief overwhelmed her.

"Are you saying that I might die soon?" she demanded, emotions flooding into her throat and voice.

A pause and then "No."

"This is not a good sign, though, is it? That my strain is drug resistant."

"Dr. Resnick said this is just part of finding the right drugs for you."

"I've studied this on the web, Mom. I know what's going on. Drug resistant people with AIDS die. They can only buy a little time at best."

She felt any hope of personal peace rush out of her like a torrent of mountain run-off. Her thoughts spun out of control. She had taken comfort in knowing she could live indefinitely on the medication. Now that hope had been obliterated, just like her hopes with Michael.

And, this time, she knew what she would be facing. The first time, AIDS came at her like a headline, confusing, surprising, but not burdened with nightmare, not then. But since then she had seen the images of its victims, had learned of its relentless path of ruin through their lives.

This time, she could feel her soul shrink in terror. Words struggled to form in her mouth, but her young mind did not have the words to describe the depth of fear, of nightmare, that immediately filled her when her mother said the words "drug resistant."

She reached for a prayer. "Oh, dear God, please, no," she gasped, her eyes wide.

The pained, empathetic faces of her parents blossomed in front of her, bigger and bigger in her mind's eye as she unconsciously tied them to the message they delivered. They became ugly. The family room grew ugly. The kitchen grew ugly. And everything wobbled and waved like the images atop asphalt on a hot and humid day.

Her mouth suddenly drew tight, her cheeks filling with air. Then the air exploded from her mouth. She pushed herself off the couch and ran. She ran out of the family room, down the foyer and out the front door. The slamming of the storm door as it crashed back into the doorframe drove another chord of terror into her parents' souls.

Her legs stretched and reached out across the shoveled sidewalk and icy street. Her shadow cast changing shapes and lengths as it raced under street lamps. Her shoes, flat-soled hiking boots, occasionally slipped on the ice. But when she slipped or stumbled, she just kept going, ignoring this small danger.

Nearly half a mile away, she raced into a snowdrift outside St. Luke's Episcopal Church. She was not Episcopal; she just hoped that somehow God was nearby. Outside the glowing stained glass of the church, Liv collapsed to her knees and sunk to her belly in the cold snow.

"Oh, God, please don't let this be true. Please. Let me be re-born free of this sin. Please..." She bent down, her forehead touching the surface of the snow. Images of Chelsea, her breasts hanging out of her shirt, her mouth taunting, jumped into her head. She saw again the horror in Michael's face. Rage rushed up inside her. She banged her fists into her forehead, into the snow. She screamed.

"No, no!"

Seeing the church windows, she rose to her feet and screamed, "You sonuvabitch! How could you do this to me?! God, you suuuuck!"

Her voice echoed in the silent, snowy night. She heard herself and crumpled to her knees. She had never before called God a sonuvabitch. He deserved it! she thought. Yet they were words she never used, not on anyone, words she heard others use and always knew she would never say.

Crying uncontrollably, she spoke out loud. "Why God? Why are you doing this to me? It's not right, not fair. Merry Christmas, my butt!"

Ten minutes later, the headlights of the family SUV found her huddled in the snow bank, her whole body shivering with the cold and heaving with hard sobs. As Dave picked her up in his arms, she latched on tightly to him, crying softly into the soft leather of his coat, most of her emotion spent and a numbness overcoming her. Mel sat in the car, biting her finger and trying to squeeze the tears back into her eyes.

CHAPTER 35

Lokoma village, Sierra Leone
December 15, 5:35 a.m. Greenwich Mean Time

The rain stick, a long tube filled with small stones, rattled above him in the firelight. Jacob tried to move, but he had been tied to the ground, his arms frozen at his sides. The witch doctor, streaked with violent shades of red and black, wore only a loin cloth and a grotesque wooden mask. He continued to shake the rain stick angrily. Other masked dancers around him shook other instruments and pounded small drums. Their flickering shadows bounced off the walls of the thatched huts surrounding them. Loud shouts and wails filled the air.

The witch doctor's mask, by far the largest at three times the size of a man's head, had angry faces front and back. It dripped with the blood and smeared fat of enemies. Jacob twisted in his bonds to avoid the drops as the man danced over him. When the drops struck his bare skin, they burned, audibly sizzling above the din of the dancers. Jacob repressed screaming in pain because he knew his captors would do him greater harm if he did not remain quiet.

The witch doctor grunted something and waved his stick in the air. Four masked men emerged with small clay jars filled with thick paint. They streaked Jacob's face and body with reds and browns and whites. One opened the wound on the side of his temple and sprinkled crack cocaine in it. Then they placed a mask over his face. It smelled like a rotting carcass. In vain, Jacob tried to shake it off. Through its eyeholes, the witch doctor re-emerged. His hands reached for Jacob's heart and, to Jacob's horror, penetrated the wall of his chest, disappearing inside him as though his skin and bones had the consistency of muddy clay. Rather than hurt, it simply felt uncomfortable, unwelcome. Only when the chanting apparition's hands started probing did the pain begin. Jacob grunted to restrain his scream.

Suddenly, the man's hands jerked out of Jacob's chest. A loud, howling wind hurtled from inside Jacob. Three transparent spirits rode it, whirling into the night sky wailing. Jacob recognized them as Father Jim, Jesus Christ and a young woman he had never seen before. On their backs, they carried the sleeping bodies of many of the people Jacob had seen die in the last eight weeks.

Suddenly, a lightning bolt exploded. The spirits and dancers evaporated into bright, day lit jungle, filled with monkeys, snakes and frogs. Just as suddenly, the jungle collapsed into a luminescent ball of green light. The ball started spinning, accelerating rapidly. Its whistling grew deafening. Then, it hurtled through the air like a spear and struck Jacob in his solar plexus, sucking the wind out of him and doubling him up. Terror overwhelming him,

Jacob began vomiting the jungle on to the dirt beside him, the mask on his face now gone. The jungle came out of him intact, but in miniature, all of the region appearing in three dimensions, but no larger than a game board. The Karanjas' village appeared and Jacob could see that everything had returned to normal. From his perch above the miniature, he could clearly make out Hamara, Ani, and his grandparents. Seeing them alive elated him; he desperately wanted to shrink and join them.

Then, from the woods, Jacob heard the faint and distant sound of a tree branch snap. The dancers! They were coming back. The tiny people in the miniature village heard it, too. They appeared to panic and started running into the jungle.

Jacob turned his face toward the sound in the woods, shouting, "Stay away! Leave them alone."

He scrambled in the dark to find his weapon. Laying his hands upon it, he jolted into wakefulness, the weapon cradled in his arms. He looked around in the darkness. The small clay oven, the blankets where he had scattered them in his sleep. He rubbed his hands over his intact stomach and chest. A dream. A terrible dream.

Then he heard the distant noise again. A spike of fear cut through him. He pushed aside the beads at the entry to the hut, careful to do so very quietly. A dull gray sky threatened first light on the eastern horizon. They had come before at first light.

On tiptoe, he walked around the hut and found cover in the brush. He aimed his weapon in the direction from which the sounds had come. The sound grew closer, but it was odd, frightening. Not the footsteps of men, but a harsh thumping followed by a very heavy footfall and then a harsh thump again.

The brush started to move in the sight of his weapon. Between the leaves, Jacob could make out a bloodied hand holding tightly to a branch of some kind. Coming further into view, he could make out that the branch was really a makeshift crutch. Scanning to the ground, he could see that the intruder had a stump where its right foot should have been. The bloodied leg, barely covered by a nearly shredded skirt, looked like that of a woman.

Jacob removed his eye from the sight and looked at the intruder unaided. He watched as the grimace of agony on the intruder's face emerged with a cry into a smile. At the same time, Jacob's face exploded into a tearful exclamation of joy.

"Mother!"

Jacob raced to her and they embraced. Dropping her crutch and balancing on one foot, Ani pulled him tight to her. She kissed his face and forehead repeatedly. He nuzzled his face in her neck.

Ani's good leg began to give. Jacob let her collapse into him and helped her to a bench in the shadow of an enormous tree.

"What happened to your foot?" he asked as he sat beside her.

"This is how they keep kidnapped slaves from escaping."

She did not want to tell him that she had been used as a "wife." While she understood intellectually that she could have done nothing to change the course of events, self-condemnation came all too readily.

"I will kill them, mother. Where are they?"

She looked at Jacob, pleading. "There has been enough violence, Jacob."

"You don't know what I've done. I'm a great soldier."

"I don't want a great and dead soldier. I want a living, caring son."

She reached for his hands with hers. Moist and sticky, her right hand felt hot to him. She had held her makeshift crutch with that hand; the skin across the palm had blistered and been torn by the effort. He turned the hand over.

"This is very bad," he said.

She glanced from her hand to her stump and back to him. A small laugh emerged from her mouth. "Yes, yes, it is," she said, smiling.

"You're not angry?"

"Of course, I am, but I'm more happy than angry right now. I thought I would never see you again."

Jacob's face started to contort in tears as he responded.

"They told me you were dead," he said.

"Then, in spite of my wounds, I'm a very hardy ghost."

He hugged her and then quickly pulled away.

"We need to wrap that so it doesn't get worse," he said.

He went in search of a bandage. In a few moments, he returned with a rag he found. "It should also make it easier to hold the handle of your crutch," he said after securing it.

"You've changed," she said, "You've grown taller."

She smiled. He smiled. And they both laughed.

Jacob's face grew solemn. "Mama, I've killed."

She nodded her head and took him in her arms. "I know, my darling boy. I know."

"How do you know?"

"My son, the son of a chief, is very famous among the rebels. They want very much to kill you."

Jacob rested his head on his mother's shoulder. "They made us this way. They gave us drugs. They showed us movies about killing."

"None of that is your fault."

"The worst part was thinking you were dead. That and knowing that father betrayed the village."

"Who told you these things?"

"My officers."

"You mean your captors."

"Yes, the same."

Weakened from her journey, but stimulated by pure adrenaline on seeing Jacob again, she pulled him closer.

"You know that they told you at least one lie, then. Do you think there are more?"

Jacob nodded. She studied him. She saw the slit on his temple where the crack had been administered. He did not have to explain it. She had seen it all herself during her captivity. She glanced down for a tell-tale welt on his chest. Nothing.

"Praise God," she said on realizing he had probably not received the much more troublesome heroin.

"Which god, mother?"

She looked at him with eyes filled with compassion.

"Jesus Christ, of course."

"But the priest took Papa away from you."

"The priest made a decision of religion, not of God."

"I don't understand."

"Jacob, I have seen men killing in the name of Allah and I know they have killed in the name of Jesus. Yet when we read the Word of Jesus, he tells us to turn the other cheek, to love our enemies. So these men that kill in His name are using his name to accomplish their own ends, not those of Jesus. In the same way, the priest told us Hamara could not have three wives."

"So Jesus thinks it's okay to have three wives?"

"I don't know. I think God wants us to love first. From that love will come good decisions about how to live. Having many wives gives men too much power over women, but it also protects women sometimes. It gave us all a home and the protection of the chief. Still, we were often only your father's slaves."

"No one should be a slave," Jacob said.

"Only slaves to God and his love," she said. "The priest meant well, but doing well is not a simple thing to be read from a rule book. Fr. Jim just did not understand or consider the trouble it would bring. Being declared soiled did not feel good."

"You're not soiled, mother. You are a hero. And I love you very much."

She squeezed him and shuddered.

"Are you all right?" he asked.

"I'm very tired. It was a very difficult journey."

"An incredible journey with one foot!"

She smiled at her son, happy to see a little boy still lived in him. "Jacob, you must seek protection. There is a price on your head. You killed your captors. The rebel leaders are not happy with you."

"I'm a good soldier, mother. Like Rambo. Do you know who Rambo is?"

Ani reflected on the movie shown at least once a week to the small boys her captors recruited. The video always preceded hours of nearly spastic dancing, drum pounding and stick-shaking around nighttime fires, the incessant music of men and boys who sought ceremony to bring them courage and honor – and blood thirst.

She remembered the carnage caused by only one man in the movie. Now her son thought he was Rambo. Watching those boys in the rebel camp, she had prayed her son would not succumb to the same temptations, while knowing he would and probably had already.

"I know Rambo, "she answered. "He is a movie superman. You are not Rambo. No one is Rambo. You can't fight them alone. We're very lucky you're still alive."

"But, mother, I can protect us. We can stay here and re-claim our village from the rebels. I can avenge noni and nona – and you."

For an instant, sadness paled Ani's face, but it quickly grew stern. "Don't argue. Listen to me, boy. I have heard their plans, their secrets. They stole our village for bauxite. The Abo's paramount chief, our neighbor to the northeast, is plundering the land for bauxite, something for which the Liberians and their friends will pay a great deal of money. They stole our village lands for the bauxite that lies beneath them."

Jacob remembered the workers he had seen on his way to the village. "It's more than that, mother. They leveled our farm. The plateau is just dirt."

"Then they've taken away our food supply. I wish I knew why. Your father knows the Abo chief. He thought he was well-connected to the government in Freetown, but I now know that he pays the gangs that call themselves rebels to do his killing. So the rebels are not our only enemy. Our neighbor is probably the bigger enemy. He wanted your father dead so he could have our land with little dispute. That makes you his next problem if they get your father."

"I will never give our land to him. That must be why they want to kill me, but even if they kill me, our people will rise in anger."

"Unless you kill your father."

Jacob hesitated. He studied his mother for uncertainty. There was none. "How did you know?" he asked.

"As long as they thought you would kill Hamara they let you live. I'm almost sure of that. I know how they think. Once you killed him, the Abo chief comes in like a good Samaritan and saves our people from a bad succession. He gets the plateau, the bauxite and the support of our people in mining it. Hamara is dead. You're executed as a criminal."

Jacob's brow furled. Confusion circled his face before finally capitulating to the truth his mother told him.

"They had me convinced," he said. "I would have killed him and given them exactly what they wanted. They made a fool of me."

"You're a boy, son. You don't know the ways of the world. They relied on that. The remarkable thing is that you had enough courage to turn on them. You may not have understood it all, but you saw through them."

"But why did I see government soldiers and rebels both guarding the laborers in the mines?"

"Where?"

"There's a mining camp just over the next hill."

"The Abo chief must still have ties to Freetown then. Maybe this is just about the money. Maybe the government is corrupt and working with the rebels. You can't be seen by them, Jacob. Both sides probably think you stand between them and their greed. We have to get you out of here."

"I think they're afraid of the spirits here. There is no sign of them coming here."

"Even if that is true, a change in local commanders could change the superstition. That's not a risk worth taking."

"I won't go anywhere without you, mother."

Ani looked at her stump. The infection now seeped through the wrap. She would only hold him back. It would not be long before she died.

"No, Jacob. You must go alone."

"I will only go if you come with me. Otherwise, I will stay here and fight to the death."

She grabbed his jaw in her hand and prepared to repeat her demand. She studied his face as she held it and recognized the determination in it, the maturity and the fire that the trials of the last two months had burned into his soul. She knew that his will would outlast her weak body.

"I'm proud of you, boy," she said, "All right, we go together to Freetown. To find your father. We'll warn him and find protection for you."

"We'll go and get medicine for you first, Mother."

"They will have all that at the camp in Freetown. We should leave after dark."

"Right after dark."

Ani lay back on the bench. In a moment, she fell sound asleep. Jacob checked to make sure she was breathing and then arranged her legs so that they did not fall off. He found some wild coffee beans on the edge of the woods and chewed them to help keep awake while he guarded Ani, repeatedly thanking Jesus for her return.

CHAPTER 36

Refugee Camp, Freetown
December 16, 9:15 a.m. Greenwich Mean Time

"Musa!" Hamara raged. "What is wrong with you!?"

He slammed the elder into the concrete wall of the infirmary.

"Touch me again and I'll kill you," Musa, the younger and heavier man, said as he struggled to break free.

"You'll have to wait until I'm too old to fight back." Hamara held a forearm in the man's throat and twisted Musa's golf shirt in the other.

"I'll hire someone," Musa responded, conceding Hamara's superior strength.

"That should be easy enough in these times, but, until then, I'm still your chief. When I give an order, I expect it to be followed." Hamara lightened his grip.

Musa shrugged him off, stepping to the side. "You may have a death wish, but I don't. Our village needs its leaders to be here. Not sick or dead. Dealing with your daughter's malaria kept you away from the village when the bandits attacked. How much more damage do you want to do?"

"The vaccine needs to go to the women and children first," Hamara countered. "They're the most vulnerable to malaria. Not the grown men. The elders' council agreed to that. You could have waited until there was more vaccine available."

Musa's eyes reddened with anger. "And I disagreed with the rest of the council. Don't forget, too, that we agreed it was voluntary. Have you forgotten the shaking, the fevers, or what it feels like to lose control of your bowels and bladder? Leaders cannot function that way. Do you think the Americans will let us stay if we're sick?"

Hamara inhaled deeply. "I am not ready to give up on getting our land back. There is word of a further ceasefire with the remaining rebel and bandit bands near Lokoma. When real peace comes again, everything will be restored to us."

"You're a dreamer, Hamara. That's one of the lovable things about you, but it's counterproductive in this case, even dangerous. The government will re-allocate the lands in some scheme that could just as easily steal our land permanently."

"You don't trust the government?"

"Do you?"

Hamara had to acknowledge his own suspicion of the Freetown government. Historically run by a small minority of the well-to-do descendants of re-located British slaves, the central government often completely discounted the issues of the tribes that had lived in the region for centuries. A sense of entitlement prevailed in the ruling class. Wronged by slavery, they had received amends from the British. Over the nearly 200 years since, there remained an ongoing cultural sense that the slave descendants should be entitled to privilege greater than others. Rarely would someone say it outright, but even now, it remained obvious to Hamara and other leaders from the bush. It seemed ironic that those whose ancestors had lost the wars centuries ago, been captured and sold off as a profitable solution to getting rid of enemies – that those should have returned to dominate the region under the protection of their former masters, the British.

"No, Musa, I don't trust them. Still, we need to find a way to fight for our land. We should run only if it becomes clear that we won't get it back."

"Run? Is that what you call going to a land where malaria virtually doesn't exist, where the minimum wage for one hour is five times a good day's pay for our people? And there are drugs for Sara. The American government will provide them if you can't pay for them."

Hamara still sought reasons to stay. "But America has problems we don't want. Its streets are filled with drugs and violence. It has no morality. The women wear very little there. Sex is freely given. It's no place to raise our children."

Musa's eyes widened. He tilted his head and looked at Hamara as though he were crazy, as though he had been asleep for ten years.

Hamara laughed a sad laugh. "It seems part of me lives in the past, before the civil war," he said. "So do you think the real America is more like the Cosby Show or more like the rap videos?"

Musa put an arm around the chief's shoulder. "Let's find out together, my friend."

"I still need to think about it."

Musa stepped away and turned to face Hamara, hands on his hips. "Pa, I know what you're dealing with. Do you want to let your whole family die here for the sake of your misplaced pride?"

"I don't understand," Hamara responded, a tighter knot forming in his stomach.

"Mariama confided in me. She's frightened, not for herself, but for you and your daughter."

"You're way out of line talking to my wife."

"She came to me. The day after you got the report last week. I know, Hamara. No one else. Just me."

Hamara looked skyward, letting out an exasperated sigh. "I did this to them," he said.

"She didn't say that."

"I probably got it from a prostitute. Mariama passed it to Sara when she was pregnant with her. By some miracle, Emma was spared."

"It's an ancient practice, Hamara. We all did it. You didn't know. You're the one that brought an end to it with your conversion – you and your priest friend."

"But I knew it was wrong. In my heart, I knew it was wrong."

Musa jumped at the opening. "Then make amends. Get them to America where they can have medicine and live long lives."

"We're running out of time for Sara. For some reason, her immune system is weaker than that of the rest of us."

"We can sail right after Christmas. The southern trans-Atlantic route tends to be very mild at that time of year, as long as we stay south. We think we can go with lesser ships under those conditions. Otherwise, we may be months before we get sturdier ships."

Hamara considered Musa's comments, considered all the issues that swirled in his mind. "I suppose that we can take them to America and I can come back to deal with the village lands."

"Until the government stabilizes, you can't do anything anyway."

Hamara felt drained. He had held on so hard to the village, to tradition, to his understanding of duty. And now he had become his family's killer. Until now, he persisted in risking their lives for the village, for tradition. There was no village. Not for now. And if they died, there would be no tradition anyway.

His chest and shoulders tightened. He wanted to strike out and hit something. Maybe that was why he went after poor Musa, but that certainly had not helped matters.

What could he do? He had very little money left, enough in a bank account to buy food for a few months, assuming the value of the Leone did not collapse in another inflationary spiral. His family's legacy, its wealth, its food – everything – came from the village. To concede that it was gone, that he had failed his family and everyone else in the village – he had doggedly resisted that logic, waiting for a miracle in an environment over which he seemed to have no control at all.

Without the village, the base of power and the things he knew, Hamara questioned his ability to put his family's life back together, let alone that of the entire village. What kind of work could he do in either America or Freetown? Who would want an old man in his forties without formal training for anything but village chief? He could farm, but he would need money to buy land.

Yet he could accept all that. He could not accept the loss of his wife and children. The uncertainty of Jacob's fate already cast his spirit in constant turmoil, his sleep deeply disturbed. His head swam at the nightmarish thought that his recklessness seemed destined to cost Mariama and Sara their lives. And what of Ani? Had he not only thrown her out of his home, but killed her, too – either through AIDS or through her capture by the rebels? Would things have been different if he had been in the village the night of the attack?

"Hamara, are you still with me?" Musa interrupted the chief's reflection. Hamara nodded at Musa, but only made brief eye contact. He needed some kind of divine guidance on this matter. The distractions of all the issues he faced made it difficult to focus on any one of them at one time, let alone God or prayer. The priest had said turn your worries over to Jesus Christ. There was a verse out of the book of Matthew that he liked to quote but, like so many other things, Hamara could not recall it. Something about dealing only with the things of today, that tomorrow would take care of itself. That proved a concept difficult to accept for a chief accustomed to control.

"Am I still the paramount chief, Musa?" he blurted.

Puzzled, Musa responded, "Of course. Like it or not, you're the one to whom everyone still turns for direction."

"Why not God?"

"God's a concept. You're flesh and blood. Some of them even act like you're divinely appointed."

God. A concept? The thought struck Hamara hard. He, more than any of the Lokoma, needed God to be more than a concept. He needed God to be an active, intervening savior – just like Fr. Jim promised.

"We need something more substantial than me as a bulwark for faith, my friend," Hamara said.

"Do you not want to be chief anymore?" Musa said, uncomprehending.

Hamara grunted a small laugh. "No, I am the chief. For now. But we all need something bigger than me. Something more than a concept."

"The Muslims have Sharia law. It keeps the people in line and gives them some kind of order to rely on. It brings the community in line under its leaders."

Hamara rubbed his eyes. "Musa, it's time that I let go of my ambitions and turned everything over to God to work out. We need to trust God to work out the best in each individual."

"Which God? Allah or Jesus?"

"Only Christianity respects personhood. A blending of community and individuality is central to Christianity. Think of the Christian Trinity: three persons in one God."

"You place too much faith in individuals," Musa challenged. "The community has to be bigger than the individual."

"If that were the case, Musa, I would choose to stay and fight for the village, for the community of our ancestors and our descendants. The individuals of today should be insignificant in light of all that."

Musa paused, as if to absorb this last insight. "I stand corrected," Musa said at last. "We should indeed be thinking about individuals. Without their survival, there are no descendants."

"Then you see it my way?" Hamara said.

"Certainly."

"And we will trust God to show us the way? We will concede our pride and put this in the hands of the Lord?"

"Have we any choice?" Musa responded.

"You answer that," Hamara directed.

"No, Hamara, we have no choice."

Musa folded his arms. Hamara could see that he had clearly irritated his lieutenant. He wanted Musa to give in to the priest's concept of God. Hamara knew that Musa thought the spirits of the rainforest had not liked it before. Those spirits, if they existed, were no more inclined to like it now. Hamara knew that Musa felt that the priest could not have been killed soon enough.

"Make sure we sail before the New Year, Musa," Hamara said. "We can't afford to waste any time."

A grin spread across Musa's surprised face. "It will be done," he said.

The two men shook hands, each holding eye contact long enough to demonstrate strength.

The image of Jacob flashed in Hamara's mind. He determined that his family would sail, but he personally would not go until he found his son.

CHAPTER 37

Aldrich Mountain Lab
December 16, 10:20 a.m. Mountain Time

Jim hid behind a pile of trade journals he had moved into place to block a security camera's line of sight. Looking at his watch, he saw he had been here 15 minutes this time. Too long. He would be missed soon. He clicked exit for the e-mail program and without waiting for that to finish entered Sheila's company-assigned log out code. He pulled the flash drive from the USB port and shoved it in his shirt pocket.

Footsteps.

Jim froze. The e-mail program still churned through its exit routine; the logout routines had not even started yet. If the screen was still active, Mike would know he had been in Sheila's files. He would search him and find the flash drive. That would surely blow his cover and kill any chance of getting documentation back to Christus.

The footsteps continued in the direction of Sheila's cubicle. Come on, Jim silently instructed the computer. Come on.

He could power off the monitor, but if the log out hung up, he would not know. The next time the monitor was powered on, it would be discovered that someone had been into the files.

Take the chance, he thought as he pressed the power button on the monitor.

The footsteps stopped. When Mike peered over the cubicle, the monitor had turned black and Jim held a picture of Sheila and Jennifer in his hand.

"What are ya doin', boy-o?" Mike asked.

"Why haven't you shown me this picture?"

Jim offered a challenge to re-direct Mike's thinking.

"How's that?"

"The security photo you provided of Jennifer doesn't do her justice. And this one looks a good bit more current. Should make her a lot easier to find."

"I guess I didn't even realize it was there."

"It was shoved up behind the monitor. Someone probably would have had to sit here to see it."

"We've left it alone. This cubicle will go intact to Sheila's successor when we find him or her. Plus it's kind of a shrine for the other employees. Wanted to make sure they thought we gave her enough respect."

Jim put a hand in his pocket to make sure the flash drive did not slip out as he stood up. "Wouldn't want anyone to suspect ya rubbed her out."

"No. No, we wouldn't want that," Mike said, taking a quick look around.

"Was it necessary?"

"She was askin' for it, if that means anything to ya."

"Sure, ya have to do what ya have to do."

To hide his lie, Jim tried not to look at his brother. Mike hesitated a beat before speaking, waiting for the eye contact from Jim that finally came.

"C'mon, boy-o," Mike said. "Boss wants to see us."

The brothers found Claire McQuaid's office door ajar when they arrived. Claire stood at the window, chewing on the tip of a pen. She may have been looking at the fresh powder covering the mountains or she may have only registered it sub-consciously as she thought.

Mike rapped on the door as he stepped inside. Claire did not react at first so he rapped again. This time, she turned.

"Michael," she said. "Good. I've been waiting for you two. Come over."

They joined her at the enormous window. She returned her eyes to the snow and kept them focused out the window while she talked.

"Snowflakes fascinate me," she said. "Always have. Even as a little girl, my mother would catch snowflakes with me. Mother said no two were alike. In those few seconds from the time a snowflake landed on my hand until it melted, we would study it, trying to commit its characteristics to heart so that we might compare it to its successors."

She paused, glancing quickly at the men. She squinted in the bright sunlight reflecting off the snow.

"Did you ever study snowflakes, Farley boys?"

Mike responded, "When we were very small. We -"

"Must not have been an easy thing to do," she interrupted. "How can you appreciate such things of beauty living in the midst of so much hatred?"

Mike grew wistful. "There were good times to be had, especially before it all killed our mum."

"Can't be easy to lose a parent," Claire empathized. "Especially one so young."

"Very difficult," Mike said.

"You're quiet, Father," she said to Jim.

"Just paying attention, Claire. Trying to understand where you're going with the snowflake analogy."

"Oh, good. A student."

"Always."

Claire opened her mouth, inhaled and then clinked her teeth together repeatedly before speaking.

"Well, Father…"

"It's Jim now. No more Father."

"The snowflakes. No two alike." She faced out the window again. "Just like people. When one dies, it can never be replaced. Kind of like a parent. Like your mum, boys. The violence and the hatred made that happen. And what causes the violence and hatred?"

The men shrugged.

"Too many people struggling for too few resources, for starters. Moreover, we don't have the best mix of people. The less educated propagate like rabbits while the educated have few children. The kinds of people that make for a civil world are becoming a smaller and smaller segment of the population. The others, many genetically impaired, threaten to create a collective consciousness built on only the basest things. Francis Galton, Darwin's cousin, talked about this 150 years ago when he first proposed eugenics. Fools like Hitler gave it a bad name, but there is a place for it. Everyone, even the basest of us, deep down wants to elevate the race."

She turned back to the men. "Do you understand where I'm going with this?" she asked.

"No," Jim said.

Mike shot him a nasty glance. Claire walked across the room to a large leather wing chair in front of the fireplace. She sat down.

"Join me on the couch," she commanded, waving to the couch across from her.

Mike and Jim did as ordered.

"Didn't you get an understanding of all this in west Africa?" Claire asked.

"Of what?" Jim responded.

"It's disease there," she explained. "Killing people and making inferior the quality of what little life they have. It drains the society of its resources, destroying productivity and national morale. Ultimately, it creates fertile ground for society's lowest common denominator to rise. Isn't that what happened in Sierra Leone?"

Jim shifted uneasily on the couch. "In part," he responded. "But the situation is much more complex than that. Given the right or wrong circumstances, aren't we all at risk to become the so-called lowest common denominator?"

"There but for the grace of God and all that," Claire said disdainfully. "C'mon, Father. You know better. Get out of the Christian 'everyone is equal in God's eyes' thing. You can't possibly expect a good God to provide the same treatment to a mass murderer as he would to a woman who spends her life immersed in her prayers."

"That's the thing about forgiveness. Christ brought redemption to all of us, no matter how big a sinner one might be. If we want it."

"Father, you have your head up your backside. There are unforgivable sins."

Jim thought he had better reinforce his cover a bit. "It's just Jim, Claire. I'm not a practicing priest anymore."

"How about Sean? Why not that?"

Jim felt himself tense up. "It's been Jim for a long time. Sean went away."

McQuaid leaned forward, studying the priest. "No," she said, "I don't think so. Sean's still here. I can see him."

Jim averted his eyes, looking at the fireplace. The woman seemed slightly crazy.

"Look at me, Sean. Tell me why you changed your name."

He closed his eyes to gain fortitude and turned back to her. He knew he had to pick up the tone of the discussion. He did not want to make McQuaid an open enemy.

"Little bit of a run-in with the British police when I was a teen," he answered. "Local priest helped hide me out, put me in a seminary under an assumed name. Next thing y'know, I'm buyin' the whole program. Until the last few years, that is."

"Mike says you've killed."

"That's right."

"Before the seminary? Or since?"

"Before."

"But you're ready to do it again?"

Jim hesitated. Everything in him wanted to answer no, but his cover depended on his perceived commitment to return to his old ways.

"I've learned life is cheap," he said, trying to maintain eye contact. "I'll do what I have to do." Her words had made him acutely aware of his shame. She saw it in him. He needed to push back at her, push back with Christ's love, and see past his shame to touch her.

"How can that be? You just spent 20 years committed to averting violence, to loving everyone. Forgiveness, remember? I don't understand."

In her green eyes, he saw the unexpected. Undefinable softness competed for a home amidst pain and dark emptiness. The emptiness seemed almost willed, determined to push out the encroaching goodness. In the dark depths of her pupils, the devil himself seemed to lurk, touching Jim's deepest well of fear. Yet the softness pulled him in, made her seem familiar, made his heart ache for her in some inexplicable way.

"What is it you see in my eyes, Sean?" she said as the black pupils in her eyes seemed to dilate and redden.

Jim blinked. He contemplated his hands, hands that had held newborns at baptism, that had comforted the dying, that had pressed the flesh of the Lord into the hands of others, that had planted a bomb that killed innocent people. He shifted his gaze to the fire, staring at the flames. He could feel the heat on his face, a slight sweat breaking out on his neck. He called on Christ for strength. He tried to remember that God offered infinite forgiveness. The Irish landlord's car exploded again before his eyes. The toddler hugged her father. The teenaged daughter clung to him and her sister. The wailing filled Jim's ears.

He cringed, his breathing labored. He felt weak inside, the strength sapped from him. He begged Christ to fill him with strength. He called on reserves of faith, of hope, built through decades of service and penance.

Slowly, he turned his head and re-focused on Claire, her face set firm in judgment. "Some of us find it hard to live with forgiveness," he said quietly, directly. "Perhaps we can't forgive ourselves."

Claire seemed to flinch. She tapped an index finger on her lips as she absorbed Jim's response.

"Are you speaking about me?" she asked.

"No."

Inhaling deeply, she placed her hands on the arms of the chair as though to go.

"How about you, Claire?" Jim interrupted before she could get out of the chair. "Have you ever killed?"

He wanted to understand her, to find the source of the softness, to convince himself that it was more than illusion.

Claire sank back down. She smiled wanly. "What if I said that I have?"

"I wouldn't believe you," he said. "Once you've killed, the taboo is gone. You understand how easily it can be done, how survivable the consequences. Once you get there, you understand that killing remains an option for you. If you had killed, you would understand that."

"What about Sheila?" Claire countered. "You're aware of that little problem."

"Hiring people is not the same as doing it yourself. Too impersonal."

Claire tucked a shoulder into one corner of her chair as she pondered her new security officer. She began slowly nodding her head. "It's been surprisingly personal, intensely personal. Every time I pass her cubicle or discuss her work, it's personal. She isn't here anymore. It didn't have to be that way. I raised her in this business. Like a daughter."

Her eyes reddened as they blinked back the fleeting threat of a tear. "So people like you are always killers, then," she said, suddenly regaining her composure. "Find Jennifer and do your job, then, IRA man. Mike, get him out of the lab. I don't want him back here until he's done what he has to do."

"I'll make sure of it," Mike said.

Silence ensued for a long moment. The room made no sound save the soft crackle of the fire.

"What are you two waiting for? You're dismissed, Farley boys."

Mike nodded to Jim. They got up and headed toward the door.

"One other thought," Claire called out, staring into the fire as the men reached the door. "You should know this. What we're doing here involves getting rid of thugs like you. Your time's almost over. Technology is going to make this a much more civil place. You're going to go away like the dinosaurs. What we're doing here will make certain of that."

After the men left, Claire sat behind her desk. She pressed a series of buttons, locking the room down and bringing up the big screen to play her video once again. She popped three Excedrin migraine in her mouth. Putting on her earphones, she pressed "start" on her desk and then turned the volume way up. The recently added security camera video of Sheila's garroting caused her to curl up in her chair. She kept rewinding it until she knew she could take it, until her horror subsided and transformed into clinical fascination.

CHAPTER 38

Freetown, Sierra Leone: Outside Refugee Camp
December 16, 5:40 p.m. Greenwich Mean Time

His shoulders ached from the pressure of his mother's arm as she leaned on him throughout the long, muggy journey through the jungle. Just as the makeshift crutch had torn blisters in his mother's hand, the skin near his neck had been rubbed raw by the chafing of his mother's arm on one side and the strap of the heavy Kalashnikov on the other. He tried to hold one hand in front of them to push away the dangling webs of green worms that seemed to overrun the trails at this time of year.

They stopped frequently to rest. Ani's leg throbbed more and more painfully. The pus draining from it came faster now, quickly making the wrap wet and heavy. Jacob would carefully unwind it, soak it in a creek, wring it out and then find a clearing where it could sit in the sun and dry. He would use another cloth to wash Ani's leg itself. Each time, he hoped for improvement. Each time, he saw only more discoloration and more swelling.

"I did this," he said at one point.

Ani spoke through a grimace. "That's nonsense, Jacob."

"If you had not come to warn me, your leg would have healed."

"The rebels move camp constantly. They would have dragged me along at their pace. It would have been much worse. And I wouldn't have my son with me."

"You could have died coming to me all alone in the jungle."

"I was never alone. Open your heart. Trust that whatever happens to us is as God wants it. If we are open to God, if we listen, then whatever happens to us is the right thing. You cannot have regrets with faith."

Jacob did not respond. He silently finished putting the wrap back on. *Where are you, Jesus?* he thought. *I see only evil around me. Except my mother. She's good. Very good. You need to take care of the few good ones like her.*

They finally reached the refugee camp shortly after sunset. The cicadas and other insects of the night clicked and sang in full throat as mother and son hobbled toward the gate.

"You need to come in with me. It's the only place you can be safe."

"To be safe, mama, I need to keep moving so they cannot find me."

"Don't you want to see your sisters and your father?"

"I have nothing to say to Papa."

"Then come see your sisters and Mariama."

"I'm a soldier. A woman can't give me orders."

Ani shook herself loose and hopped away from him. She pondered him, looked at the muscle that had begun to re-shape his small body, saw the weapon hanging from his shoulder. And she saw his eyes, not the eyes of a killer, but the wide, wet eyes of a wounded child.

"I love you, boy," she said. "You can be a soldier with a mother if you want. Or you can be jungle animal with a gun. If you won't listen to me, you don't want a mother."

Jacob let the weapon, its strap having formed a painful groove in his skin, slide off his shoulder. Ani's face bore a determined look anchored by the soft brown eyes for which Jacob had yearned during their long separation. The condition of her leg caused him to fear losing her again. His lower lip began to tremble, but he could not bring himself to answer her. Instead, tears betrayed him. Ani held her arms out and he stepped into them, bawling into her shoulder.

Jacob knew where his family stayed in the camp. He took Ani around the outside perimeter of the fence to a spot where they could observe the family. Though many of the families in the camp stayed in a combination of tents and three-sided cardboard lean-to's, the Karanjas now had a corrugated aluminum hut that, though still very small, was much larger than most of the other homes in the camp. It also had three glass-less windows with mud cloth drapes hung by nails. From their elevated spot on the edge of the jungle, Jacob and Ani could see through one of the low windows. Mariama sat on Sara's bed holding her hand. From this distance, Sara looked more fragile than ever. She did not react to Mariama's conversation, seemingly listless. Emma brought her mother a cup of something and Mariama tried unsuccessfully to get Sara to drink from it.

"I can't believe she still has malaria," Jacob whispered.

"It's not malaria, Jacob. The rebels said she has AIDS. They said that the whole family might have it."

Horrified, Jacob challenged, "AIDS comes from sex. Sara can't have that."

"There are other ways to get it, particularly if your mother has it when you're born."

"How can you know this about our family? You haven't been with them."

"My captors kept careful track of the chiefs and their families. They don't want anyone to become strong and threaten their control."

Jacob thought about Sara, remembered holding her as a tiny baby, remembered playing with her. She completely trusted her older brother. Adored him. And he adored her. Tiny, fragile, wide-eyed. Completely trusting. The last time he saw her he fed her ice chips, trying to help fight her fever.

"Is she dying?" he asked.

Ani slipped to the ground to rest. Jacob joined her.

"In Sierra Leone, someone with AIDS has no hope," she said.

She thought of Sara, Mariama and Hamara. She worried for Emma and herself. If Hamara did indeed have it, then he was certainly the carrier. And almost certainly the virus was in Ani's blood.

"Is there hope somewhere else?" Jacob asked.

"I have heard there are places where medicines can keep it from killing you."

"Where?" he said, feeling a surge of hope.

"England. The United States."

"We should take her there. To America."

She took Jacob's hand and held his gaze. Her hand felt very hot. "It's too late, son. Even if we could get her help there, she wouldn't survive the journey."

"So what do we do? We can't just let her die."

"That's not our decision. What we can do is help her find peace and be happy in her last days."

"There must be medicine here in Sierra Leone. Drugs are everywhere in this country. There must be some that actually help people. The government leaders would have medicine if they were sick."

"Probably so," she agreed. "How would we get it?"

"We find it and steal it."

"No, Jacob. They'll kill you."

Jacob looked toward the camp. "They're trying to kill me anyway. I might as well have a good reason for dying."

Ani pulled him close to her and rocked him. "Don't talk this way, boy. Don't talk this way. Your mother needs you. Promise me you won't do anything stupid."

In the warmth of his mother's embrace, Jacob mumbled, "I promise."

Fearing Jacob would be recognized, mother and son waited for darkness before approaching the camp infirmary. Light from the concrete block infirmary's few small windows let them know that people still worked inside. To avoid the guards, Jacob found a hole in the fence that he had noticed on a prior visit. Ani had wanted Jacob to take her to visit Hamara first, but she had fainted just before sunset. Jacob feared she could wait no longer for medical attention.

As he carried her, he could feel the heat from the fever on her skin, her breath warm and sour with sickness.

"Just a little further, mama," he said, fighting the urge to panic.

Ani mumbled incoherently.

Jacob did not knock on the door, but instead walked right in, his mother on one shoulder, the Kalashnikov dangling from the other. The reception area had only a small fluorescent light in one corner. At first, Jacob saw no one, but then he heard the sound of hands clapping softly. The sounds came from a nun, dressed in white robes, who hobbled up to him.

Seeing Jacob's face, the nun jerked her head back in a flash of recognition.

"Sister, my mother needs help."

The nun grunted, opening her mouth to show she had no tongue. She closed her mouth and her eyes fixed on him making him very uneasy.

"This is my mother. Please help her. They've cut off her foot."

The nun looked at Ani's leg and nodded. She pointed to a cot and nodded for Jacob to move Ani there. Once Ani was settled, the nun placed a hand to her forehead. Pulling her hand away, she shook it as though to say "hot."

Gently, she unwrapped the leg wound and studied it. She smiled at Ani reassuringly, but Ani only moaned.

The nun turned to Jacob and motioned for him to go. She looked very familiar to him.

"No, I'm staying with my mother."

The nun shook her head rapidly and pushed him toward the door. Instinctively, he lifted his weapon. The sister calmly stepped back, her eyes on his.

"Do you have medicine for her?" Jacob asked.

She firmly nodded her head "yes."

"Do you know Sara Karanja?" he persisted. "A very tiny, sweet little girl."

The nun nodded affirmatively.

"Is there medicine for her?"

The nun's face darkened with sadness as she nodded no. She folded her hands as though to tell him to pray for his sister and his mother.

Then Jacob remembered the nun, remembered from the fog of the drugs and the darkness of a night he wanted to forget, a night when he ran back to the rebel camp confused and horrified, only to be greeted as a hero with the other boys and their cruel leaders.

The nun, seeing his recognition, held her hands open in a gesture of why.

Jacob dropped the barrel of his weapon toward the floor. He feared her, feared what she knew, feared her judgment.

The nun's eyes softened. She touched Jacob's chin and gently tilted his head up. She pointed toward the ceiling.

"God?" he questioned.

The nun nodded. Jacob looked at the stub at the end of her right leg and then to his mother's stub. The images spun in his head. He saw the blood and pus that oozed from his mother's leg, the white stump of bone peeking out from the goo. He recoiled from the pain he imagined.

He pondered the nun, felt again the splatter of hot blood that the rebel leaders refused to let him wash from his legs for days afterward. The muffled screams of that night bombarded his hearing. And the gurgling, the awful gurgling. Even the rebels had spared his mother her tongue.

Jacob dropped to his knees before the nun. "I'm so sorry," he said, tears choking his words.

The nun dropped awkwardly to her knees beside him. She pulled him close, their tears mingling.

Footsteps could be heard outside. The nun gently pushed him away, gesturing for him to go. He pulled his dirty hands down his face, streaking it as he dried his tears. He helped the nun stand.

As he started to turn away, the sister grabbed his shoulder and held out the cross hanging around her neck.

"I don't understand," he said.

She took the cross off and placed it around his neck. She placed a hand on each of his shoulders, looked back and forth between his face and the cross, and then nodded as if to say the cross was a good fit.

"What can I do to make it up to you?" he asked.

The nun shook her head as if to say "nothing," and then looked heavenward. When she saw Jacob follow her eyes up, she turned back to Ani, shaking her head with concern.

"Please help her. And my little sister. "

The nun nodded urgently.

Voices came from the reception area.

"I'll come back. With help. I promise."

The nun pushed him toward a back door.

As he slipped into the night, Jacob gripped the cross. He half expected it to burn a hole in his hand.

Freetown: Inside Refugee Camp
December 17, 3:15 a.m. Greenwich Mean Time

Hamara's eyes flapped open. He found himself staring at the tin ceiling of their tiny hut in the darkness. The wheezing and slight snoring of Mariama, Emma and Sara filled the small space. He pressed the backlight on his watch, an extraordinary luxury to Hamara. 3:15. Another fitful night of sleep.

Thoughts raced through his mind. How had he let this happen? What if he had been there for the raid? He envisioned himself bravely rallying the villagers and running the rebels off. He should have directed a war ceremony, pulled out the drums and the rain sticks.

Or what if he had taken Jacob to Freetown with them? No, the boy did not want to go, but, Hamara could, as his father, have insisted. Did he not want the boy to come? Or did he just resent his loyalty to Ani.

He should have moved the whole village out days earlier. They could have moved to a refugee camp then. Everyone would still be alive. Everyone would still be together. Jacob. Ani's parents.

Faces of the dead and missing marched through his mind's eye. He pictured himself convincing the elders to move everyone out. He pictured the rebels arriving at an empty village, their blood-lust unquenched.

Then, last night, Ani showed up. She said that Jacob had brought her. He thought they both had been killed. The amputation of her foot broke his heart, but his enormous relief predominated. Ani had told him of Fela's treachery, of the Abo chief's association with bauxite and the rebels. She told him of how Jacob had been turned into a killer.

Hamara rolled sideways on his cot. He covered his eyes with his hands. He just wanted to go back to sleep. He knew Fela to be greedy, but he did not know that his greed could turn to war-like ambitions. The man had been financing the criminal rebels in the area to build his business and his wealth.

And for that little bit of temporal wealth, he decided to destroy nearly two centuries of legacy and tradition for hundreds by driving out the Lokoma villagers.

I should have seen it coming, Hamara thought. I should have armed our people and fought.

But he knew they would not have been able to fight off the entire strength of the rebel forces and their allies. He knew that, in the end, without the central government intervening directly on his behalf, the village would have been taken. Only many more lives would have been lost.

He tried to find comfort in prayer, but other thoughts distracted him each time he started. "God, help me," he finally prayed. "Please take these problems away from us. Let me sleep. Let me feel good in prayer."

But his mind fought back in the other direction. What can I do to fix things? he thought. Go to the central government. See Minister Tombu. He seemed like a good man. He had met the minister on two other occasions, including when officials from around the country celebrated the "end" of the civil war at a ceremony at the State House.

Hamara's head pounded and his stomach curdled with nausea. He could not lie still any more. He looked at his watch. 3:21. He got up from the mat and walked outside.

He started to look up to the stars, but he saw something move in the shadows by the window near Sara's bed.

"Who's there?" he whispered angrily as he turned.

A boy stepped from the shadows into the starlight.

"Jacob?"

Jacob began backing away. He did not want to face his father, the father he had been assigned to kill. And he could not stay in the camp he had raided.

"Don't go, son. I want to see you."

Hamara slowly walked toward him. Jacob raised the Kalashnikov and his father, stunned by the sight, froze in place. The barrel pointed directly at Hamara's chest. Ani had told him that Jacob had been charged with assassinating him, that she had tried to convince him how misguided that was. Hamara inhaled deeply, recaptured his composure and whispered, "No matter what happens, I'll always love you, son."

He closed his eyes. He no longer controlled his destiny. How fitting that the son whose mother he had discarded would be his final undoing. For no one else would he have surrendered so readily, if at all.

"I have to go, Papa."

Hamara opened his eyes. The barrel had moved away.

"Why did you come?" Hamara stepped toward him. Jacob backed up, re-aiming the weapon at his father.

"I'm leaving," he said, his voice thick. "I left something for Sara. I have to go now."

Jacob turned and ran down through the avenue of tents. Hamara took chase. Jacob dove to the ground, scuttling through a small hole in the camp fence. Hamara tried to get through it, but could not. By the time he raced out through the front gate, his boy had disappeared again. He cursed himself for being too old and too big to catch him.

"Dear, God, please take care of him."

On the ground inside Sara's window, he found AIDS medicines, clearly stolen from the hospital, a capital offense under martial law.

"Thank you, son," Hamara whispered as both fear for Jacob and hope for Sara surged inside him.

CHAPTER 39

Fort Collins High School
December 17, 8:12 a.m. Mountain Time

Liv swallowed a deep gulp of frigid morning air. Sticking a gloved thumb under the shoulder strap of her backpack, she pulled it up to lessen the strain. Foggy breath emerged from her mouth as she walked down the path to the main entrance of the high school.

Sitting in the car, Mel waited for Liv to turn and wave good-bye as usual. Not this morning. The new Fuzeon injections had not yet begun to restore her energy. Liv had barely moved out of her room since Saturday night's debacle. As her energy levels declined, so had her spirits. She had been forced to sit out volleyball again and she did not have the energy for friends after school. Mel feared this was the beginning of the debilitating depression about which Paul Resnick had warned.

Mel had encouraged her to stay home yesterday, to watch movies and pick up her spirits. But getting her out of bed to return to school today had been a major chore. Mel finally convinced her by pointing out that she might not even get to sit on the bench for the regional finals night after next if she did not show up for school today.

Liv had mumbled an obstinate "fine," sitting up on the edge of her bed. It seemed she always woke up nauseous anymore; she gave her body a minute to adjust before trudging into the bathroom to brush her teeth.

As Liv disappeared behind the high school's doors, Mel turned over the ignition. She asked God to watch over her little girl today, to help her feel happy. As Mel pulled out, a man in a Honda sped into the lot and cut her off, nearly hitting her left front fender. A guy in a hurry to drop his kid off and get to work, he did not seem to care about anyone else in the lot.

Always men, Mel thought. Think they're more important than the rest of us, all the little housewives. She watched his impatient face as he nearly shoved his son out of the car.

"Asshole. You asshole!" she shouted, gesturing animatedly within the closed windows of the SUV.

She slammed her fist on the horn. The bastard calmly gave her the finger. That really pissed her off. She undid her belt and opened the door. A gust of cold, wet snow helped her get hold of herself. She dropped back into her seat, wiping the wetness from her face. She never lost her composure like this. She despised it when people did. What was she going to do? Get out and fight him?

She blew out and then inhaled deeply. Let it go, she thought. Let it go. Losing control will only hurt me, not that jerk.

She drove out of the lot ahead of the guy, still trembling. When he sped past her on the road a moment later, she could not resist the temptation to lay on her horn one more time. Startled, the guy jumped in his seat and slowed down to catch his breath. Now, she could see his mouth churning with expletives. Unable to keep from grinning, Mel waved mischievously as she sped by.

Liv dealt with her own frustrations in class. Behind in everything, she struggled to keep up, particularly in geometry where she had no idea what the difference between a complementary and a supplementary angle was. In chemistry, they had started the unit on kinetics while she was out and she quickly found herself lost in k-cals. English proved a relief as the class discussed *Catcher in the Rye*, a book she read in an effort to keep up while lying in bed. The depressing angst of the self-centered Holden Caulfield had aggravated her own emotions, but now it lifted them as she not only understood the subject, but received kudos from her teacher for her answers in class. For the first time since finishing the book, she did not aspire to be a deaf-mute as Caulfield did.

Walking the halls proved slightly traumatic. She waited for someone from the Christmas party to assail her about what happened with Chelsea. And she expected Chelsea to pop up any minute and lay into her. If she ran into Michael, she did not know what she would do, probably melt into a locker or something.

As other kids passed her in the hall, she cringed at every sideways glance and listened for her name to be mentioned in conversation. Did everyone think she was gay now? She should not have missed school. Her absence raised questions and provided an opportunity for rumors to run out of control.

Then it happened. Michael appeared in the hall ahead of her. He had just come out of a classroom door and turned in her direction. She quickly turned the other way, hoping to disappear into the girls room before he saw her, but as she turned, she banged into another girl and her books tumbled out of her arms. The other girl sneered and said, "Excuse you!" Embarrassed, Liv stooped to pick up her books, scattered all the way across the hall. She hurried to get them before Michael got this far, but she failed.

As she scrambled across the floor, a hand put two of the books in front of her face. She looked over to see Michael.

"I hate when that happens," he said, smiling.

With his help, she quickly found herself standing up again with all her books in her arms. "Thanks," she said, struggling to avert his eyes, but drawn to them nonetheless.

"Are you all right?" he asked.

She wanted to tell him no, but she knew if she started down that path, her emotions would get the better of her, embarrassing them both. "I'm fine, thanks."

"Have you been sick?"

"Just a virus. I'm all right now."

"I thought maybe it was that party," he said. "Chelsea made me pretty sick with the way she acted and all."

Liv's eyes widened "In what way?" she asked.

"She's a very gross drunk."

"Right."

"I can't believe the way she treated you."

"Right. I guess that's what friends are for."

"I don't think she's much of a friend, Liv."

Liv shrugged. She wanted to ask him if he was still okay with her, if he understood that she was anything but gay, to make sure he didn't think she was sick. And maybe try to explain it if he did. Except she had no certain explanation, not even for herself. Still, she could try.

But not here, not in front of the whole school.

The warning bell sounded.

"We'd better get to class," Michael said.

"Right," she said, glancing up at the clock above the lockers.

Michael turned to head off, but hesitated. He turned back to Liv who stood virtually paralyzed in joyful bewilderment.

"See ya later," he said.

"You, too," she said, nodding her head.

As she hurried to her class, she chastised herself for her total lack of verbal skills. How many times had she just grunted "right?" Did he still like her or was he just being nice? Liv dropped into her seat in history class exhausted, but exhilarated. He spoke with her. She had not expected even that much.

CHAPTER 40

Fort Collins: Churchill's Pub
December 17, 5:10 p.m. Mountain Time

U2's "I Still Don't Know What I'm Looking For" played, its incessant tribal drumbeat pounding in the background. Churchill's Irish Pub, its landmark shamrock in bright green neon hanging on the outside, had a very light crowd tonight. On a Thursday, nine days before Christmas at 11 o'clock at night, Churchill's was virtually empty.

Fr. Jim sipped his beer and played with a dark brown crust, all that remained of his Reuben sandwich save a few strands of sauerkraut scattered on his plate. He wondered if the music was mocking or supporting him.

He had come up into the mountains with their snow and sub-everything temperatures, but found they were actually quite pleasant. Ten degrees in the dry Colorado air did not seem quite as cold as forty degrees in humid Rome. The winds were certainly far more intense here. A 50 mph blow rolling over the mountains onto the foothills could be death defying.

He had started his search at the Holiday Inn then visited every hotel in the area, from Boulder, an hour south, to Cheyenne, 45 minutes north, and Estes Park, 45 minutes west. No one recognized her picture.

Her car remained parked outside her apartment, not having moved in weeks apparently. Her credit card records showed no activity. She had pulled $1,897.23 from her savings account the first week of December, evidently all the savings she had. Somehow, she must have managed to survive on that since. Unless she already had been killed. Unless his brother and Claire were setting him up somehow.

He checked rental car records for the Front Range as well, just in case she had figured out how to rent a car without a credit card. She might be able to do that with cash at some of the smaller outfits, but all of them would require a driver's license. Another dead end.

Earlier in the afternoon, at the city's public library, he uploaded to Christus the files he had copied from Sheila's computer at the Aldrich lab. Once Christus reviewed the files, he could find this distasteful assignment finished. Seeing his brother again had been very hard on him. He no longer saw in him the misguided patriot, an illusion he had carried all these years. Instead, he saw in his brother a cold-blooded killer and mercenary who knew no other life. He wanted to redeem him, to get him on the right track, but that would take blowing his cover, something he could not do until he received the all-clear from Christus.

The most troubling part of the assignment had been completely unexpected. He felt compelled to understand Claire McQuaid, to help her. A bizarre one-way kinship had formed in him. At times, he thought he saw the devil himself in her. Still, she touched a part of his soul that wanted to reach out and hold her, protect her. That odd inviting softness on the green fringe of her pupils. He wondered if it wasn't the soft side of temptation, a delicate enticement from Satan. Maybe the self-destructive side of him wanted this, the part that still had not forgiven him.

Getting back to the lab had one major obstacle. He needed to do something about Jennifer. He prayed about it regularly. He did not want to kill her, but part of him had started to accept the trade-off of her life for the millions that could be saved by stopping the Aldrich.

Could he do it? He had witnessed so much killing. And at the very outset of his life, he had no reluctance. Lifting his eyes heavenward, he asked for guidance, but he only heard the din of U-2's music. How would he do it? He studied his hands. He felt a need to do it with his bare hands, to punish himself by making it as personal as possible. But that would make it only more grueling for the woman. It needed to be quick, painless.

And what of the last rites? She deserved an opportunity to do a final preparation for her soul. He frowned at the irony of Jennifer's killer first offering her the sacrament. But he would do it, as incomprehensible as it would seem to her. He would do it because he always did the right thing, no matter the cost to himself.

"Father, let this cup pass from me," he mumbled over his beer, wanting only to drink more of it to numb his mind.

He knew where he would look for her next. He had secured a copy of the organization chart from her last job at Prodeus.

"To you, Jennifer," he said in a low voice as he raised his beer back to his mouth. "May the Holy Spirit keep you safe from this madness."

CHAPTER 41

Fort Collins: Clement's Cul-de-sac
December 18, 6:20 p.m. Mountain Time

The SUV's headlights splashed over the double garage. Liv pressed the remote button on the visor. She waited while the garage door ground noisily over its rails. She and Jennifer had spent the last hour at the climbing gym as Liv, feeling stronger day by day, worked to re-build the tone in her muscles after the layoff and the diminishing effects of the medication. Tomorrow night's regional volleyball match kept her focused. While she did not expect the coach to give her much playing time, she wanted to be ready.

Once inside, Liv pressed the button to close the door. They made it a practice to stay in the Expedition until it was down to minimize the risk of Jennifer being seen, a concern Jennifer seemed only to have in the neighborhood, but not at the rock gym, When the door thundered upon hitting the concrete pad, Jennifer scrambled from her hiding place on the floor. She threw open the rear cargo door aside and jumped out.

"This is starting to feel foolish," she said. "No one's after me anymore."

The garage light spilled on to the face of a pale, wide-eyed Liv.

"Liv. What is it?"

"Somebody's out there. A big guy in a leather jacket in a Mercury Marquis."

"So?"

"It's 11 o'clock at night and he's looking this way. People don't just park in our little street for the night."

The two women walked through the interior door into the house. Jennifer proceeded immediately to an upstairs bedroom window. She wanted to get a first-hand look at the guy in the car.

"Does he look familiar?" Liv asked.

"No, but I can't get a good look at him through the windshield."

Liv tried to peek over Jennifer's shoulder.

"Wait, look!" Jennifer said suddenly, pointing across the street to the left.

Dave and Mel emerged from behind the neighbor's house, coming off the path that followed the creek. Jennifer and Liv moved their attention back and forth from the Clements to the man in the Mercury.

"Should we warn them?" Liv suggested.

"No, no. I think we're all better off if the bad guys don't know we're on to them."

They watched Liv's parents cross the street not far from the car that surveilled them. They proceeded up the walk to the front door of the house. As they did, Jennifer poked Liv.

"Look," she said, pointing to a man emerging from the bushes by the trail entry. "Never mind, it's just a jogger."

The man wore a dark blue warm-up suit with orange fluorescent patches so that he could easily be seen by passing cars. Joggers were not uncommon at this hour along the trail, even in the depths of winter. He bent over behind a big pine and began stretching.

Liv heard the jangle of keys and then the crack of the front door as it opened. Ever since she could remember, that combination of sounds had comforted her, telling her that one or both parents were back home from a day at the office, a business trip, or maybe just shopping.

She skipped down the stairs to greet them, a big smile on her mouth but worry in her eyes. Jennifer followed.

"Hi, Mom," Liv said, throwing her arms around her mother.

"Daddy," she said as she went to hug her father. She liked the cool and slightly bristly feel of his face, fresh from the chill of the outside air.

"Quick. Close the door," she said.

Jennifer did it for them.

Liv stepped back and spoke slowly for emphasis, "Somebody's watching the house."

"No," Dave said, having seen no one himself.

"Here," Liv whispered, waving them over to the blinds. She pulled them back barely enough for her parents to see. They looked just in time to see the jogger get into the passenger side of the Mercury.

"Oh, my God," gasped Liv. "He was following you on the trail."

They watched the activity at the car. After the jogger got in, there was a long pause before the vehicle's headlights came on and the motor cranked up. It pulled away and turned out of the neighborhood.

"Looks like your spy was just here to pick up his friend after his jog," Mel said gently.

"No, Mom. Why would a jogger get a ride?"

Dave, who could vaguely remember what it was like to get out and jog on a regular basis, explained, "The man probably lives someplace where it's not easy to run. Maybe there are too many cars or something. So he drives over here to where we have a nice trail and some peace."

Jennifer put a hand on Liv's shoulder. "Makes sense to me," Jennifer said. "I've caused us all to get a little too paranoid."

"C'mon, time to head up to bed," her mother encouraged. "You have school in the morning."

As the women went to their bedrooms, Dave stepped back into the frosty night. He watched the Mercury's lights disappear around the corner. Awfully late for jogging, he thought.

Fr. Jim turned to his passenger. "Did you learn anything?" he asked.

"They're worried about their daughter," Mike answered.

"Nothing about Jennifer."

"No."

"You amaze me, Mike. You hide in the weeds to listen to a couple's private conversation. You drive down from the mountains to check up on me. Don't ya have better things to do?"

"I don't trust those people," Mike said. "Claire has real issues with the man. He's pushing her for a cure for his daughter."

"What's wrong with that?"

"She thinks he suspects something."

Jim sighed in exasperation. "Jennifer's the target, not innocent people."

"There are no innocent people," Mike said.

"Isn't that from Rambo?"

Mike smiled. "Good job, little brother. One of my favorites. First Blood." He drew out the word "blood" for emphasis.

"I'm not goin' to do your dirty work if ya don't trust me, Mike."

"What are ya tellin' me, Sean?"

"I'm telling' you to go back up to the lab and let me alone to do my job."

"Ah, I need to be back in the mornin' anyway, but you owe me. I got you this job. I put myself on the line for you. Get it done. If you really have it in ya."

"Don't worry about it," Jim insisted.

"My bet is that if you get inside that house you'll find something that tells you where she is. If you do, it means Clement might know things he shouldn't. That'll tell ya what ya need to be doin'."

Jim pulled up to a red light and turned to glare at his brother.

"It's the way the game's played," Mike said. "You know that and you know we don't have any choice."

Jim knew his brother's rules for damage control on a mission like this. No witnesses. No loose ends.

"Kill Dave?" he asked.

"The whole damned family. If ya don't do it, I'll find someone else. Thirty-six hours I'm givin' ya. Noon Saturday. After that, the devil take ya. Or your God if he'll still have ya."

As Jim pulled out, he unconsciously pressed the gas pedal too hard and the Mercury skidded momentarily on the ice.

"Careful, little brother," Mike said. "People are dependin' on us."

CHAPTER 42

Fort Collins High School Gymnasium
December 19, 6:17 pm. Mountain Time

Twenty-four hours later, Liv squirmed in the bleachers right behind the Ft. Collins bench. The scoreboard showed the Eagles down one game and behind 7-10 in the second. She still supported the team, but she deeply wished she could play. She felt at her neck for the little blemish forming, like the ones she had seen months ago in pictures on the web. She pulled the turtleneck up tighter.

Liv followed the ball's arc from the back court of the Longmont team. It sailed toward their forward on the front line. She leapt high into the air, preparing to spike the set-up into the midst of the Fort Collins defenders. Suddenly, the Longmont girl flipped upside down and crashed on to the floor. Beneath her was a teammate who had inadvertently submarined her in pursuit of the ball. The cheers of the fans turned to complete silence and then whispers as the coach and others from the Longmont team gathered around the prone girl.

CHAPTER 43

Clements' Home
December 19, 6:55 p.m. Mountain Time

The toe of one shoe precariously gripped the brick wall on the back of the Clements' home while the other balanced on a slippery, barren tree limb. Jim chipped the ice away from the windowsill to get a better hand grip. After putting the small pick back in his belt, he slowly ran the beam of the penlight along the edges of the second-story window. No alarm contacts. At least, none that he could see. Mike told him that alarm companies and homeowners often economized by not alarming small second story windows. He gambled that was the case here.

Slipping a pocket knife in between the top and bottom window, he snapped back the latch. He quietly eased the window up. He waited thirty seconds, prepared to scale back down the tree quickly if necessary. No alarm. He grabbed the ledge with both hands and thrust his body across it. He crawled inside, easing on to the bathroom floor.

He had watched Mel and Liv Clement leave in their SUV an hour earlier. Dave had not arrived home yet, but Jim was betting he would go directly to his daughter's volleyball game. His information told him the man always attended the games, but often arrived only in the last few minutes. Apparently, he had a difficult time extricating himself from his work in the evenings.

Jim wandered the upstairs, discovering three bedrooms, one clearly the master with a king size bed and a wedding picture on the dresser. Another had a great deal of pink in it and clothes scattered around the floor. Make-up and accessories covered the dresser and a faint smell of nail polish hit his nose. Clearly the teenage girl's room.

The third room had a large table in the center with a sewing machine atop it. No one could sleep here, he thought. Part of him hoped he would find nothing. Another wanted to find Jennifer and be done with her. He had heard back from Christus that the upload of Sheila's files had encrypted segments they had not yet deciphered. Jim might need to get back into the lab to complete the information.

So he was not done. He needed to get back in the lab, but Claire would not let him back without a dead Jennifer. She, and perhaps the Clements, stood between him and the ability to save millions of lives.

He tiptoed down the stairs to the main floor, listening for sounds that indicated anyone may have returned home. He kept his penlight pointed down so as not to have it seen through the front windows of the house. Wandering through the first level, he discovered the kitchen, a dining room, a living room, a study and a family room. Nothing indicated the presence of an extra person in the home. He thumbed through a message pad near the kitchen phone. No mention of Jennifer.

The small beam of his light bobbed around in the dark searching for the door to the basement. He knew there had to be one because the house had a window well on the western side. Approaching a door off the kitchen, he eased it back trying to minimize its squeak.

"Oil your doors, Dave," he whispered in frustration.

Pointing the penlight through the doorway, he scanned soup cans and jars of white flour and uncooked rice. The pantry.

A distant thump sounded. A car door? He walked to the front window and carefully peered outside. Nothing. Walking to the garage door, he pressed an ear to it. No sound. He started to open the garage door, but stopped when he realized it would trip the alarm. He noted another door beside it. It had to be the basement.

Cracking the door, he looked down a flight of plank stairs to where light shone across gray concrete at the bottom. Probably a utility light of some kind. The steps would be noisy. He placed a foot on the first step very carefully and quietly, proceeding cautiously to the bottom where the wall ended. He stretched his neck around the corner and saw the source of the light. A door slightly ajar led into what looked like a finished room of some kind. He stepped into the narrow hall between the steps and the room, drawing closer to the doorway.

A woman's bare feet with red, manicured toenails lay on a white duvet near the foot of a queen size bed.

Jennifer, he thought. Why had she not heard him? He looked for movement from the feet. Nothing. He waited another beat and a foot moved side to side.

He reached into his coat and pulled out the 9mm pistol his brother had provided. Silently sucking in a deep breath, he approached the doorway. He had hoped that he would not find her, that he could continue to put this off. Now, too much was at stake.

Peeking around the threshold, he observed a woman sprawled under a thin white sheet on the disheveled bed. Only a freckled, white shoulder and her feet peeked out from beneath the sheet. She appeared to be sleeping, her breasts rising and falling in slow rhythm. Glancing at a v-like swell and dip in the sheet just below her smooth and flat stomach, Jim felt a surge of animal attraction, one that long experience had taught him to suppress.

He stepped on to the room's carpet and studied the woman's face. Jennifer Winters. Dear Jesus, he prayed, help me to do the right thing.

But another thought rumbled into his head, one that said he did not need to talk to God about this. The less he thought about it, the better off he would be. He knew it was the right thing. He had reasoned it out over and over again in his head. Otherwise, he did not get back in the lab; he did not get the information needed to stop this genocide. He had once killed for a far less noble cause.

The color of alabaster, her still, glowing face below a mane of thick red hair struck him at that moment as more beautiful than the finest sculptures of the Vatican. Porting him 25 years back in time, Jennifer's coloring reminded him of the landlord's daughter. He felt the urge to kiss her, not shoot her. To caress her, not maim her. To be her forgiveness.

He knelt down on the floor beside her bed, his face even with hers. He needed to wake her. She needed a chance to make peace with God. As a priest, he needed to do that much. He could justify a killing in this case, but he could not justify throwing away a soul. He lived to save souls. If he could insure the salvation of her soul, he reasoned, her earthly life became a secondary issue, even irrelevant if one accepted the thinking of Thomas a Kempis and St. Francis of Assisi.

He slowly reached across and gently caressed her shoulder. He meant it to wake her, but the feel of her silken skin aroused him. He closed his eyes as he shivered. Jerking his hand back, he pressed it against his forehead.

God forgive me. Give me strength, he thought.

Jennifer stirred slightly, turning in his direction, eyes still closed.

"Mmmmm," she purred.

The temptation to love, not to kill, overwhelmed him. He rose from his knees and stepped back into the corner of the room. He would never finish this if she opened her eyes, if she spoke to him. Such a thing of beauty. A thing he had avoided his entire life. And now, his passions aroused to kill, they sought another more natural path with this woman, the scent of her perfume now filling his head.

There can be no final confession, he thought. He did not have the strength. It must be God's will to finish this now.

Jim pointed the gun at her face, her angelic, inviting face. He walked around the bed. He could not destroy her image; he would shoot her in the back.

A clanking sound. Metal against porcelain. A toilet flushing. He had not seen the room in the corner, a light shining from beneath its door. He quickly raced back into the hall. He heard the bathroom door open.

"Jennifer?" a man's voice whispered.

Fr. Jim felt himself trembling. His pulse had skyrocketed and stayed up. He would never be able to aim the gun accurately. And with two of them, they might overpower him or get away. He had not planned to kill two. He could not kill two. He had rationalized Jennifer. He had no choice. But he had the opportunity to save any others. So far. He had told himself that he would move the body if he found her at the Clements. He would spare the family.

But now someone else had entered the equation. Who? He could not just kill him outright. He had not prepared himself for that.

On tiptoe, the hit man-priest hurried up the stairs back to the main floor.

Back in the guest room, Jennifer turned to her companion.

"He meant to kill me, didn't he?" she whispered, her breathing rapid, "I can't believe they would really do this."

He nodded affirmation. She sighed and looked down, the sheet wadded in her tense hands. It had been all she could do to keep from screaming and kicking while the intruder had surveyed her.

She looked back to the man. "Why did you take so long to come out? What if he just pulled the trigger?"

"I know the type, Jennifer, They always take their time."

"I've never been so scared in my life."

"You're a brave one to lay still through that," he said. "Now I have to follow him and prove who's behind this."

"It has to be Eldridge."

"We have to prove it or Claire will never believe it. He's hired his own people and this guy should lead me right to them."

"Be careful."

"You should know that I recognized him. He's a priest. Jim Reilly. Do a search on him. A troubleshooter for the Vatican. They're in this with Eldridge. This is about stopping progress."

"My God. It's true."

"Stay out of sight and lock it down behind me."

With that, he left the room.

On the main floor of the house, Jim pondered the gun in his hand. He had come very close. Very, very close.

"I'll take that as a sign," he said, lifting his eyes up.

He wanted to throw the gun down, to leave it behind. He contemplated leaving it for the Clements. They would need it. As far as he knew, they had no weapons.

Through the walls, he heard the garage door grind open. As quietly as possible, he took the steps two at a time until he returned to the open second story bathroom window. He sat in the windowsill and began to turn around to make the short climb down to the tree limb he used coming up.

Something had changed. The tree limb seemed lower. He ran his penlight up the length of it. It landed on a fresh break against a heavier limb that supported it. The combined weight of the snow and Jim had been too much for it.

Lord, help me, thought the priest. He climbed back in. Maybe he could slip down the stairs. He had not heard the door from the garage to the house open yet. Maybe he had not heard the outside garage door after all. These houses were so close together that it may have been the neighbor's garage.

Then, he heard footfalls from the foyer downstairs. Glancing back to the open window, he pulled his gun and unlatched the safety.

CHAPTER 44

Fort Collins High School Gym
December 19, 7:08 p.m. Mountain Time

The Eagles game ended well. With Longmont's top player out with a concussion, Ft. Collins came back and won the final two games, 15-13 and 15-11. Liv walked over and congratulated her teammates.

Mel came up and hugged her. As Liv returned the hug, she looked over her mother's shoulder.

"Where's Dad?" she asked.

CHAPTER 45

Fort Collins, Clement home
December 19, 7:14 p.m. Mountain Time

From the foyer on the main floor of the house, Dave heard the scraping from upstairs. He reached for the light switch, but decided to operate in the dark. He knew the house. An intruder probably would not.

Could Liv or Mel already be home from the game? Not Jennifer. She was downstairs.

"Liv? Mel?" he called.

No answer. If it were one of them, they would answer. He stepped quietly onto the first of the steps that led to the bedrooms. Halfway up, he stumbled in the dark and latched on to a handrail. It squeaked. He held his breath and did not move.

A thump came from the hall bath. From where he stood, he could see that the bathroom door stood open. Carefully covering the last few stairs to the landing, Dave struggled to keep from breathing heavily and loudly. He could feel his pulse racing in his ears, his heart slamming against his chest wall.

Click. A metallic sound. Again from the bathroom. Call 9-1-1, he thought. Reaching into his pocket, he realized he had left his mobile on the center console of his car.

He took a soundless step toward the master to get to the landline phone. He thought better of it. The intruder could use the time to race downstairs and get out the front door. For the moment, Dave had him cornered in the bathroom.

He inhaled quietly and deeply. He charged into the bathroom, slamming the door back against the linen closet. He whirled around. No one. He grabbed the porcelain soap dish from the sink. The window was open. He moved toward it when he noticed the closed shower curtain. If he leaned out the window, someone standing in the tub could nail him.

As he reached for the plastic shower curtain, his heart did somersaults, bouncing off his chest and back. With a single motion, he yanked the curtain aside and thrust with the soap dish.

No one.

He rushed the window. A silhouette dangled from a branch that hung precariously from another. He watched a large man bounce on the branch until it broke away. The man swung down, crashing into a snowdrift below.

"You! Stop!"

But the man ignored Dave's shouts as he half-crawled and half-limped out of the yard. Racing down the stairs, Dave leapt over the last three and threw the front door open. He had the sonuvabitch. The man could barely walk, let alone run. Dave could catch him easily.

Charging into the frozen night, Dave jumped over the snow-laden junipers that lined the front stoop. As he did, the motion detector turned on the floodlights, casting his long shadow across the stark white landscape. Another larger shadow loomed rapidly behind him. He did not remember crumpling into the snow drifted against his home. The blow to the back of his head took care of that.

CHAPTER 46

Cul-de-Sac Behind Clements Home
December 19, 7:36 p.m. Mountain Time

Shivering, Jim limped into the driver's seat of his car. His felt for swelling on his left ankle. Tender, but very little swelling. Nothing broken then. Just a sprain. And not even a bad one.

So Clement and Jennifer had a thing for each other. Disappointing. Very disappointing. The whole good guy thing in Lokoma probably had everything to do with money and virtually nothing to do with helping people.

Still, Jim did not want to shoot the man. When he leapt for the branch, he risked his life to avoid that possibility. Had he just put off the inevitable? Pillow talk would certainly have brought Clement fully into the loop on what Jennifer knew.

So had anyone pulled into the garage? Maybe the mother and daughter had returned home. Had they seen anything?

Jim drove the car around the block to the Clements' cul-de-sac. He drove slowly toward the house behind a black SUV. It turned into the Clements' driveway and he recognized it as the family's Ford Expedition. The garage door opened, revealing Dave's Volvo in its place. So why had Dave not pursued him. He could have caught him.

Then Jim saw the answer. Dave's body lay sprawled in the snow beneath the bushes in front of the living room window. A small, steaming crimson puddle stained the snow beneath the man's head.

Jennifer finished buttoning her jeans, not bothering to tuck in her shirttail. She slipped into the dark, unfinished area of the basement. The snow on the concrete floor that had fallen in through the window well chilled her bare feet. As instructed, she secured the window well's lock. Footsteps overhead caught her attention.

Returning quietly to the guest room, she leaned against the door jam and listened.

"Dave?" Mel called.

"Daddy?"

The basement door opened.

"Jennifer?" Liv called. "Are you down there?"

"What?" Jennifer said in a voice meant to sound like she had just awakened. "Liv? Is that you?"

"Have you seen my dad?"

Rushing to the steps, Jennifer answered. "No, wasn't he at the game?"

"Mom," Liv called. "He's not here."

It made no sense to Mel. Dave's car was in the garage. She started to head back down the stairs to Liv when she felt a cold breeze on the back of her neck. Looking over her shoulder, she could see that the window in the hall bath stood open. Dave's phone went into voice mail after four rings; Mel pressed the "end" button. Cautiously, she climbed back up the stairs and stepped into the bath. Flipping on the light, she found snow inside on the windowsill and melting on the floor.

Her stomach clenched and she caught her breath. "Liv," she called, not moving an inch. "Are you all right?"

No answer.

"Liv!"

"What is it, Mom?" the girl called from the foot of the stairs.

"Liv, don't move!"

Jim's training kicked in. He parked the car on the street in front of the Clements' neighbors. He did not know what happened to Dave, but he needed to see if he could help him and, if not, anoint him with the last rites. He knew him to be a practicing Catholic. Clement deserved at least that much even if his adultery with Jennifer may have made it pointless.

And if he were seen? A risk worth taking? Was there too much at stake otherwise?

Jim mumbled a short prayer and decided to do the right thing. The Lord would take care of the rest. He touched the holy water vial that hung secretly around his neck and opened the car door.

The door slammed violently back against his shoulder, throwing him across the seat.

"Get your bloody ass back in there!"

Mike shoved Jim across the seat and slid behind the wheel.

"What in the name of the Lord were you tryin' to do?" he raged as he turned the key in the ignition and began to drive away. "Don't answer because I know exactly what you were doin'. You're still a bloody priest, Sean. I guess ya can take the priest out o' the church, but ya can't take the church out o' the priest."

"I have to help him," Jim responded.

"That's not an option. Your carelessness left me no choice but to stop him."

Jim looked at his older brother between narrowed eyes. "You did it? You were there?"

"If he caught ya, it would have really complicated things. Especially since he knows who you are, little brother?"

"It was you?"

Mike pulled up to the red light at the intersection around the corner from the Clements'. The turn signal clicked rhythmically. He looked at Jim.

"Yes, it was me. Ya had me worried for a minute downstairs. I thought ya might actually try to kill her."

"I don't understand."

"I thought ya could never do it, Sean. I counted on it."

"Then, I nearly disappointed you."

Mike nodded, twisting his mouth thoughtfully. "And that makes ya more dangerous than I ever imagined," he finally said.

In the distance, a scream of "Daddy" echoed in the night as Liv discovered her unconscious father.

Public Offerings continues in

Public Offerings Book Four:

Children on the Altar

Enjoy the free excerpt that follows

Learn more at www.PublicOfferings.net

Follow at www.Facebook.com/PublicOfferings

EXCERPT:

PUBLIC OFFERINGS BOOK FOUR

CHILDREN ON THE ALTAR

CHAPTER 1

Port Loko, Sierra Leone
December 20, 9:52 a.m. Greenwich Mean Time

The ashes and mud smeared on his face hid ten year old Jacob Karanja amidst the brush that lined the outside of the modern glass and stone building in Port Loko. He lay prone, cradling a rifle nearly as long as he was tall. Sieramco, a subsidiary of a Swiss company, housed its executive offices here. The company had closed the offices when the civil war had made it untenable for its white Swiss managers to stay in country. The closing had impoverished Jacob's Lokoma tribe. For decades, the tribe mined bauxite for a subsistence living while Sieramco's executives and shareholders grew wealthy on the sale of bauxite for aluminum production in the West. Without Sieramco's administrative and transportation infrastructure, the economies of scale made further bauxite mining a money-losing business for the Lokoma.

Jacob understood none of this. Fela, the Abo chief, understood it well. So did Adrian Guerra who viewed reviving the local economy as an important part of his and the World Bank's mission. Fela and the Abo offered a means to consolidate the bauxite lands, creating enough concentrated revenue to either attract Sieramco back to the country or to allow a new company to start up with sufficient scale to achieve sustained success. And Chief Fela planned to do so at the expense of the Lokoma.

That much Jacob understood.

Visiting Abo village, pretending to be just a little boy there to play, Jacob had learned Chief Fela would be in Port Loko today. He did not need to understand the business issues or rationale. He only knew that Fela had somehow been behind the invasion of Lokoma village, behind the murder of his grandparents and the dislocation of his family. No system of justice could be relied on to fix the matter. Jacob thought it likely that the government somehow had a hand in supporting the chief.

Fela exited the former headquarters building with Adrian Guerra. While Guerra wore a white Hawaiian shirt, Fela wore robes to the ground, a length of cloth wrapped around his head into a cone. He had made the pilgrimage to Mecca, making him a haji in the Islamic community. Jacob had asked his father about that once, wondering why men would wear such clothes in the humidity and heat.

"It's a statement," Hamara had told him. "For most, it's solemn, well-meant. For some, like our friend Fela, it's more like a dog marking his territory."

Guerra's presence with Fela only confirmed Jacob's suspicions that the government and the Abo worked hand-in-hand. Guerra always represented himself as someone close to the Leonean leadership and his body language made it clear he was catering to Fela.

Working to choke down his anger in order to remain steady, Jacob peered through the rifle sight. Fela, moved unsteadily into the crosshairs as he approached his chauffeured Mercedes in the parking lot. Holding his breath, Jacob squeezed the trigger. As he did, a military jeep drove across his line of sight. The bullet hit the metal around the windshield, ricocheting loudly. Fela, Guerra and the other men dropped to the pavement. Five shouting soldiers piled out of the jeep and raced toward Jacob, rifles and pistols positioned to fire.

Jacob remained flat on the ground for several seconds, stunned. Then, fear and experience rushed in. He calmly aimed his rifle, taking down two soldiers with deadly accuracy. The three others took cover. Jacob used the opportunity to slip down an embankment and race down a pre-planned escape route. He put the rifle into a slot in a tree trunk that he had identified earlier. Pulling a towel out of the same slot, he wiped the camo off his face as he ran. Climbing an embankment, he raced into a crowded open-air market, just another unruly child annoying the merchants.

Loud shouting erupted behind him. People started scattering to the sides. Pounding footsteps on the pavement. A line of people wound into a large white tent. Jacob scooted into the middle of the line, disappearing behind a large woman in a bright kaftan. The soldiers stopped outside the tent, yelling at each other in the Abo's Krio dialect. Jacob understood most of it. One of them described the shooter as a boy. Another disputed this, commenting on the assassin's accuracy in taking down two of their comrades. No child could shoot that well.

"Move along, boy," the large woman said as she pushed him by the scruff of the neck.

He tried to shrug her off, but she clamped her hand on his shoulder.

"You wanted to break into queue. You pay the price." The woman smiled, a glimmer of mischief in her eyes. He tried to shrug off her grip one more time.

"If they be lookin' for you, boy, you best stay wid me."

One of the soldiers poked his rifle into the tent and peered around. Jacob pushed close to the woman now and she held him to her enormous bosom as though he were her own.

The soldier looked straight at Jacob, but Jacob didn't see him with his head buried in the folds of the woman's dress. Not seeing a lone boy, the soldier left.

"Thank you," Jacob said, starting to pull away again.

"Stay here, boy. Give the soldiers more time to go. Anyway, you look well. Keep it that way."

She shoved him toward a woman in a white smock. She rubbed alcohol on his arm with a cotton ball and nudged him gently toward a man with a large syringe. Fear surged through Jacob. He hated needles. I have to be a man, he thought.

As the needle penetrated his skin, tears dribbled out of his squinting eyes.

"Now you won't be gettin' no more malaria," the big woman said as she wiped the tears from his face with her big sleeve.

CHAPTER 2

Peggy's Cove, Nova Scotia
December 20, 7:27 a.m. Atlantic Time

Little Marie lay under her covers playing. The cry of gulls outside her window, braving the frigid North Atlantic winds of Peggy's Cove, awakened her just after dawn. Her Barbie doll leaned over the keyboard of the smartphone and pressed on the keys, typing an imaginary message. The phone's screen remained as blank as it had been for over six weeks now.

"Save us," said Marie. "Smoke is filling our cabin and people will die and lose their eyes."

"Don't worry," Marie said in a deeper voice. "We will send someone to save you."

"Oh, no," Marie said in her normal voice, the one she assigned to Barbie. "No. It's too late."

Marie plunged Barbie headfirst into the mattress. "I'll save you, Barbie. I'm Marie. I'll go on the beach and save you."

Then for no clear reason, Marie curled up and started crying.

A gentle hand touched her shoulder. "Marie? Are you all right, sweetie?" It was her mother. She pulled back the covers. As she felt the movement of the blanket, Marie scooped up the phone and pushed it underneath her stomach so her mother would not see it.

Annette Louve saw the tears and the fear on her eight year old's face. Jack still slept so he was not the problem this morning. Anyway, he had been sober for a month thanks to Father LaBonte's efforts, and, of course, the shock of the airplane tragedy.

"Marie, why are you crying?"

"Go away, Mama. I need to be alone." Nothing about this behavior added up to Annette.

"Look at me, please, dear. Now."

Marie turned her head to face her mother. As she did, her chest rolled revealing the edge of the phone.

"What's that?"

Marie curled up again, but her mother's hand was beneath her extracting the device. "Where did you get this?"

Marie sat up on the edge of the bed, prepared to run. Annette read her intentions and blocked the doorway with her body.

"Well?" Annette said, waving the phone at Marie.

"Don't break it, Mama. It's important."

"And why is that?"

Her lips curled into a cry as she explained, "It's from the plane crash."

"The plane crash?"

"Yes," she said tearfully.

"I don't understand," Annette said as she turned the device over and over in her hand.

"I found it on the beach when I wasn't supposed to be there. I thought Daddy would hit me."

Annette crouched in front of her daughter and hugged her. "Oh, honey. Daddy was having a very hard time back then. He would never touch you now. He loves you very much. We both do."

Marie whimpered, her head tucked into her mother's shoulder. Annette pulled back abruptly.

"Now, how do you know this is from the plane crash?"

Marie chewed her lip as she pondered her mother. "It told me," she blurted out.

"How did it tell you?"

"I could read it," Marie spoke very sincerely. "Until its battery died. "

With a face full of concern, Annette put herself at Marie's eye level. "What did it say to you?"

"It said somebody crashed them on purpose."

Annette's heart raced. This could not be real. Marie was imagining.

"Did it say who that somebody was?" she asked, feeling flush.

"It said that the answer was inside it."

Annette turned phone over in her hand again. She thought they had a charger for it. "Jack," she called quietly and then very loudly, "Jack!"

Five hours later, the family sat in the rectory of the windblown church at the top of the cove.

"Why did you bring this to me?" Father LaBonte asked.

"The note on the phone is very specific," Jack said, sitting forward on the couch between his wife and daughter. "It's my fault that it didn't appear sooner. Marie was afraid of me."

LaBonte place a hand on Jack's forearm. "So what does this note say?"

"It asks that we take it to a parish priest, to someone not beholding to the United States government, that the US government could not be trusted."

"What about our government, the Canadian government?" the priest asked.

"Too friendly with the Americans I figure."

"What else does it say?"

"I don't know, but the phone has a storage card in it with a list of document files on it. Most of them are password protected, though, but a reminder popped up after we re-charged it. It said that the phone's owner was supposed to be at a meeting at some lab this past October. One short note without a password names the lab. Says it is guarded by an extreme IRA faction…"

"IRA? Irish Republican Army?"

"The same, Father. I think this guy thought the IRA sabotaged the plane."

The priest navigated the phone and found it was named Evan's Phone. He searched contacts for Evan and found only one. the owner's name and address appeared briefly on the opening screen. He turned it off.

"We can start by confirming that this is really from the flight, I suppose," the priest said.

"How can we do that without involving the authorities?" Jack asked.

"We'll just have to get an old paper and see if…" The priest paused while he turned the box back on and read the name and company on the opening screen again. "We'll just have to see if Dr. Evan Conger of the World Health Organization died on that flight."

CHAPTER 3

Fort Collins: Clement home
December 20, 11:12 a.m. Mountain Time

Dave did not want to wake up the next morning. His head still pounded, but medication and sleep diminished the intensity to a bearable level. Opening his eyes did not seem like a good idea.

Liv carried a tray into the room at 11:12. She did not know whether to bring breakfast or lunch. She opted for oatmeal with sliced bananas. Dave ate oatmeal for his health; bananas had potassium, good for his heart. Coffee and a newspaper still in its plastic also sat on the tray.

Before Mel headed off for a closing, mother and daughter, eating a quick breakfast of hot tea and English muffins, worried that the hit on the back of the head had done more serious damage than the emergency room physician thought.

Jennifer remained sequestered in the guest room where Mel had instructed her to stay after the break-in. The intruder had seen her. If not a run-of-the-mill burglar, the man posed a clear threat to the well-being of the entire household. Mel wanted to believe the man to be just a burglar. Jennifer insisted that she thought he was. Mel's sixth sense picked up a level of anxiety in Jennifer that suggested she knew more than she admitted.

"Good morning, sweetheart," Dave said, his eyes still closed.

"It's almost afternoon, Daddy," Liv said, "Were you planning on sleeping all day?"

"I would love to."

"Does it still hurt?"

"It's not too bad right now. I think if I stand up it will start all over again."

"You're supposed to stay in bed all weekend so that shouldn't be a problem."

Liv picked up a pillow and Dave sat up in bed as she stuffed it behind him. She put the tray down over his legs. Fearing that the sloshing, overly full cup of coffee would spill its steamy contents in his lap, Dave risked burning his tongue, taking a quick sip.

Her hands free, Liv felt for the cell phone in her jeans pocket. Earlier that morning, at Mel's instructions, she had programmed "9" as the speed dial for 9-1-1.

Dave saw her patting her pockets. "Is the alarm on?" he asked.

"Yes, sir. Mom gave me a full security briefing before she left."

Liv's wording caused Dave to smile.

"Security briefing? What are we? The CIA?"

Liv blushed. "It seems to describe it," she said.

"I don't think there's anything to worry about. Some dumb burglar that didn't realize we had a house guest."

"What if it's the people that are after Jennifer?"

"If they exist, they're professionals. They would have finished the job."

Liv's shoulders relaxed. Her dad made sense. The bad guys would not have just visited and left.

"Do you want to watch TV?" she asked, picking up the remote from the nightstand.

"I'd rather not. The noise might be too much. We can read the paper."

He pulled the newspaper out of its plastic and handed Liv the front section.

CHAPTER 4

Liv's Diary
December 20, 10:47 p.m. Mountain Time

Tonight, I feel as good as I can remember. It may be too much to hope, but the doctor might have found a medicine that works for me.

Life has been very busy. Of course, life may be short, too, if the medicine stops working like all the others did. Mom and Dad try to keep my hopes up, but I know from reading online and from my response to the meds that I'm probably going to die from this sooner or later. Not eventually like everybody else. But soon for some reason.

I've spent a lot of time feeling sorry for myself. The other night was the end of that, though. A week ago, Chelsea embarrassed me beyond hope in front of Michael. She made me an untouchable. He hasn't said so and he's been nice, but… I don't know. I cried so much that my eyes stayed swollen for almost the entire week. Everyone at school probably knows by now. If I were them, I'd be scared of me.

But seeing Dad lying in the snow bleeding opened up a whole new level of pain. I thought he was dead. I've never been so scared. It was so sad, so horrible. I had no idea how much I love him. There has been so much resentment from me about his work or how he acts.

We were covered in snow, but I held his head in my arms. We rocked. He didn't know it. He seemed to barely breathe. His blood dripped on my sweats. I didn't care. I only knew how much I loved my Daddy, how hard he had worked for us. I don't think I ever realized he could get hurt until then. He's always the strong one, the one nothing bothers.

Mom told us that I screamed loud enough to wake the dead when I found him. Dad said that must have been why he woke up. I saved him, he said. Even laying there in the emergency room, covered in blood, his eyes barely able to open, he made me laugh. That's the Daddy I remember and love. That's why I hate it so much when he's gone.

So I'm not feeling sorry for myself anymore. When I pray from now on, I'm going to thank God for my dad and my mom. I already started today. I thanked him for the time I've had here and how good that time has been. Sure, I prayed for the AIDs to go away. Still, I think that may not be what God has in mind for me. It's the first time in a long time that I just thanked Him. I paused for a long time on the words 'thy will be done' in the Our Father. I said them again and again. I think I mean them now… finally. It takes a lot of pressure off. I wonder if God feels the same way.

Here's my prayer tonight. God, thank you again for saving my dad. I feel strong tonight. I don't know if I'll still feel so good tomorrow or the day after or the day after that. Whatever happens, please let me know how to handle it and what you want me to do. Please, God.

Clement Home
December 20, 11:24 p.m. Mountain Time

Mel simultaneously tapped on the door and cracked it open. She caught Liv quickly sliding something under her bed. "Sweetie, time to get to sleep. You need your rest."

Liv popped up and gave her a mother a long, tight hug. "Are you okay?" she asked.

"Am I okay?" Mel responded, surprised. "You're the one we need to worry about, Miss Energizer Bunny."

Liv pressed her head into her mother's shoulder, a small smile creasing her lips. "Don't worry, Mom. I'm doing so much better."

Mel placed a hand gently on Liv's head and slowly stroked her hair. Dave's injury had frightened her, too. He seemed so unconquerable, so determined and bull-headed. Seeing him lying helpless in the snow had made her feel vulnerable, exposed. It terrified her. Worse, it shamed her to think that she thought first of herself at that moment.

It had caused her to re-visit her priorities. On what foundation had she built her life? What kind of relationship did she and Dave have? She needed to take care of him. Spending the next morning and half the afternoon at the office seemed absolutely the wrong priority. But she needed to earn a living. And Liv did a great job of playing nurse.

Liv's hair felt like it needed washed, but Mel decided not to bother her with that tonight. She would wake her early in the morning instead. Liv did not seem to find much peace lately. For now, she should be able to savor it.

So should I, thought Mel. A wave of fear shivered through her, the constant foreboding that had seemed only to intensify since the diagnosis.

She pulled Liv closer.

CHAPTER 5

Loveland, Colorado: Josie's Café
December 21, 9:20 a.m. Mountain Time

Dave's wooziness assured him that he should have stayed in bed this morning. The call surprised him. He thought the priest still kept himself busy in the mountain villages south of Freetown. This morning, however, Fr. Jim walked through the door of Josie's. A little ruddier because of the Colorado cold, he still poured sincerity from his eyes.

"This is a real surprise, Father. It's great to see you again. I'd heard that either bandits or rebels had killed you."

"And here I am in the flesh, Dave. Your PDNA is what brought me here."

"How?"

"I know you have a house guest."

Dave's hands tightened on the edge of the table.

Fr. Jim leaned toward him and spoke quietly. "Relax, if you work with me, it won't bring you any more harm."

"What harm?"

"I'm the guy who broke into your house."

Dave tilted his head and studied the priest. He felt his heartbeat accelerate. "You're what? You're the guy that damn near killed me?"

Jim held Dave's gaze. "No, I didn't hit you."

Dave thought of Jennifer's comments about a rumored Vatican plot. "One of your fellow priests then. What are you guys? Jesuits, right?"

"No, I'm just a simple missionary that stuck his fingers in too many electric outlets when he was a kid. Can't seem to break the habit."

"So who slugged me? And why the hell were you in the house?"

"Dave, listen. Revenge is the last thing you have time for. Things are not what they seem."

CHAPTER 6

Liv's Diary
December 21, 11:05 p.m.

What a night. Not a minute of playing time for me. Plus we lost. We only won one set. Coach said I'd missed too much practice time to put me in, unless we built up a good lead. I have no doubt he blames me for losing the match against Poudre when I passed out. On the way home in the car tonight, I asked Mom and Dad if I should have told the coach the truth. Thought maybe I made a mistake. They had the right idea. If the coach knew about the HIV, he probably would have wanted me off the team.

I don't hate him. I just…

It was our last match for the season, but… for me… it probably was my last chance ever. I'm feeling really weak again. For the last week, I'd been feeling stronger and stronger. Then today, I woke up feeling a little nauseous and dizzy. By the middle of the day, I had a killer headache. By game time, I had four acetaminophen in me and two ibuprofen so the headache was under control, but I still wasn't right. So the Fuzeon shots worked for a while, but I think the HIV's already building resistance. I told Mom when we got home. I'm such a baby. Cried hard for ten minutes. Mom didn't. She was good. Said I was probably wrong. This is just a dip, that it was way too soon to tell. She thinks it may even be my body adjusting to the drugs. I want to believe it, but it's hard to stay positive all the time. Both other times I had drug resistance, I felt just like this at the beginning.

But I'm still strong enough that I could have played tonight. It's weird how important that seems when I'm literally facing death.

Then there's Michael Winston. He didn't show up for the match at all. Chelsea's little drunken thing must have gotten to him after all. So, first Chelsea gives me HIV and then she drives my boyfriend away.

Confession: We played stupid kid games three years ago. Middle school. Everybody does stupid stuff in middle school. It is so embarrassing now. But Chelsea liked it. A lot more than I did, I guess. But if she gave me HIV, then she should have it, too. She could be a carrier. Has to be. Because that is the ONLY way I could have picked this up. I need to tell her and tell my parents before she spreads this to a lot of other people. For the longest time I didn't because I thought it was too long ago to be the cause. Why completely embarrass myself for something that might not have happened? But what I've read lately says it could have happened then.

So, there it is, dear diary. No boyfriend. A best friend that totally betrayed me. Oh, yeah. I'm dying, too. How cool is that?

I'll tell you how cool. So cool that I'm not going to let it happen. I'm going to find a way to fix my life myself. I don't know how, but I will beat this stupid thing. I pray about it EVERY day. God will help me. I know it. If he doesn't… Well, if he doesn't, he isn't so loving, is he? I'm having a much harder time with "thy will be done" tonight than I did last night.

At least, I think Daddy's head is okay now. Not sure, though. He went out this morning for a meeting after Mom and I both told him it was too soon. He came home acting weird. But not like he gets about work. Much more intense – as if that were possible. Might be just his head still recovering, but I don't think so. Something's up. Something big. Or bad.

CHAPTER 7

Clement home
December 22, 5:10 a.m. Mountain Time

Sitting in the darkness in the Clement's family room, Jennifer closed the app and put her phone down. She had been there since 3:30 when she woke with a start. She thought she heard something scraping at the basement window over the guest room. It may have been part of her dream, but she did not want to risk it. So she moved upstairs where she felt safer.

She listened again for the noise. She heard the drip of the kitchen faucet, the hum of the dishwasher in its dry cycle, the quieter hum of the ballast of the fluorescent light over the sink.

She got up from the couch in the family room and walked toward the kitchen. She carried the TV remote with her and entertained turning the TV on. No, she thought, I need to hear everything.

The hit man could come back at any time. Mike had not contacted her since his visit the night of the break-in. Why had the hit man not come back? He had to know she was there now.

Click!

Jennifer jumped. What was that? She listened intently. The fans of the heating system blew, explaining the clicking sound as they switched on.

She dialed 911 on her phone, but did not tap the call button. Instead, she let her finger hover over it, just in case. She walked over to the sliding glass doors and pulled the drapes tighter, making certain to leave not even a slight crack for someone to look in. She headed toward the front door where she again confirmed the alarm was on and working.

Back in the kitchen, she put her phone down and pulled two butcher knives from the drawer. Returning to the family room, she sat back down in the couch, but did not pick up her phone again. She did not want to risk being distracted. She could not afford to be surprised.

APPENDIX

PUBLIC OFFERINGS

ABOUT THE AUTHOR

With the *Public Offerings* series, Bob LiVolsi won the Writers League of Texas prestigious manuscript contest for best thriller. In the same competition, Bob was also a finalist for best narrative non-fiction. He started his career as a journalist and was managing editor of the Daily Kent Stater at Kent State University in the aftermath of 1970 shootings. There, he won the national Sears Congressional Internship for his investigative coverage of racial tension on campus.

A high tech executive on teams that took two companies public, Bob applied his experiences in the mercenary world of high-stakes investment to *Public Offerings*. As a vice president with Hewlett Packard and in his roles in building new companies, he traveled the world partnering with large corporations, governments and other international organizations. Bob is currently CEO of VRI, a humanitarian vaccine systems company. He has a certificate in vaccinology from the Pasteur Institute in Paris, and he has been a mentor for a vaccine formulation company in the National Science Foundation's regional Innovation Corps program. His and his wife's private support of missions in the Middle East, Sub-Saharan Africa and Central America brought him closer to the day-to-day challenges presented by disease, poverty, war and tyranny. In the mid-1990s, he began online communication with a missionary priest in Sierra Leone where he learned about the horrors there not yet reported in the western press. The priest disappeared and was assumed killed. He became the inspiration for Fr. Jim Reilly in *Public Offerings*.

Bob lives with his wife of 35 years in Austin, Texas. He is writing *Courtship of Innocence*, the sequel to the *Public Offerings* series.

CHARACTER SUMMARIES

Clement Family, Fort Collins, Colorado

Dave Clement

> Dave is the father of Liv Clement and husband of Mel Clement. As VP of Operations and Business Development at Prodeus, he is the main driver of partnerships to deploy the Portable DNA Analyzer (PDNA) with malaria vaccine pilot in West Africa. Dave is the likely successor to Ed Hepp as CEO of Prodeus. Claire McQuaid, Executive Director of Aldrich, relies on Dave's partnership and his relationships in the pharmaceutical industry and with international aid organizations

Liv Clement

> Fifteen year old daughter of Dave and Mel Clement. Liv is a good student and volleyball player at Ft. Collins High School where she is a sophomore. She is on anti-retrovirals to manage HIV. She insists to her parents and doctors that she has participated in no risky behaviors that would lead to HIV. She has not had a blood transfusion, another possible source of HIV. She keeps her HIV very secret; her friends, teachers, and coaches do not know she has it. She frequently writes in a diary to help her cope

Mel Clement

> Liv's mother and wife of Dave Clement. Mel works as a mortgage broker, but now seldom goes into the office, working from home to be present for Liv. Mel is frustrated with Dave for constantly prioritizing work over family and feels he is not doing enough to help find answers for Liv's HIV.

Aldrich Institute, Colorado

Claire McQuaid

Executive Director of the Boulder, Colorado-based Aldrich Institute. She has spearheaded the development of the malaria vaccine to be tested in Sierra Leone with the Lokoma tribe and others. Claire's body is disfigured from wounds incurred when she was young. She is passionate about her work and feels a duty to change the world on a grand scale. She helped put Ed Hepp and Prodeus in business where she sits on the board. She plans to have Dave Clement replace Ed as CEO when Ed's Parkinson's disease advances to the point where he cannot carry the CEO workload. Importantly, Claire relies on Dave to smooth the way for cooperation with locals in Sierra Leone and with significant allies such as Evan Conger at the World Health Organization (WHO).

Sheila Stratemeier

Lead developer for the malaria vaccine at the Aldrich Institute. Sheila works out of the Aldrich's secretive mountain lab in northern Colorado's Rawah Wilderness, high up in the mountains near the Medicine Bow Range. Sheila is troubled by the alternatives that Claire and the Aldrich are considering for deployment of the malaria vaccine; Sheila and Jennifer Winter, who works for Dave Clement at Prodeus, are close friends going back to the days when they were protégés at the Aldrich Institute fresh out of grad school.

Eldridge Perry

Director of Drug Discovery for the Aldrich Institute. Eldridge works out of the firm's mountain lab in Colorado's Rawah Wilderness. Sheila Stratemeier and Jennifer Winter both reported directly to Eldridge when they worked there together; he is still Sheila's manager today. A very secretive and mysterious man, Eldridge compartmentalizes work assignments among his researchers and developers so that no single one of them has a complete picture of the company's plans and strategy.

Lokoma Village, Sierra Leone

Fr. Jim Reilly

Irish missionary priest who serves the people of Sierra Leone. Fr. Jim feels a special fealty to Chief Hamara Karanja and the Lokoma tribe. He baptized Chief Karanja and the tribe members when they converted from a local tribal religion three years ago. He is itinerant, traveling from village to village and often saying Mass outdoors. Dave Clement and Fr. Jim have been friends since Fr. Jim gave a fundraising sermon at Dave's church in Colorado eight years ago. Since then, Dave and Mel have contributed funds and time to help the Lokoma through hard economic times during the civil war in Sierra Leone.

Hamara Karanja

Paramount chief of the Lokoma nation in the northwest mountains of Sierra Leone. Hamara considers Dave Clement a friend through Dave's efforts to bring medical missions to the Lokoma, bringing items such as eyeglasses and prescription medicines. Hamara is married to Mariama Karanja who has given birth to two daughters: Ketta and Sara. Ketta died recently at age seven from malaria. Sara is five and her family dotes on her, particularly since the loss of Ketta. Hamara's oldest child Jacob, age 10, is his son by his first wife, Ani. Hamara was married to both Ani and Mariama simultaneously, but had to choose one when he converted to Catholicism, as polygamy is outlawed by Church law. He chose Mariama. Jacob holds this against his father.

Jacob Karanja

Hamara's oldest child, Jacob was born to Hamara's estranged wife Ani. Age 10, he lives with Ani, his birth mother, in the chief's compound along with Ani's parents, Mariama and his sister Sara. Jacob aspires to be a chief like his father and seeks ways to demonstrate his manhood.

International Aid Organizations (NGOs)

Adrian Guerra

The West African Country Director for the World Bank, Adrian is based in Freetown, Sierra Leone, the capital city. Adrian visits Lagos, Nigeria, to persuade Dave Clement to place the malaria vaccine pilot in Sierra Leone, not strife-torn Nigeria. Adrian wants Chief Karanja to move the Lokoma people to sell their ancestral land to another tribe ostensibly to get the Lokoma to more reliable medical care and safer environs away from the criminal bands that still wander the bush, years after the official end of the civil war. Chief Karanja is against such a move, believing he owes it to his tribe and to their ancestors to keep the Lokoma where they are. Adrian has to sign off on the World Bank funds needed to subsidize the malaria vaccine project in Sierra Leone. Dave's long-term relationship with him helps make that happen.

Evan Conger

Director of sub-Saharan tropical diseases for the World Health Organization (WHO), Evan is a reliable and experienced hand in health care administration and drug discovery. He served as Executive Director of the Aldrich Institute until the President of the United States tapped him to be Surgeon General. After serving in the administration, he could not go back to the Aldrich where Claire McQuaid was doing an effective job as his replacement. Instead, he took the job at WHO, hoping to make a difference there, particularly with regard to malaria. He started the malaria vaccine research at the Aldrich and is working with Dave Clement to bring the pilot project for the vaccine to Sierra Leone. WHO's endorsement of the effort will be critical to its deployment and its financial success. Evan and Dave have known each other for years and have a close, trusting relationship. Evan is the kind of man everyone looks up to as a mentor.

Author's Note July 2014

On the next page is a short bibliography where more information can be found about what the situation on the ground is really like in West Africa. Much of the developing world remains in turmoil, facing daily trials that those in the developed countries may rarely, if ever, encounter. Thanks to the Gates Foundation, The World Health Organization, Doctors Without Borders, pharmaceutical firms (big and small) and others, including many small faith-based NGOs, help is reaching many of the people. But not nearly enough. And stability is extremely difficult to maintain.

Some true-to-life facts mentioned in the Public Offerings series:

- Many in the region really believe that vaccines are a western plot delivering HIV and infertility.
- One in five children in Sierra Leone dies before age five.
- So-called rebel bands still roam the bush even where civil war has ended, and civil wars are still ongoing or brewing. Maiming, murder and rape are common in these situations.
- The Boko Haram in Nigeria and extreme elements of both Christian and Islamic groups in the Central African Republic keep life dangerous and short in their respective countries.
- A form of AIDS that kills at an accelerated rate has been discovered in West Africa.
- There is, in fact, evidence that a malaria vaccine may cause more virulent strains of malaria: Mackinnon MJ, Read AF (2004) Immunity Promotes Virulence Evolution in a Malaria Model. PLoS Biol 2(9): e230. doi:10.1371/journal.pbio.0020230; http://www.plosbiology.org/article/info%3Adoi%2F10.1371%2Fjournal.pbio.0020230
- Sierra Leone, according to many studies, remains the poorest nation on the planet.

Public Offerings continues in

Public Offerings Book Four

Children on the Altar

You can buy each of the four books in the Public Offerings series at your favorite book store in either eBook or print format.

Or you can purchase all four books and get the complete Public Offerings series in a single volume at your favorite bookstore, including the Amazon Kindle bookstore at http://goo.gl/MdkLFY

Public Offerings Book One: Birthright

Public Offerings Book Two: The Price of a Life

Public Offerings Book Three: Killer Priest

Public Offerings Book Four: Children on the Altar

Public Offerings Complete: All Four Books in One Volume

Learn more at www.PublicOfferings.net

Follow at www.Facebook.com/PublicOfferings

www.ingramcontent.com/pod-product-compliance
Lightning Source LLC
Chambersburg PA
CBHW060144130626
46556CB00006B/2481